Wildcrest Witches Romance

The Complete Trilogy

HEATHER SILVIO

Panther Books

Panther Books: Worldwide.

Visit the author's website at https://www.heathersilvio.com
Contact the author at: heather@heathersilvio.com

Cover design by Getcovers

ISBN (Print) 978-1-951192-26-6
ISBN (E-book) 978-1-951192-25-9

BOOKS BY HEATHER SILVIO

DOCTOR DANGER MYSTERIES

Hazard in Hawaii (#1)

Spirits in Savannah (#2)

PARANORMAL TALENT AGENCY

Lights, Camera, Action (Episode One)

Reset to One (Episode Two)

That's a Wrap (Episode Three)

An Unexpected Sequel (Episode Four)

Jumping the Shark (Episode Five)

The Season Finale (Episode Six)

Paranormal Talent Agency Episodes 1-3 Collection

Paranormal Talent Agency Episodes 4-6 Collection

Paranormal Talent Agency Episodes 1-6 Collection

NON-SERIES FICTION

Not Quite Famous

Beyond the Abyss

Courting Death

NONFICTION

Special Snowflake Syndrome

Happiness by the Numbers

Stress Disorders: A Healing Path for PTSD

Love's Misfiring Magic

CHAPTER ONE

SHELLY

Shelly Newsome's goal tonight had been to win back her ex-boyfriend, not send him to the emergency room. Yet, there they were. At least the six-story sprawling Wildcrest Hospital complex was state-of-the-art. That was thanks to Mia Fynn filming her movie about witches here. When it became one of the highest-grossing films of all time, map-dot-sized Wildcrest experienced a boom in tourism. The fact that the town, located in the wilds of Nevada, actually provided a safe haven for supernatural beings met the definition of exquisite irony in Shelly's book.

If only the doctor would stop looking like he was trying not to laugh. He avoided making eye contact, no doubt because that would push him over the comical edge. Shelly sighed. Of course, Dr. Benjamin Wright was her best friend, so she supposed it was only natural.

"I don't know what happened," Shelly said, pacing a circle on the bland linoleum between two rows of plastic chairs, trying not to let the beige walls close in. "It wasn't a complicated spell, I didn't think." Her history with spell-making was by no means stellar. But she meant what she said to Ben. "I'm not sure what went wrong." Anxiety zinged through her, the taste of bile in the back of her mouth. "You're sure he's going to be all right? The way that he grabbed his throat, struggled to breathe." She suddenly had a hard time catching her breath.

"Breathe, Shelly."

She inhaled, held to a four count, exhaled. Repeated. Ignored the scent of noxious hospital disinfectant that threatened to overwhelm her nasal passages. Ignored the buzzing of her cellphone in her pocket. She knew it was her mother calling. Again. "Thanks. I've never seen someone turn that shade of purple." The blood drained from her face. "I could have killed him."

"You didn't." Ben leaned in and lowered his voice. "I knew he'd be okay when they brought him in. You never had anything to worry about."

"Thank the Goddess." She breathed a sigh of relief. All witches' magic had specific inclinations that typically surfaced during puberty. Ben's ability was to sense the physical health of others – both good and bad – and intuitively know what they needed, whether traditional or magical intervention. So, if he said Ethan was never in any real danger, Shelly believed him. If only she could get a grasp on her own magical aptitude.

Ben's cellphone buzzed and he raised his eyebrows at her when he saw the caller.

Of course, her mother was calling Ben. Shelly gave a small shake of her head. She'd call her mother back when everything felt more settled.

"I guess what they say isn't true, that a way to a man's heart is through his stomach," Ben said, and now he outright laughed, the sound bouncing around the small, thankfully empty, waiting area. Shelly refrained from reading him the riot act. When you've known someone your entire life – and were best friends since he took the blame for a minor car accident in high school even though it was your fault – you cut them a little slack. A little.

"Gee, thanks. That's very supportive." She collapsed into one of the green plastic waiting room chairs, dropped her head into her hands. "What if I'd seriously hurt him?" She mumbled through her fingers.

"Look at me," Ben said. She didn't. "Shelly Newsome, look at me right now. Please."

Shelly raised her head, her hazel eyes meeting his brown ones. "At least you said please."

"Tell me what happened."

Horror filled her as tears flowed. Ben's smirk fell and he pulled Shelly into a hug. She leaned into the embrace, her hands clutching at his familiar scrubs. Warmth enveloped her. He held her until the tears slowed then stopped. "Ethan broke up with me this morning," she muttered into Ben's shoulder. "He says he's moving out at the end of the month. In five days."

Ben pushed Shelly to arm's length, eyes wide in shock. "He broke up with you? Why didn't you tell me sooner? And why were you baking him a magical dinner if he's leaving in five days?"

She broke eye contact. "This morning, I thought… I thought he was going to propose," she whispered.

"Oh, Shelly."

"Yeah, yeah, I know."

"Didn't you tell me you thought something was missing?" Ben asked, confusion clear on his face. He ran a hand through his short brown hair.

A flush crept up Shelly's neck. "Let me explain." She fiddled with the bottom of her t-shirt, rubbing the soft cotton fabric. "I thought what was missing was me hiding the witch side of myself from him."

Prior to *Witches in the Wild* filming there years ago, the supernatural beings in town mostly kept that quiet. Once the movie shot to success, they could live openly to a certain extent because the normals and the tourists thought they were playing up the movie angle for tourist dollars.

That wasn't entirely wrong, of course, but the tongue-in-cheek approach had masked the truth. And, then once the Las Vegas city council officially recognized the existence of supernaturals last year, even more beings decided to live openly. Shelly had chosen not to share her witch nature with Ethan in part because she didn't identify as a witch. Why would she when she couldn't cast basic spells?

"I thought that when he proposed," Shelly continued, "the promise of taking our relationship to the next level would give me the prompt to tell him the truth."

"Why did you think he was going to propose?"

She tilted her head back, long black hair hitting the seat bottom. "He said he had something important to talk to me about." She shrugged. "After five years together, what else could it be?"

"He broke up with you instead."

"Yep."

"Now I'm even more confused. If he broke up with you this morning, why would you be making him—" He stopped with a shake of his head.

He knew her too well.

"You were trying to win him back." He grimaced when she nodded. "But why?"

"He's the one."

"Even though there's no spark?"

"Yes." Shelly picked at her cuticles. "It's a slow-build relationship."

Ben snorted.

"All right, I get it. Five years is a long time to build."

"What happened at dinner? I assume you weren't trying a love spell."

"Of course not!" All witches knew that love spells were verboten. Free will didn't allow for that. But that didn't mean they couldn't nudge other directions. Her brow furrowed. "I was making vegetable lasagna, his favorite meal. I wanted to make sure that the positive feelings were as strong as possible, so I added saffron to ensure a good mood, plus included a magical enhancement. To boost it."

Ben's eyes twinkled. "That explains his symptoms."

"I'm so glad," she said with an eye roll.

"No need to be sarcastic."

"Sorry. I know you're trying to help."

He thought for a moment. "Interesting that Ben had the exact opposite response. Sadness, irritability, asthma attack."

Now Shelly gave him the side eye. "Uh huh, I get it."

"I just find it interesting that your magical enhancement worked in the opposite direction," he repeated with a shrug.

"Why can't I be a better witch?" Shelly groused.

Ben half-smiled. "I don't know. Maybe the Goddess was trying to tell you something."

"That I shouldn't cast spells," she said, defeated.

Ben closed the space between them and opened his mouth to speak, but another voice overrode his.

"Shelly, honey. Is everything okay? Jenny from book club called to tell me she saw you in the ER."

Ah, the beauty of the small town. Shelly stood to face the owner of the husky voice. "Hi, Mom."

CHAPTER TWO

BEN

Ben's jaw had snapped shut at the sound of Grace Newsome's voice; she commanded whatever space she entered. After she passed the final row of chairs in the small room, he joined Shelly in embracing her mother, awed as always that someone's mother could be so cool.

Not that Ben didn't love his mother, but she was quieter and laser-focused on the family business, Wildcrest Witches International. Yep, their family business was running the coven's corporate entity. Welcome to the 21st century of practicing witchcraft. They even considered taking the business public after Las Vegas passed their resolution, but thankfully, that impulse passed. His mother, the Chief Financial Officer, wasn't a witch, but her facility with numbers was nearly magical.

"Shelly, Ben, I'm glad I found you both," Grace said into Ben's chest. She was short like her daughter, but rail thin where Shelly had curves that made a man want to— He slammed that line of thinking down and concentrated on the firebrand before them.

"Hi Grace, we're fine, as you can see," he assured her, worry lines clear on her face.

Grace shook her head, causing the halo of shoulder-length curly red hair to bounce around her face and her dangling earrings to jangle. "Thank the Goddess. When Jenny called, and neither of you answered your phones, it was all I could do to contain myself." Her purple eyes filled with tears. When Ben was in high school, he'd assumed those were contacts, but no, her eyes were purple. Shelly explained that the color related to her mother's magical inclination to recognize the happiness potential of others.

Shelly and Ben exchanged a guilty look. They'd both seen her mother's calls, but the woman could be excitable, and they had wanted to make sure that Ethan was good first.

"I'm so sorry, Mom," Shelly said, hugging her mother again. "But, Ben's right. You can see we're fine." She swallowed. "Though Ethan is being treated."

"Is he okay?" Grace asked, politely, as if discussing a stranger.

"He's going to be perfectly fine," Ben answered the question. "He'll be released in about an hour." Had Shelly told her they'd broken up? He'd always wondered what Grace thought of Shelly's boyfriend – ex-boyfriend. She never seemed fond of him. Or maybe that was wishful thinking on his part.

"What happened?" Grace asked.

Shelly placed her hand on his upper arm. "I'll explain it, Ben." She stared at the ceiling for a moment. "Ethan reacted to a spell."

"What did you do?" Grace managed to ask the question without sounding accusatory at all.

Shelly still reddened. "I was trying to increase his feelings of wellbeing."

"Let me guess? It did the opposite."

"How did you know?"

Shelly's mother leaned into the green plastic chair next to her, fingers wrapping over the top. "When your magical abilities first manifested, that happened all the time."

"Why don't I remember that it did the opposite?"

Grace's fingernails tapped out a staccato beat on the chair back. "I have no idea."

"Wait. Is that why you bound my magic until I graduated high school?" Shelly's voice definitely sounded accusatory. "I thought it was because you wanted it to mature." Now, she sounded sad. Ben's heart ached for her.

"Can't both of those things be true?" Grace asked with a tilt of her head.

Emotions played across Shelly's face as she considered her mother's question. Then the uncertainty cleared and her grin lit the room. Ben smiled automatically in response. Her ability to remain positive had always drawn him to her.

"Yeah, for sure," Shelly agreed with her mother. "Guess it didn't work as well as we'd hoped. Do you think it'll mature by the time I'm thirty?"

Grace shrugged. "Darling, I have no idea."

"Do you want to see Ethan?" Shelly asked.

"Of course," she answered, though again Ben noted a lack of genuine interest. Hmm.

"Let me know when he's ready to be discharged, so I can take him home," Shelly said to Ben, her voice hitching on the final word. Grace's eyes narrowed in response.

He assured Shelly he would, then watched the women exit the public side of the waiting area, weaving past the rows of empty chairs toward the automatic sliding glass doors. Grace's flowing patchwork skirt swirled around her legs and Shelly's jeans did wonderful things for her backside. Someone snickering behind him caught his attention. Ben turned to face the man standing in the doorway of the medical staff entrance.

"Can I help you, nurse?" Ben asked in his most condescending doctor voice. The owner of the snicker belly laughed.

"When are you going to tell Shelly you've got it bad for her?" Nick Moore asked, mischief in his dark blue eyes.

Ben sighed. "It's complicated."

"Dude, you've wanted her since high school. It's time to uncomplicate it."

"Yeah, and I've been in the Friend Zone since high school," he reminded Nick.

"That's entirely your fault. You had many opportunities."

"Not hardly. She dated what's-his-name, Will, all through high school, then moved away from Wildcrest to go to college," Ben said, as though Nick, his best male friend, didn't remember all of that. The supernatural support found in their tiny corner of Nevada meant that few left. Those who did invariably returned.

"Ancient history, my man," Nick disagreed.

"And then she met Ethan senior year of college. I still can't believe he agreed to move here with her when they graduated," Ben said. "You'd think our small town was too small for the city slicker."

"C'mon, Ben. Ethan's not a bad guy. You know that," Nick said.

Ben cringed. Nick was right. Just because Ethan had what Ben wanted – and threw it away. "This stays between us," Ben said in a lower voice, "but Shelly told me Ethan broke up with her this morning."

"Now's your chance!"

"I started to, but then Grace arrived."

"Fine. When you get Shelly alone again, now's your chance." He enunciated the repeated phrase.

Ben hesitated.

"What?" Nick asked in exasperation.

"You know what. What if I say something and lose the friendship?" The thought of not having Shelly in his life…

"What if you say something and she jumps into your arms?"

Ben lifted an eyebrow at the image of Shelly jumping into his arms. "I'm too tall for that," he said with a chuckle.

"Joke all you want," Nick said, then glanced back into the room behind him. Another nurse beckoned to him from near a blue privacy curtain inside one of the half-dozen glassed-off rooms. Nick clasped a hand on Ben's shoulder. "Don't blow this."

CHAPTER THREE

SHELLY

"What's going on, Shelly?" her mother asked when they stepped away from Ben. She stood with her hands on her hips, almost like a petulant child.

Shelly smiled. "What makes you think something is going on?" They had stopped outside the sliding door for Ethan's triage room. Shelly reached to open it, and Grace placed her hand on her daughter's.

"Shelly. Honey. You almost never use your magic. Yet you did tonight. What's going on?"

At the repeated question, Shelly pulled her arm back from the door and hung her head. "Ethan broke up with me." The dam broke. Shelly explained everything that had happened. When she finished, Grace pulled her into a tight hug.

"Oh, darling. I'm sorry." She led her a few steps away from the door to a set of green plastic waiting chairs up against the wall. Shelly idly wondered why every section of the emergency department looked the same to her.

"Thanks, Mom." She perched on the edge of a chair, her leg bouncing.

"How are you feeling now?"

"I'm okay." *How are you supposed to feel when you accidentally nearly kill your recent ex?* Shelly's fingers began tapping out a beat on her bouncing leg.

"Relax, darling. Ben said Ethan will be okay. No harm, no foul."

"This time," she said darkly. "What about next time?"

"Maybe don't try your magic like this?"

"Hmm."

"That's not an insult to your magic," Grace assured her.

"I know, Mom. It's not my… area of strength. I think that's how you've put it with your clients?" Shelly's mother was a life coach for supernaturals. And, apparently quite good at it. Her magical inclination to sense the happiness of others and guide them toward increasing it was a perfect fit for that vocation.

"Have you thought about what you really want?"

"What do you mean?"

"How's your website design freelancing going?"

The unexpected segue caught Shelly off-guard. "Pretty good," she said, a slight stretching of the truth. Okay, that was a lie. Despite her misfiring magic, her magical inclination appeared to be sensing the magic of others and seeing the order in the chaos. Design seemed a good fit, and she was trying to parlay her experience with one of the biggest marketing companies on the west coast into her own small business. Except it'd been slow going. She wasn't about to be homeless or anything that dire, though she was pinching her pennies.

"Prior to the breakup, how was your relationship with Ethan?"

"Pretty good," she said again. But maybe Ben was right. Maybe that missing spark was more of an issue than she was willing to admit.

"What have you learned from your decisions to date?"

"That I'm tenacious?"

"Yes! You go after what you want."

"Okay…"

"That's what you need to do now."

Her mother made that pronouncement with utter conviction, but it confused Shelly. That had been her plan. She was going after what she wanted. Ethan. And it flamed out. Spectacularly. Because she sucked as a witch. Her lips thinned into a line of displeasure. Grace placed her hand on Shelly's still-bouncing leg.

"Just be sure you're going after the right things."

"Is there something you want to tell me?" Despite usually being straightforward, to the point of being blunt, every now and again Grace would speak in riddles like that. Like there was something Shelly was missing. Except, like a good coach, and within the bounds of her magic, she wouldn't give her daughter the answer.

Grace grinned. "I trust you'll do what's best for you." She stood, stretched her arms over her head. "I'm glad everybody's okay, but I'm exhausted. And, I'm sure your father is waiting up."

Shelly glanced at her watch; it was after midnight. "Give Dad a hug for me," she said, standing next to her mother. "Thanks for coming down to check on us."

"I love you, darling."

"Love you, too." Shelly watched Grace walk past the nurses' station in the middle of the room toward the exit, mind racing to uncover the subtext of what she'd been told. She knew her mother. There was definitely subtext. With a sigh, she entered Ethan's room, closing the door behind her.

Her breath caught in her throat at the sight of Ethan Platt, her boy— ex-boyfriend, she corrected herself. Even pale and hooked up to machines monitoring his vital signs, the man was a vision. Blond hair. Cheekbones that could cut glass. Long eyelashes women were envious of, and always commented on... even in front of Shelly. She bristled a little at the memory. He'd shocked her when he'd approached during senior year of college. Shelly was what people called cute; he looked like a Greek god in search of his goddess. He'd turned out to be down to earth though. They'd always gotten along great. Well, until the last year.

Beeping increased on one of the machines, drawing her attention. Ethan's head moved to the side. "Ethan?" She asked softly, in case he wasn't really waking up.

His eyes opened, the blue vivid in his face. "Hey, Shelly. Did I fall asleep?"

"You did. How are you feeling?"

"Much better." His voice was gravelly, but his smile was full wattage. "Ben said I can leave soon?"

"He did. I can take you home?" Asked, rather than assumed.

Ethan's smile slipped a fraction. "That'd be great. A ride back to the apartment."

The word change struck like an arrow to her heart. "Right. The apartment."

"But no more home-cooked meals," he teased, maybe to take the edge off.

It worked. She chuckled. "You got it." She approached the bed, hesitating to touch him. "Let me talk to Ben. I'll be right back," she said brightly, instead.

"That sounds good, thanks." Ethan's eyelids were already drooping.

Guilt surged. She knew it was late, but still, this had to be an aftereffect of her misfired spell. She closed the door gently behind her and set off in search of Ben. A quick search, since he was now reviewing someone's chart at the nurse's station in the center of the room.

"Is that Ethan's chart? He'd like to know if he's cleared for me to take him back to the apartment." It saddened Shelly that she'd already adopted the word change. *What about my mother's recommendation to go after what I wanted?*

"It's not his chart; I've already taken care of it." He gestured to the side. "I believe Nick is wrapping up some final notes before we officially release."

"Thanks, Ben," she said. "You're such a good friend. I don't know what I'd do without you."

His eyes dropped to the chart he was reviewing. "Glad I could help."

"Mom told me I should go after what I want," she blurted out and he met her gaze.

"You always should."

"She also said I should be careful continuing to use my magic."

He quirked an eyebrow.

"Okay, okay, she said not to use my magic."

"That sounds more like it."

"How can I help Ethan see we belong together without magical assistance?" she asked, more to herself than to Ben.

"Ethan's what you want."

Shelly couldn't tell if Ben was asking or agreeing with her, so she chose not to address it. "I know I can't do a love spell. And, even a smaller spell to increase wellbeing misfired. How do I show Ethan I care?"

"Should magic be necessary to show someone you care?"

She waved a hand dismissively. "When time is of the essence, you use what's available to you. I have only five days. Four, really." Ben's expression remained neutral. "Is there something you want to tell me? Mom was speaking in riddles, too." He must have heard the frustration in Shelly's voice.

"I just want you to be happy."

"Ethan makes me happy." She thought Ben sighed.

"What's your plan?"

"I'm not sure." She frowned, glanced around the room. Glass-fronted triage rooms filled most of the four walls, with space for a public door and a medical staff door, plus a handful of the hard, plastic chairs. Blue privacy curtains inside each triage room concealed the wheeled hospital beds and monitoring equipment. The antiseptic smell that defined the hospital filled her nose. The sound of beeping, crying, and muffled conversation reached her ears. She focused on all those things while Ben finished reviewing the charts, waiting for her to figure out her next steps.

She snapped her fingers. "I've got it. It's brilliant. You can help me!"

Ben's eyes narrowed. "How can I help you?"

"You're a much better witch than I am. You can help me craft spells to show Ethan how much I care. After all, what are friends for?" Relief flooded her now that she had a solution.

Ben cringed, his lips thinning for a moment, before he offered a half-smile.

She didn't understand why he appeared less than enthused. *He'd never bonded with Ethan, but why wouldn't he want to help me?*

CHAPTER FOUR

BEN

Ugh, the Friend Zone. Still. Why wouldn't I want to help my best friend? Gee, I don't know. Because she's going after the man who just broke up with her? Although, if Ben was honest with himself, he wouldn't want to help her go after any man who wasn't him. Not that he said any of that to Shelly. She was so excited; and he meant what he'd said. He wanted her to be happy. She deserved to be happy. He'd have to ignore the sinking feeling in the pit of his stomach.

"Of course, I'll help you."

With a squeal, Shelly grabbed him in a hug, the chart he'd been reviewing a welcome barrier between their bodies. If he was going to be in the Friend Zone, then he needed to focus on helping his friend. Just because Ben thought they acted more like roommates around each other didn't mean Ethan would be a bad guy for Shelly.

"Thank you, thank you, thank you," she said. "You won't regret it."

Her excitement infectious, he laughed. "I'm sure I won't. But you might." Ben wanted to eat the words when her smile slipped.

"What does that mean?"

Should he take Nick's advice to tell her how he felt? What if she dumped him as a friend and continued to try to win Ethan back? Then he'd lose everything.

"Ben? What does that mean?"

He shook his head. "I'm only teasing. You know the old saying… be careful what you wish for…"

"You just might get it," they completed in unison. It had been a joke since they were kids, waiting and waiting for their magic to manifest, only for Shelly to learn hers wasn't so controllable. She'd been inconsolable after several near misses where people had almost gotten hurt, including a ridiculous car accident when they were sixteen. She'd thought it would be hilarious to cast a spell to take control of Ben's car and then set up a game of chicken to freak him out. Except what had happened was she'd lost control of her own car – nothing responded to her, not the steering, the brakes, nothing. And they'd had a front-end collision.

Luckily, they were only in a parking lot, so the slow speeds meant neither were hurt.

But the thought that her misfiring magic could have had serious consequences shook her hard. She didn't try using her magic again for almost six months, finally tempted when she saw a cat stuck in a drain and didn't want to wait for help to arrive. Of course, by then, her parents were prepared to bind it when it misfired again. She and the cat were fine, but that was it for magic.

Her frown lines smoothed out and she grinned. "I'm not saying everything's perfect."

"Nothing's perfect."

"Exactly." She nodded. "But, Ethan and I… we had something… have something. Whatever. You know what I mean."

"I do." Ben wanted her to look at him the way she looked at Ethan, but he also understood that she wanted to make it work.

"Start in the morning?" She checked her watch. "Um, later in the morning, I mean. Text me when it's a good time?"

"Don't you have client stuff scheduled for tomorrow?"

"Nothing I can't work around," she responded vaguely.

"I'll need to grab some sleep once my shift is done, so let's say lunchtime? Ish? I'll text you." Plus, he needed to return an unexpected voicemail from Las Vegas. Chief Resident at a major metropolitan hospital? In Sin City? He hadn't been looking to leave town. In fact, he'd hoped to get the position there at Wildcrest Hospital; but they'd been awfully quiet about which resident would get the nod. And if it wasn't going to work out with Shelly— no, he wasn't giving up yet.

"Lunchtime-ish sounds good."

"Nick will be in Ethan's room soon with the discharge paperwork. You guys should be on your way in no time," Ben explained in his professional doctor voice.

"Thanks, Doctor Ben. For everything." She gave him another hug.

He didn't want to let her go, but released her when she stepped back.

"I'm looking forward to tomorrow," she said.

"Me too."

She walked the few steps across the linoleum, slid open the sliding glass door to Ethan's room, and finger waved to Ben before disappearing on the other side of Ethan's blue privacy curtain.

Ben's plan differed from hers. He would help her, like the best friend he was. But, while she hopefully began to see him in a different light, he'd also hope her plan failed completely. Then he'd throw caution to the wind and tell her how he felt.

CHAPTER FIVE

SHELLY

Sleep eluded her the rest of that night. Thus, Ben caught her mid-yawn when he opened the door to his house before she could knock.

"It's a good thing you aren't trying to sneak up on anyone," he said, stepping to the side to allow her room to enter. He smelled nice; she wondered if it was the sandalwood shower gel he liked.

"Your brothers aren't home?" she asked, not seeing their cars parked out front.

"They're both at work. Aaron started his new job today," Ben said to her before leading her toward the kitchen. She followed him through the foyer to the kitchen, marveling at the remodel. When the brothers bought this house, its cracked tile flooring, outdated kitchen, and stained gray walls needed serious TLC. In the past six months, they'd worked tirelessly on it. Now it was a masterpiece with dark laminate wood flooring gleaming beneath newly painted soft white walls and recessed lighting.

"How exciting! It's at the new realtor's office, right?" She sat at one of the high stools surrounding the new quartz-topped kitchen island. She glanced around for Ben's familiar, Cookie, but didn't see the calico beauty anywhere. Cookie may have been the reincarnation of one of Ben's long-ago ancestors, but she was still a cat who liked to nap during the day.

"Yep. I can't believe my kid brother got his realtor's license." Ben shook his head, his back to Shelly while he opened the stainless-steel refrigerator, brought out a bottle of white wine. He grabbed two long-stemmed glasses from the cabinet. "I figured we could use some liquid libation for brainstorming the spells to use."

Shelly clapped in delight. "Perfect. Ooh, is this that new Riesling you mentioned? The drier one?" She spun the bottle to read the description on the back.

"I picked it up the other day, was saving it for the right occasion."

The wistful tone of his voice caught her attention. She glanced up at him. He immediately broke eye contact.

"Did you want something to eat?" He faced the pantry next to the refrigerator, but she could see the tips of his ears turning red.

"What's up?"

Ben turned back around, now holding a bag of tortilla chips. "What? Nothing." He set the bag on the counter with a big smile. "Chips and salsa. I know they go better with margaritas."

"No, it's perfect," she told him, still off kilter though not sure why. Her chest tightened with the uncertainty and she refocused on her best friend instead.

Ben filled their glasses, tore open the bag of chips, and dumped a healthy amount of medium-spice salsa in a blue and white patterned porcelain dish before taking the seat beside her. He held up his wine glass.

"To finding the right spells," he said.

"To finding the right spells," Shelly repeated, mirroring his glass with hers. Then savored the wine as it slid down her throat like a, well, fine wine. Ah, there was a reason a crisp Riesling was her favorite.

"What were you thinking for this grand plan?" he asked before popping a chip into his mouth.

Her fingers drummed on the island. "I'm not sure. It's more that I know what I can't do."

"Well, right. No love spells. No increasing wellbeing spells." His eyes cut to her, a devilish smile playing on his lips.

Shelly gave him a shove. He pretended to almost fall from the stool. "Yeah, yeah. Smart aleck. Other than those two."

They sat in silence for a moment, thinking about what else they could do that would be effective without violating the witch's code. The coven followed the standard code of "Do what you like so long as you harm none." But, the definition of harm could be fluid, and they wouldn't want to inadvertently land on the wrong side of it. A meow came from a back bedroom. Shelly jumped to her feet.

"Is that my Cookie?" She headed down the short hallway to the front bedroom. "Cookie?" A meow greeted her seconds before the calico cat came into view, curled into a ball on Ben's bed. She slow-blinked at Shelly, who kneeled beside the bed, scratching behind the cat's ears. Cookie purred in response. "You should come out to sit with us later," Shelly told her and the cat nodded.

It was an odd, but interesting, fact that all familiars could understand all witches, but each witch could only directly communicate with their own familiar. That way they could act as the advisors they were intended to be for their assigned witch. Thus, Cookie's nod, since Shelly wouldn't be able to understand the cat's thoughts.

Ben's familiar, like her own, had appeared when his powers first manifested at puberty. Cookie was so sweet-natured, unlike Shelly's familiar. She inwardly chuckled, though make no mistake, she adored her fox, Rose, despite a bark that sounded like the fox was imitating a tiny, yappy almost-dog. Plus, Shelly was the only witch she knew with a fox for a familiar.

"Are you going to stay in there loving on Cookie all day, or are we getting to work?" Ben asked from the kitchen.

"I'm coming, I'm coming," she said, giving Cookie a final kiss before rejoining Ben, who was still eating chips as though she had never left.

"Any ideas?"

Shelly slowly submerged her chip in salsa. She then removed the chip so fast that she spilled some on the countertop. Her eyes gleamed. "Yes, actually. What's the main issue between me and Ethan?" She popped the chip in her mouth.

"Is this a trick question?" Ben answered with a raised eyebrow.

"No," she replied, indignant.

"Then I'm not sure."

"It's that he doesn't know what he has, right in front of him," she said in triumph. She'd figured it out.

Ben tilted his head. "That's the issue?"

"Yes! We're meant to be together, but he can't see it for some reason."

"It's tough when somebody can't see what's right in front of them," Ben agreed, downing the remainder of his glass of wine in one swallow.

"Exactly," she agreed. "We're looking for a spell to help

him see what's in front of him," Shelly continued, talking through her thought process.

Ben poured another glass of wine.

Shelly stood from the stool and paced in front of the counter. "We need a spell to open his eyes." She stopped. "Help to see what has been unseen," she said, trying to use the formal spell-casting language she was so bad at.

Ben laughed. "Ah, I get it now." He thought a moment. "I can do that; a combination of spells for awareness, focus, and increased intuition ought to do the trick. Shouldn't be too hard, to be honest."

"Too hard for me, though, right?" She teased him.

"Yeah."

Shelly rolled her eyes. "What ingredients do you need?"

Ben frowned. "We should make a list. I'm pretty sure I don't have everything we need on hand. We'll have to go shopping."

She grabbed a small pad of paper and pen from a drawer next to the pantry, then held the pen aloft, at the ready. "Okay, go."

"Frankincense and jasmine for increased intuition."

She scribbled these as Ben considered what else they needed.

"Crystals for focus. Probably citrine and carnelian are best."

Shelly nodded, though she couldn't even remember what a carnelian crystal looked like.

"Rosemary for focus, as well, and marjoram and poppy seed for awareness." Ben's tongue protruded slightly, something he'd done his whole life when he was concentrating. She hid her smile. "And, I think we'll be okay with just a white candle," he said, nodding as though completing some internal debate with himself. "That's it."

"Okay," Shelly agreed and handed him the list. "What do we need to buy?"

Ben's eyes bounced between the list and various points in the kitchen, no doubt visualizing where specific ingredients resided. "The crystals, frankincense, and jasmine."

"Time for a visit to the apothecary," she sang out.

Ben matched Shelly's smile. He loved her grandparents almost as much as she did, and they'd been the proud owners of the Wildcrest Wizardry apothecary for decades. "Time for a field trip," he agreed.

CHAPTER SIX

BEN

Spring in the desert varied little. Today, the sun shone in the cloudless afternoon sky, though the temperature was mid-60s. And it completely matched Ben's positive mood. Spending time with Shelly always brightened his day. He was glad they were able to get together more days than not, even with his busy hospital schedule.

By turning his head, he could see the top of hers as she walked beside him along the path to the apothecary. He resisted the urge to wrap his arm around her shoulder when she shivered.

"Are you cold? Do you want my jacket?"

Her head tilted up to meet his gaze and she smiled

crookedly. "And have it reach my knees?" She looked ahead again. "It's not that far of a walk."

"If you're sure."

"I am." She pointed toward the rocks off the side of the concrete sidewalk. "Did you see him?"

Ben peered but must have been too late. "See whom?"

She hurried a few steps ahead and looked down at the rocks, hands on her hips as she bent over a bit. "Aww, he must have gone back underground."

"Chipmunk?"

"I think so. They're so cute. I love that they live along this path."

Her infectious enthusiasm got to him. He couldn't count how many times they'd walked the half-mile to the apothecary on the sidewalk that ran alongside the wash, or dry creek for storm drainage, between his street and Wildcrest's small downtown. Yet, he knew that Shelly delighted in the desert wildlife – and occasional housecat – that they'd see.

"Thank you," she said.

"For what?" Ben asked, still searching for the chipmunk that undoubtedly had gone underground as she surmised.

"For helping me get Ethan back. I know you've never really liked him."

His neck flushed at her words. He thought he did a better job at hiding his feelings. He certainly hid other feelings well.

Her fingers touched Ben's arm. "I'm not trying to make you uncomfortable. I just… you know how much it means to me. You're a good friend."

Goosebumps rose along his arm where her fingers grazed. "Best friends," he responded, squelching the desire to pull her into his arms. Being relegated to the friend zone hurt, but the thought of losing her hurt more.

Shelly squeezed his hand, leaving it cold when she released. Was it his imagination that she held on longer than was necessary? Their eyes met for a long moment and then her steps quickened away from him.

His phone rang before he could hasten to catch her. She stopped when she heard him answer the phone. "Hey, Dr. Casey."

"Do you have a minute?" Dr. Casey Hayes asked.

"Of course," he answered eagerly. When the Chief of Staff of the hospital called, one made time; especially when one wanted to be promoted.

"I apologize for the delay in getting back to you, but I wanted to be the one to tell you." She exhaled audibly. "You should let Las Vegas know you're considering their offer."

"I'm not getting the Chief Resident position." He said it matter-of-factly to his boss, but frustration surged. He'd been certain this was his path, to stay with his family and friends.

Shelly's mouth twisted, matching Ben's.

"It's not set yet, but they're looking hard at another candidate," Dr. Hayes continued.

"Jason?"

"I'm not at liberty to say, but he would be a competitive candidate."

Ben could read between those bright lines. Dr. Jason Lawson, his fellow resident and pseudo-rival, was the front runner for the position he wanted. "I appreciate the call." Ben swallowed that sharp pang of disappointment and disconnected.

"That was Dr. Hayes?"

"Yep."

"Is she really giving the position to Jason?"

"Well, it's not her position to give," he reminded Shelly. "But, yeah, she told me to consider Vegas."

Shelly's eyes widened. "You're seriously considering leaving?"

He shrugged. "If I had a reason to stay…"

She rolled her eyes. "Oh, I don't know. Your parents. Your brothers. Your friends."

They resumed walking along the concrete path, the desert alive around them. Ben focused on the shrubs, birds, and lizards – tried to ignore that she didn't specifically list herself, but used the generic *friends* label. "We'll see," he finally told her.

As they exited the wash a few minutes later, the backside of the businesses on Main Street appeared before them.

Yes, their main drag was not-so-creatively named Main Street. Of course, that was decades ago, so you couldn't really fault the founders. Ben and Shelly came up behind the apothecary and walked between it and the grocery next door. Reaching the street, they turned to face the two-story beige stucco building. Actually, Shelly had informed him once that it was really taupe, not beige. Sounded good to him. All he knew was that it was stucco. In the desert, stucco abounded.

Wildcrest Wizardry catered mainly to tourists who wanted "spells" but those in the know could get real spell-casting ingredients – and a great latte. Or so said Shelly, who admitted she was addicted to them. The apothecary store was large and bright, with a sweet, gentle lavender scent, and very well-organized by types of ingredients and spell intentions.

It was mid-afternoon in March, so Ben didn't expect too many tourists. But there would be some, based on the tour bus parked out front. There were always a few people, hoping to get an inside scoop about the witches of Wildcrest.

Shelly reached the door before him and pulled it open, stepping aside so he could enter.

"Proof that chivalry isn't dead," he quipped as he stepped past her. Her laughter followed him in.

"Hey guys," a bubbly voice greeted them before the door could even whoosh closed.

"Hey Rebekah," Shelly responded, wrapping the tall blond store manager in a quick hug. "Are my grandparents here?"

"They're at the post office checking on a delayed delivery. You'll probably miss them."

Even though the post office was only across the street, it was a small-town post office, with only Miss Jerri working. And, like every small-town cliché, she loved to chat with her customers.

"That's okay, I'll be back this afternoon."

Before he could ask Shelly why she was returning later, she'd hurried down the candle and crystal aisle. With a slight wave at Rebekah, who'd returned to the cash register, Ben followed Shelly.

"What do you think of this one?"

The sparkle in her eyes told him she was teasing, but he ignored that and took the dragon candle from her with mock-solemnity. "Yes, yes," he intoned. "This is perfect."

Shelly giggled.

He replaced the candle on the shelf. "I think we're good in the candle department."

She pointed to several rows of shining crystals. "Do you see the citrine and carnelian crystals?"

He watched her eyes scan the various crystals on display. Her mouth turned down at the sides for a moment as she searched. Ben wondered if she was thinking about how she struggled with crystal-based spells too.

"Here's a citrine," she said, handing him the yellow quartz before returning to consider the sparkling crystals.

He reached forward with his other hand, but she beat him to the stone he had just spotted.

"That's what a carnelian crystal looks like!" She gently lifted the palm-sized red-orange stone off the shelf, then turned the stone around.

"That's a beautiful choice," he said, his gaze on Shelly instead of the glassy, translucent crystal.

"It feels warm." She sounded surprised.

Her comment surprised him too, though really it shouldn't have. "Just because you have challenges controlling your abilities doesn't mean you don't have any," Ben reminded her. Shelly's look of gratitude elicited a flash of sadness for his best friend. Being a witch defined them. To be without that connection to their identity – he couldn't imagine.

They heard the sound of rubber soles behind them and then a hesitant question. "Excuse me?"

Ben turned toward the voice and found a middle-aged couple wearing matching outfits. Being completely honest, he liked tourists for their money, but also because they were fun to play with. Ben imagined it was like his familiar Cookie playing with a mouse. On second thought, that was kind of violent.

"Do you live here?" The female half of the couple looked between Ben and Shelly, trying to answer her own question. He returned the favor, inwardly chuckling at their yellow fanny packs and wide-brimmed floppy hats.

"We do," Shelly answered. "Can we help you?"

"Brian and I took the tour this morning," the woman continued. She, of course, referred to the bus tour that hit all the locations from *Witches in the Wild.* "This was the final stop, and they said you could get supplies for real spells here." On the word spells, her eyes widened, as if she couldn't quite believe what she was saying.

"You can," Shelly assured her, without a hint of irony. "That's what we're doing."

"No, you're not," the man disagreed. His stance, with hands jammed in the pockets of his cargo shorts, suggested the tour had not been his idea.

"Didn't you know that movie was basically a documentary? As in nonfiction," Ben told them. The woman's intake of breath confirmed for Ben she wanted to believe, but the man's expression soured.

"That isn't nice, making fun of the tourists," he said in a huff.

"Oh, Brian, they're not making fun of us."

Ben felt bad hearing the sincerity in her voice, and decided to try complete truth. "We're really not. Though I was joking about the movie," he amended his statement. "But witches do live here. It's just that nobody believes us."

Shelly shrugged when the couple looked at her for confirmation. "It's true."

"That's so neat," the woman said in a soft voice.

Her husband shook his head. "They're playing you, Jean."

Shelly placed a hand on Jean's shoulder. "I promise we're not." She leaned to whisper into the older woman's ear. Jean nodded along with whatever she was saying.

"Thank you so much," Jean enthused. "I'll try that." She pulled her husband toward an aisle with various dried herbs.

Ben narrowed his eyes at Shelly. "What did you tell her?"

"I just made a few suggestions for some herbs that could help improve his mood." She poked him in the chest. "And you know, since she doesn't have any actual power, that at worst, nothing will happen." She grinned. "But at best, the placebo effect will give them a lovely evening."

"Come on, Shelly," he said with his own small smile, before following the couple into the herb aisle.

Shelly quickly located the frankincense and jasmine, on the other end from where the tourists were peering at the choices. They exclaimed quietly to themselves after searching the internet on their smart phone. Ben assumed they were researching the magical properties of the items. He smothered a wider grin. Shelly was right. Let them have their fun. It was sweet of her to try to help.

Jean gave Shelly a little wave as the couple departed the aisle, the tourist clutching a handful of wide, flat beans.

Vanilla for love and as an aphrodisiac, if Ben had to guess. He wondered if he should grab some for him and Shelly. The impish thought arose before he could squash it. His mood instantly soured. If they brought any home, it would be for Shelly and Ethan, not him and Shelly, he had to remind himself.

CHAPTER SEVEN

SHELLY

On the walk back to the house, Ben was uncharacteristically quiet. At first, Shelly didn't realize he was providing monosyllabic answers, since she wasn't too talkative either, thinking about him leaving. It was different when they both left for college; they were on an adventure, together but apart. This time, the sense of loss… and he hadn't even left yet. It saddened her that she wouldn't see him all the time, and she wondered if that could be how he was feeling. "Is everything okay?"

"Of course."

"Are you sure?"

"Why wouldn't it be?"

"You've been quiet."

"I'm not allowed to be quiet?"

The guilty look on Ben's face following the comment suggested she must have looked wounded. And, indeed, his retort stung. She was only checking in with him, not criticizing. "You know you are," she said.

A desert rabbit caught her eye and she watched it start to hop away, then pause when it realized she and Ben were only about ten feet from it. Shelly halted; Ben walked another couple of steps before catching on and stepping back to her.

Shelly loved that her community had built itself around the desert like that, instead of bulldozing it all down for construction. The small wildlife flourished in these pockets of desert, especially the brown desert cottontails with the long ears. And the ears on the one they watched stood up straight, seeming a third the size of its narrow body. The rabbit eyed them, its white whiskers twitching. She wondered if it was deciding which was the bigger threat — the two of them on the sidewalk path, or the homes that lined the wash? In a dash, it raced away and disappeared, probably into an underground burrow among the rocks and shrubs.

"Sorry if I snapped at you," Ben said.

"Did something happen that I missed?"

A small sigh sounded. "Must be the tourists."

"Must be," she agreed, though really, she didn't. Since

when did the tourists rattle Ben? Confusion flared brighter. Maybe it was just the call from the chief, she decided. Ben would tell her how he was feeling when he was ready, because that's what best friends did.

They rounded the corner from the wash sidewalk and headed the final distance to Ben's green stucco house. She took a single step up the short three-step concrete staircase, and stood to the side of the turquoise door so Ben could unlock it. He shifted the apothecary bags from his right to his left hand.

"Do you want me to get those?" she asked.

"No, I've got them." He fumbled with his keys in his right hand and they fell to the concrete floor.

Too quick for him to object, she leaned down and snatched the keys off the floor. "Guess you need my help after all," she sang out.

Ben was still chuckling when they entered the house and headed straight for the kitchen. Standing side by side, they emptied the bags and lined up their supplies next to the arrangement they'd made before leaving.

"Do we have everything?"

Ben's warm eyes met hers and he placed his hand over Shelly's on the counter, giving it a gentle squeeze. "We have everything," he assured her.

Whatever weirdness had happened on the apothecary trip seemed to have dissipated.

"What do we do, oh wise one?" she asked.

"I'll walk you through it," he answered, and got to work. He lit the end of a small bundle of sage and waved it before him, cleansing the space of any negative energy. He blew it out when finished and they both inhaled deeply of the pungent aroma.

"First, I'll set our candles up for the directions." He placed four white votive candles in a diamond before him, intoning the power of the North, East, South, and West as he did so. He lit the candles then blew out the match.

"Now, I'll place our crystals in the sacred space." He placed the citrine crystal first near the West candle. "For detailed focus." The carnelian crystal he placed opposite, closer to the East candle. "To increase visionary focus."

"Now I'll mix our herbs together in the pewter bowl. This will allow their energies and purpose to intermingle." He placed a small amount of rosemary in the bowl. "First, the final ingredient for improving focus."

"Next, we'll add the frankincense and jasmine to increase intuition of what is before Ethan." Ben's fingers nimbly grabbed a pinch of the first and a dash of the second.

Shelly wanted to joke that she knew how to do spells, they just didn't work right for her. But she didn't. She enjoyed listening to his voice. Besides, interrupting a witch's spell-casting could be disastrous – even more so than her own disastrous magic.

"Finally, we'll add the marjoram and poppy seed for

awareness, so that Ethan may become aware of that which is before him." He reached for a spice, his hand hesitating. She almost broke her silence then, watching his hand hover there for a moment, before passing the spice by, and selecting a different spice, marjoram maybe. Or was that the poppy? She frowned when she realized she wasn't sure which he'd grabbed. Unusual for Ben to almost make a mistake like that. She started to ask what happened, but he was continuing the spell.

"Together, we'll focus on Ethan to receive that which we are sending. We ask you, Earth Mother, to show him a vision, to hear the unheard, help him learn what is before him, and give him the awareness to recognize its presence." Ben lit a match and set the concoction in the pewter bowl on fire. A crisp, woodsy aroma rose with flame as the herbs charred. He closed his eyes. "So mote it be." His eyes opened at the same time the fire extinguished.

"So mote it be," Shelly echoed, inhaling the lovely scent with its hint of sweetness.

Was that her imagination, or did a tingle race through her body?

Ben blew out the candles from West to South, at each one repeating, "We visualize the spark of the spell."

"Visualize Ethan and what you want him to see and understand," he instructed her.

She closed her eyes, surprised when she saw Ben's face instead of Ethan's. Mumbling under her breath, she asked the Earth Mother to show Ethan what she saw for him. A future with her. Shelly's eyes opened.

"Done," Ben concluded.

"Awesome, thank you."

"You're welcome," he said, meeting her gaze with an undefined look in his eyes.

"What's with the funny look?"

"I'm funny looking?"

"Seriously."

"Thinking about work, is all."

"Hmm, okay." She didn't push. He'd tell her about it when he was ready, though she wondered briefly if that was related to what happened after the apothecary visit, too. She checked her watch and gasped. "Is that the time? Ugh, I'm going to be late meeting Laura."

"Laura Harkin? I thought she didn't like you."

"She doesn't. I guess I'm that good," Shelly said with a big fake grin. "She wants me to redesign the coven's website."

"And you don't want to do it?"

She nibbled on her lower lip. "I'm reluctant to do it."

Ben chuckled.

"She doesn't like me," Shelly repeated his words. "Why would I want to work with someone who doesn't like me?"

"Why did you accept the job?"

"She's the head of IT for the coven's business, and I like the coven?"

"I'm sure that was part of it," he agreed.

"I need the work," she admitted.

"Is there a reason you can't do the job?"

"Nope." She knew where he was going, since this was the same process he used to help his medical students move through challenges.

"Then commit to doing the work," he said with a grin.

She gave a mock salute. "Yes, sir."

"Have fun. Check in with you later."

Shelly hugged Ben goodbye, his muscles hard underneath the medical school t-shirt. He must be working out more. She practically skipped to the car, excited to get through her meeting with Laura so she could be home when the spell opened Ethan's eyes and he saw what was right in front of him.

CHAPTER EIGHT

BEN

Ben watched Shelly slide into the driver's seat of her bright orange VW bug. She'd bought that neon monstrosity five years ago because it'd been on sale and looked lonely on the car dealership lot. A smile crossed Ben's face at the memory and he closed his front door.

Walking to the kitchen, his body betrayed him, teasing him with the lingering feel of Shelly against him in that final hug before she left. *What was I doing?*

Ben knew exactly what he was doing. A guilty flush crept up the back of his neck. His hand grabbed the spices off the countertop. Shelly had almost questioned him during the spell casting. He could see it in her eyes when he'd hesitated in selecting the next ingredient in the spell. She knew he didn't make mistakes like that.

But it hadn't been an almost-mistake.

"What are you doing, little brother?"

The deep baritone startled Ben. "Noah, what are you doing here?"

Noah Wright, Ben's big brother, was basically an older version of him. Their father's genes were clearly dominant. Noah offered a wide smile. "Left a document in my bedroom that I need for a meeting later." He gestured toward the front door. "Was that Shelly I saw leaving?"

"You know it was."

"I'd recognize that car anywhere." Noah opened the refrigerator. "Since I'm here, figured I'd have a quick snack. What were you two up to?"

"Now why would you think we were up to anything?"

Noah's eyes scanned the spices still on the counter. "That sure looks like a spell was being cast."

"You would not be wrong."

Noah laughed. "What did Shelly rope you into now? I heard about Ethan ending up in Emergency."

"Of course, you did." Ben replaced another ingredient in the cabinet. "Ethan broke up with Shelly last night." Ben hadn't meant to tell Noah, it just slipped out.

"I assume you immediately told her how you feel."

Ben's jaw fell open and the brothers' eyes met.

"Little brother, everyone in this family knows you've

got it bad for Shelly. You always have." He said this with ease, knife sliding through the apple on the plate before him.

"But, I never—"

"You don't have to."

Hopelessness surged, as he considered the implications of his feelings being so obvious to everyone but Shelly. "If all of you can see it, why can't she?"

"That would be too easy, right?"

Ben chuckled. "Yeah, I suppose."

"Am I to assume by your response that you didn't tell Shelly?"

Ben broke eye contact, gathered the remaining spices to put away. "The timing wasn't right."

"Why not?"

"Shelly has a plan."

"I'm sure she does." A slight scrape sounded and Ben turned to see Noah sliding onto a stool, preparing to eat the sliced apple and peanut butter before him, a smile playing on his lips.

"That's what we were doing. Casting a spell to get Ethan back."

"I know you aren't reckless enough to cast a love spell."

"Shelly's plan is to nudge Ethan back in her direction."

"That seems like something she would do. How'd you get dragged into it?"

"She asked." Ben sat on the stool next to Noah.

"You're helping her try to win back her ex?" He quirked an eyebrow. "I know Ethan's a nice enough guy, but they have zero chemistry. Please tell me you have another, secret plan that doesn't involve just waiting for her to come to her senses."

That flush creeping up Ben's neck increased. "Okay, that was my original plan."

Noah's laugh boomed around the kitchen.

"But I thought of a… different plan."

"Do tell."

"I realized while casting this afternoon's spell – to help him see what's right in front of him, by the way."

Noah snorted. "That's ironic."

"Anyway. I realized that my superior witch skills—"

"If you do say so yourself."

"—could come in handy," Ben continued, ignoring the interruption.

"How so?"

"I can cause her spells to backfire."

"And send Ethan to Emergency again? This doesn't seem like the wisest approach."

"No, no, not enough to hurt him. Of course not." Ben glared half-heartedly at his brother. "You can't honestly believe I'd do that."

Noah held up his hand. "I'm just teasing. Go on."

"I could cause the spells to go just enough wrong to be unsuccessful. Instead of doing X, it'll do Y. Though maybe not that precise. Similar to what happened when Shelly's spell did the opposite," Ben continued, thinking aloud about how to make the plan work.

Noah eyed Ben.

"What?"

"That's why you're red-faced. Feeling guilty that you're lying to the woman you claim to have feelings for."

"What? No!" The look of trust on Shelly's face flashed in his mind. Yeah, Noah was right. Not that Ben would admit that to him. "This is all for the greater good."

"You don't have to defend yourself to me, little brother. I think it's hysterical."

"So glad you're enjoying yourself."

"Thanks." Noah's smile slipped a fraction. "Just be careful."

"I am," Ben said with confidence, though felt shakier inside.

"If this goes sideways, I predict it will do so spectacularly."

"I told you, I won't do anything to harm Shelly. Or Ethan."

"That isn't what I mean."

"Yeah, I know."

CHAPTER NINE

SHELLY

Wildcrest Wizardry was both the apothecary and the best place in town to get coffee. Shelly loved the small coffee bar at the rear of the store. Not that she was biased at all, given that her Nana and Papaw owned it. She ran a hand along the top of the wood table before taking a sip of her latte. Her eyes kept straying to the door to the apothecary, making her unsure if choosing a seat with a direct sightline from the chair through the shop was the best choice.

"You need anything else, sweetie," a soft voice said at her ear before the owner came into view from behind her.

She smiled. "No thanks, Nana. I'm just waiting for a client."

Nana tilted her head, a lock of her short black hair falling over her eye. She swept it back. Shelly's neutral comment must have been said with an edge. Nana's purple eyes narrowed – a family trait that somehow missed Shelly's generation – and she frowned. "What client?"

"You'll see in about five minutes."

Nana set a blueberry muffin in front of her granddaughter. "To tide you over." With that, she returned to the counter, moving with the grace of a former athlete, which she was. And without magical enhancement. She was short and thin, like Shelly's mother, but had the wiry muscles of a runner. She still started every day with a two-mile walk before joining her husband and their store manager, Rebekah, to open the store and coffeeshop.

The air around her stilled and Shelly stifled a sigh. She might have misfiring magic, but even if she hadn't seen Laura, her finely attuned magical senses told her the redhead had arrived. Head held high, almost-genuine smile on her face, she stood to face her nemesis. Um, client.

"Shelly! So good to see you. Thank you for meeting me." Laura Harkin, probably six feet tall, short red hair slicked back, undoubtedly like some celebrity with whom Shelly was not familiar, and dressed in what certainly seemed to be an expensive fitted black sweater dress. Shelly wondered if Laura drove to Vegas to shop or if she was confident enough to buy online. Her magic gifted her the ability to manipulate matter in small amounts. Maybe she could reshape anything she bought to fit?

Shelly extended a hand which Laura gripped. "Of course. Always happy to meet with a potential new client." They sat across from each other, Laura placing her large handbag on the hand-carved wooden table between them. She rummaged within, pulling out her laptop and a pile of papers. Shelly recognized the initial ideas she'd emailed Laura.

Laura stared at Shelly, unblinking and unsmiling.

Audibly swallowing, Shelly wondered if that was a glint of satisfaction in the client's eyes, before chastising herself that Laura wasn't out to get her. She needed to bring it down a notch.

"Tell me about your ideas for the website," Laura demanded, pushing the pile of papers closer.

With a deep breath, Shelly jumped in. The designs for the coven website were fantastic, if she did say so herself. To the uninitiated, literally, it would just look like a Wiccan social club. And it certainly had aspects of one. But the initiated would have access to more magical coven business. Shelly had always found it amusing how the non-magical citizens in town knew, but didn't really know, they were surrounded by witches. Wildcrest was unofficially the country's most supernatural town. But not everybody believed, despite the movie and the Las Vegas resolution. They just enjoyed the money the tourists brought.

Laura nodded throughout the presentation. Shelly

found herself feeling hopeful that it wouldn't be as bad as she'd feared, trying to work with her frenemy (*did people still say that anymore?*) Then Laura opened her mouth.

"Generally, I like it. Just a few tweaks and it'll be there." She smiled, her cool blue eyes appraising. Like a shark.

And with that, the gloves came off. Shelly had never heard so many ridiculous demands. Laura wanted the colors changed a smidge on every page, every font choice. The photos were good, but not quite what she wanted, so she wanted all of them replaced. By the time she got to her complaints about the *Contact Us* form on one of the final pages, Shelly was ready to pull her hair out at the roots. Or Laura's. Didn't really matter.

But Shelly didn't. She even kept herself from sighing throughout the three-hour meeting. Yep. Three excruciating hours of being told that every single thing about the new coven website would need to be tweaked. She might have told Laura to shove it, and kept the money already paid for the initial concept pages, but she had friends in the coven. And they were ultimately paying Shelly an insane amount of money for this redesign. Beggars couldn't be choosers when a business was struggling. But Shelly thought she finally figured out why Laura hired her in the first place.

"You hired me just so you could torture me, didn't you?" Laura's eyes bugged at Shelly's question, and Shelly could have sworn she heard someone coughing to cover up laughter behind her at the counter. Her mouth dropped open to take back the question.

Laura recovered faster. "Why would you think that?"

She backpedaled. "Apologies. I misspoke. I'm still surprised you wanted to hire me for the job." Shelly couldn't believe how upfront she was being. "We weren't exactly friends in high school." Not that she'd ever really understood why Laura picked on her; she just knew the woman had done so for years.

Laura arched an eyebrow. "High school was over a decade ago. Some of us have moved on."

Shelly's face flushed.

Laura sighed. "You're the best in town," she said, her mouth twisting like she'd tasted something sour, "and the coven board of directors wanted to hire someone local."

"Of course." That explained the hire. And the attitude. But she'd need to be more careful. She couldn't just express how she was feeling like that, and risk crossing a line the coven board couldn't pull her back over from.

Laura snatched at the scattered pages remaining. "I think that's enough for today."

"I would agree, since we went over every page of the website."

Laura's blue eyes narrowed. "Sarcasm, really?"

"Of course not. Just clarifying why we were finished." Shelly offered an almost sincere smile.

Laura stood, towering in her stiletto boots, even after

Shelly scrambled to stand beside her. "I'll expect the redesigns tomorrow."

A response died on Shelly's lips. Her mind swirled with objections, but nothing she could say in polite company.

"You can accommodate, right? I'd hate to have to report back to the board that you can't." She smiled without showing teeth. "The initial designs are fine; you're just tweaking."

Shelly swallowed back an angry retort and went with sickly sweet. "That's absolutely no problem at all, Laura. Meet you back here tomorrow, same time?"

With a regal nod, Laura spun on her heels and strode away from the table.

Shelly reconsidered that Laura truly hated her. How could she possibly get the redesign done by tomorrow afternoon?

CHAPTER TEN

BEN

"When's the last time you two ate here?" Ben asked his parents and gestured at the trays on the plastic table. "Hospital food is not usually what people choose for lunch if they don't have to."

"Couldn't really say." Ben's father, Elijah, boomed out the statement. He didn't have an indoor voice. His patrician good looks drew attention anyway, but when he opened his mouth…

"That's not why we're here, of course," Ben's mother, Esther, added. Her long brown hair was done up in an elaborate hairdo – a French braid, he believed Shelly had explained once – with teal ribbons wound throughout. She wore no makeup, but her sparkling brown eyes and smooth skin didn't need enhancement, or so Shelly had also explained to him. These were his parents. He didn't pay attention to such things.

"You guys asked for this meeting." Ben lifted his eyebrows to prompt them to explain themselves. Not that he didn't enjoy spending time with his parents, especially for a break mid-hospital shift like this, but he hadn't gotten the impression this was purely a social call.

"You're spellcasting with Shelly to help her win Ethan back."

Ben sighed in the face of his father's statement. There was no point in asking how he knew. He was the High Priest of their coven, and that meant more than just leading the coven and its rituals. Ben didn't think his father could sense the energy from today's spell, but nothing happened in the coven that Elijah somehow wasn't aware of. "How do you know what the spell was for?" Ben asked instead as the question occurred to him. His parents exchanged a glance. "Noah."

"Noah," Elijah confirmed.

"He's just worried about you," Esther said and patted Ben's hand.

"Don't worry, I'm not angry at him. I know he means well." Didn't mean Ben wouldn't give Noah a piece of his mind later. Ben's phone buzzed. A number with a Vegas area code. He let it go to voicemail.

"Something the matter?"

"No," he answered his father slowly. "I've been approached by a hospital in Las Vegas to be their chief resident."

Esther looked stricken. "You're going to leave again?"

"I told them I'm considering their offer."

"I thought you got all that out of your system with college."

"Dad, it's not about getting stuff out of my system," Ben said.

"What about here?"

"I've been unofficially told that's off the table," Ben answered his mother's question. Esther and Elijah appeared nonplussed by that news. "Just wish me good luck. I haven't made a decision yet."

"Good luck," they dutifully replied in unison.

Ben's phone dinged an incoming text message. Shelly. "Excuse me a moment." He swiped the screen to read the full message.

"Everything okay?" Esther asked.

Ben laughed. "She just had a meeting with Laura Harkin. That went about as well as she'd expected."

His mother's eyebrows furrowed. "What happened? We asked Laura to hire Shelly for the website redesign." Esther Wright was the Chief Financial Officer of Wildcrest Witches International. Their witches' coven was incorporated, with employees and everything, so they could sell products through the apothecary and online. As CFO, Esther would have had a direct say in who Laura hired for the job. After all, while Laura was responsible for IT, at the end of the day, she answered to Esther.

"Laura has never much liked Shelly, for some reason. Since high school."

Ben's parents exchanged another glance, though this one he couldn't read. They'd been married long enough they spoke to each other through their eyes. He didn't think they were actually psychic though.

"What happened?" Elijah asked.

Ben relayed what the text said about Laura wanting changes to everything and the deadline for tomorrow afternoon.

His mother pursed her lips. "I'm sure Shelly can meet the deadline, but maybe—"

"I know you mean well," Ben interrupted, "but I don't think Shelly would appreciate if you intervened."

She laughed, a higher pitch than people usually expected. "She's a strong-willed one, that woman. And like a laser in her focus."

"That she is," Ben agreed. "Listen, I appreciate that the two of you are concerned about this, but you know me. Would I engage in irresponsible magic?"

An expression of surprise flashed on his father's face.

"What?" Ben asked. "Isn't that what this meeting is about? You want to caution me against using magic to help

Shelly win back Ethan." The table shook and he wondered if his mother just kicked his father to stay quiet. But he had no idea why she would do that. She spoke before he could ask.

"That's exactly why we asked you here," Esther agreed. Her hands wrapped around Ben's. "Just be careful, dear."

"Of course. Always."

Satisfied they'd gotten their point across, Elijah switched topics. Apparently, Shelly's grandparents were having trouble getting some rarer spell ingredients for the apothecary. Ben accepted the topic change, but felt off balance. He didn't know why else they would have called the meeting, if not to talk about maintaining responsibility with his magic.

CHAPTER ELEVEN

SHELLY

Ugh, this evening was so awkward. Shelly had been home for several hours working on the website changes Laura had requested. Shelly had purposefully sat at the apartment's dining room table instead of worked in hers and Ethan's shared office, and waited for him to come out of the guest bedroom. Her heart constricted at that thought. While she'd been out, he moved enough of his stuff to live out of the guest room these final days. But he hadn't come out of the bedroom. Not in hours. And there was an attached bathroom, so even that conspired against her.

A quick series of high-pitched barks drew Shelly's attention. Her fox familiar had been sitting at her feet.

Now she stood, staring in the direction of Ethan's room, the mask of dark fur around her eyes highlighting the image of her on alert. "What is it, Rose?"

Shelly couldn't read the fox's mind exactly, but they communicated through images and… well, magic. Rose was unhappy with whatever was happening behind the closed door.

"Should I go check on him?"

Rose tilted her head. If she could have rolled her eyes, she probably would have, her expression was so human-like. According to Shelly's father, her great-great-grandmother Rosalie, whose spirit had been reborn as the fox familiar, had been known in the family as a smart-aleck.

Heat suffused Shelly. Oh. Something was wrong. It couldn't be the spell. Ben had cast it and he never made spell mistakes.

Rose barked and stalked toward Ethan's door, her nearly-feline movements sleek and her body low to the ground. Shelly followed the fox, feet silent against the carpet. She put an ear to his door, but heard nothing. What had Rose so spooked? She was sensitive to cast magic, so the spell must be doing something.

Shelly tapped the tips of her fingers on the door. "Ethan?"

"I'm resting."

"Is everything okay?"

Silence.

She debated whether to knock again. Ethan's responses definitely weren't encouraging. Rose barked a third time. The fox even bared her thin, sharp teeth in displeasure. A squeak behind the door suggested movement on the guest bed.

The door cracked open. A bloodshot blue eye stared out.

"Is everything okay?" Shelly asked.

A barely perceptible grunt and Ethan opened the door the rest of the way. His pupils seemed off somehow. He blinked several times in quick succession. "Is everything okay?" he echoed. "That's a good question."

"It is?"

Ethan stepped past the two and headed toward the front of the apartment. Shelly followed mutely behind. He crumpled into one of the dining room table chairs, legs splayed, and dropped his head into his hands. She stared at the top of his blond head, then took the seat opposite him, closed her laptop so she could see him better, and waited. His muscles rippled under the black shirt he wore over khaki shorts as he inhaled deeply several times. He abruptly sat up and faced her.

"Ethan?"

"What do you see?"

Was that a trick question? "Um, I don't understand."

He ran a hand through his hair, gave his head a shake. He stared at her, unblinking. "Do my eyes look normal?"

"They seem a little bloodshot," she admitted.

He nodded.

"Are they bothering you?"

"Not exactly."

"Ethan, what is going on?"

Her stern tone did the trick and he answered. "I have tunnel-vision."

"Metaphorically or physically?" Was he seeing what was right in front of him? Just like the spell was supposed to show him. She squashed down a premature sense of happiness. It hadn't happened yet.

He looked at her askance.

She guessed it still wasn't happening. "Hey, that's a legitimate question."

He blinked rapid-fire several times again. "My vision has physically reduced down to tunnel vision. I can see what's directly in front of me, but my peripheral vision has vanished."

Oh no. A wave of nausea rolled through her. His words were almost word-for-word what the spell was supposed to do. But that wasn't the outcome she wanted. At. All.

Ethan looked at her, confusion on his face. "What should I do?"

"Um," she stalled. "Let me call Ben and see what he thinks."

The suggestion was actually pretty brilliant. As both a doctor and the spellcasting witch, he should be able to explain what was going on. And whether or not Ethan would need to visit the emergency room again.

CHAPTER TWELVE

BEN

The lift Ben felt when he saw Shelly's name on the caller ID vanished when she started speaking. He murmured in all the right places while she told her tale of woe. But he should have felt good. That was what he wanted. The spells to keep misfiring. At least he'd assured her that Ethan didn't need to go to the hospital. He knew that the tunnel-vision interpretation of the seeing-what's-right-in-front-of-you spell would be gone by morning.

"A whole day wasted," Shelly's voice said, loud in his ear. He removed the phone from the side of his head, considered the likelihood of being overheard in the janitor's closet, and put Shelly on speaker while he hopped into the small room and closed the door behind him in one fluid gesture.

"I wouldn't call the day wasted," he contradicted.

"Why not?" Shelly asked the question in a small voice.

His guilt flared. How could he answer? It wasn't wasted for him. "No, you're right. I'm just distracted by paperwork." The lie rolled easily off his tongue and the guilt turned to mortification. Was that what he was turning into? He never lied to Shelly before this week. Would the ends justify the means?

"Is now not a good time?"

"I always have time for you," he assured her. "You have my full attention."

"Thanks, Ben, I know you're always there for me."

He heard the smile in her voice and one formed on his face in response.

"But I just don't understand what happened. You did the spell, not me. This never happens to you."

"True," he agreed, for lack of anything else to say.

Shelly gasped and Ben bolted up from the sturdy white basket he'd been sitting on. The velocity of that motion caused him to bump his shoulder into a row of brooms and mops hanging on the wall. The "what?" in response to Shelly's gasp was drowned out by the cascading of those brooms and mops onto him in the small room.

"Ben, are you okay?"

He heard Shelly's question from the phone thankfully

still clutched in his hand and he brought it to his mouth. "I, um, might have made a tiny mess. I'm gonna put you on a shelf while I pick the mops and brooms up."

"You're gonna what... while you what...?" Now she laughed, full-bodied and genuine. "Thank you, I needed that."

"My clumsiness?" He hung a flat mop, sponge mop, and dust mop back on the wall, marveling that there could be so many varieties. "So glad I could entertain you."

She snorted.

Ben stilled. "Why did you gasp?"

"Right! Is it possible that my own misfiring magic somehow... infected yours?"

"No, I don't think."

"But it's possible."

"Anything is possible."

Shelly laughed. "We can always rely on my mother for a pithy saying."

"She's not wrong." Grace loved that particular phrase; if she had a catchphrase, that would be it.

"No, she's not," Shelly agreed. "Do you think it's possible?"

He hesitated, hand resting on the final dustpan.

"Ben?"

"I don't know if something like that is possible," he answered as honestly as he could, given the huge lie that started the mess. A bark sounded in Shelly's background.

"What does Rose say?" And could Rose sense his lying? Shelly's familiar seemed even more sensitive to the use of magic than Shelly herself.

"She's not sure."

Relief washed over Ben, followed by guilt that he felt relief. This was already ridiculous and they still had the rest of the week. "What's the plan?"

"After today's wasted day," she repeated and Ben let slide, "I'm no closer to convincing Ethan to stay with me. I still have Wednesday and Thursday. Maybe Friday morning, depending on when he's leaving."

She sounded so matter-of-fact, like this was a project with boxes she needed to check. He considered saying that and decided it didn't matter. In three days, this would be over, one way or another.

"The plan, then," she continued, "is to cast two more spells. Any ideas?"

"Let me think on it. Tonight's shift isn't quite as long. Meet at my place tomorrow morning around 10?"

"Are you sure I should be there? In case I'm right that my presence is interfering?"

He hung his head for a moment at her words, then recovered. "Not at all. We'll be especially careful tomorrow to counter any interference. I promise." The words nearly caught in his throat.

"Sounds great. Thank you so much, Ben. You're an awesome friend."

The call ended and he plopped back on the overturned white bucket. To be in the friend zone was bad enough, but what kind of awesome friend let someone he cared for take the blame for his actions? Ben cradled the phone, thoughts waging war in his head. It hadn't occurred to him that she would blame herself for his spells going awry. Making her feel bad hadn't been part of the plan. He was happy that Shelly was happy they were still going forward with the second chance of a spell. But the guilt threatened to overwhelm him.

This was all a lie. Even with the justification that it was for the greater good of helping Shelly realize she had feelings for him, what would happen if she found out before that?

He left the closet and resumed his shift. Those thoughts weren't helpful. He was in it until the bitter end. Now, he just needed to come up with another modifiable spell to misfire without sending Ethan into Shelly's arms, or the emergency department.

CHAPTER THIRTEEN

SHELLY

Shelly's eyes closed and she inhaled the rich scent of her mocha latte. The warmth through the cup almost too hot on her hands. Such pleasant sensa—

"Are you going to drink that thing or make love to it?"

Ben's voice cut through her reverie about coffee, and her eyes flew open at his word choice. "I'm totally going to make love to it."

The tips of his ears turning pink confirmed her zinger hit home. Of course, the flush she felt was a bit more unexpected.

"Do you know what spell you want to do?" He asked the question and turned toward the refrigerator. She watched him move a bunch of items around, but withdraw nothing. Curious.

"I don't know," she said slowly. "Maybe I should try a love spell after all."

That did the trick. Ben spun around, eyes wide. "Not a chance."

Laughter bubbled out. "I'm just teasing you."

"Do you want my help?" Ben leaned forward on the island.

"I do," she assured him, immediately contrite. "I was just trying to break whatever spell had you stuck in the open door of the fridge, rearranging stuff."

"Gee, thanks."

"What are friends for?"

"So, in all seriousness…"

"I had an idea for a spell," she finally answered his earlier question. "But, I'm not sure about it."

"What could possibly go wrong?"

"After sending Ethan to the emergency room, unable to breathe, and then causing his vision to narrow to pinpricks? Well, I don't know." She smirked.

"Let's hear it, then."

"What's happened so far," she started to recap instead. "My first spell was hit by my misfiring magic and we got the opposite. Trying to enhance feelings of wellbeing with saffron resulted in the opposite physical reaction. Trying to figuratively open his eyes to see what was right in front of him resulted in the loss of his peripheral vision for the day." She winced.

"What's wrong?" Ben interrupted her recap.

Tears filled her eyes. "I'm doing this to help Ethan realize his feelings for me before it's too late, but you should have seen him yesterday, Ben." She wiped the lone tear that broke free. "He was so scared and confused last night."

Ben came around the side of the island and gathered her into a hug. "It's going to be okay. This will work."

She wrapped her arms around his broad shoulders, accepting the offered comfort. The familiar sweet yet woody scent of his sandalwood shower gel wafted over her, increasing her sense of belonging. She leaned into the hug, tightening her grip on his shirt. A desire to kiss Ben flared.

What?!

She drew back with a shaky laugh, eyes on her latte. Suddenly, Ben's nearness provided an entirely different kind of warmth.

"Shelly?" His fingers burned her chin where they gently lifted her face so her eyes met his hooded ones. "What's wrong?"

"I…"

His fingers caressed her cheek. He leaned in. Her lips parted for the expected kiss. Disappointment surged when she felt a delicate kiss on her forehead.

Ben stepped back. He gave her the crooked smile that she loved. "We should get back to work."

"Work?"

"On the spell?"

"Right!" She had a goal. These odd feelings wouldn't interfere with that. She wouldn't let them. Would she? Should she? This was …confusing… but probably connected to all the misfiring magic flying around. If she stayed focused, she'd regain what was lost. That finally got her derailed thoughts back on track, so to speak. A wide smile split her face, confusing emotions and physical reactions placed firmly on the back burner. "My thought was to cast a spell to help Ethan regain what was lost. Me."

"Okay." Ben didn't look convinced. He sat on the stool next to her.

"We just need to work out the possible malfunctions to the spell and counter them ahead of time."

"Sure. What could go wrong?"

"Is that sarcasm?" Shelly asked with a laugh.

"Realism?"

Now they both laughed, the earlier awkwardness fading. "If the spell misfired like my original spell, then the opposite would be visited on Ethan."

"He'd lose what he has?" Ben asked.

"That's my guess."

"I'm imagining his car vanishing—"

"—his shoes disappearing off his feet—"

Ben gave a sly look. "Maybe he goes bald as he loses all his hair."

She doubled over with laughter, trying to catch her breath, the image of Ethan's luscious hair falling off his head. "This isn't a revenge spell."

"Maybe it should be."

"You'd never do that," she reminded her best friend.

He sighed. "No, I wouldn't."

"And if the spell misfired like the spell you cast to open his eyes to what's right in front of him, it would be taken literally."

"Lost items would be regained?"

"Yep. I envision every lost sock, key, mug magically appearing in the apartment by the end of the day." She snort-laughed.

"Depending on how careful Ethan has been over the years, your place could wind up looking like an episode of *Hoarders*."

"Oh, my goodness, that would be terrible indeed."

Ben belly laughed. "Even better – what if all his ex-girlfriends suddenly called, texted, emailed, or actually showed up." He widened his eyes in mock terror.

She playfully punched his arm. "Hey now, he and I have been dating for years. There better not be that many!"

"You never know how much of a player Ethan might have been in high school."

She frowned at the thought of her Greek god ex-boyfriend being a player.

"We're just joking around," Ben said.

"I know."

"Then why do you look like you sucked on a lemon?"

"Anyway, the point is we want to make sure we don't get something like either of these. Can you incorporate that into the spell?" She nibbled on her bottom lip.

"Yep. Not a problem. We're essentially doing a beacon spell, but narrowed in so that lost love is regained." He smirked. "And not other lost loves." Ben listed off the ingredients he needed, starting with the sage for cleansing and tobacco as an offering. "Lavender and passionflower for attracting love."

"Wait," she interrupted. "Isn't passionflower for friendship?"

"You are correct."

"Then?"

"Don't you want to be friends with your lover?"

"I didn't think about it that way." She stared at his back while he pulled his pewter set from the cabinet.

"That's what I'm here for." He flashed a quick smile. "And, finally, the dried rose petals."

As before, she had assembled the listed items on the island while he named them. Unlike before, just in case, she hovered over him watching closely.

"Shelly?"

"Yes, Ben," she answered, eyes still on the pewter bowl into which he'd begun depositing the ingredients.

"Look at me."

She did.

"Why are you hovering?"

"I'm being uber-careful."

"Are you now?"

She nodded.

"What exactly are you watching for? Not that I think it's what happened, but do you really think you'll be able to see your magic interfere with mine?" He quirked an eyebrow. He crushed the herbs together in the mortar, pressing and rotating the pestle to mix them completely.

"Point taken." She drank some lukewarm mocha latte.

He lit the mix on fire, intoning the spell under his breath. The fire extinguished with his final word, and he blew gently on the smoke, the commingled scent enveloping them for but a moment before lifting. "I'm finished anyway," he said with a dramatic sweep of his arm.

She giggled. "How come you aren't seeing anybody?" *Whoa, where did that come from?*

Ben's jaw dropped open.

In for a penny, in for a pound, as they said. "You're a great catch." And he was. She swallowed past the sudden lump in her throat.

Ben had an inscrutable expression on his face. "Guess the right woman hasn't seen me that way yet."

Her head tilted in confusion at his phrasing.

He winked.

Wait, was he *flirting* with her?

CHAPTER FOURTEEN

BEN

"I flirted with her, Nick. Flirted. And got bupkis." Ben continued trying to read the menu he held, but the words kept blurring. Good thing he didn't really need the menu. He and Nick were meeting for lunch in the local diner they'd eaten at a million times before.

The owner had renamed it Magic Eats after the movie exploded the town's popularity, but chose to keep the '50s décor, from the black-and-white checkerboard vinyl floor to the teal back-to-back booths along the front wall of windows.

"Tell me what happened."

He told Nick about leaning in, choosing not to kiss

Shelly on her delicious mouth at the last moment, and winking during his departure.

Nick chuckled. "You winked?"

The tips of Ben's ears felt warm. "Yeah."

"You definitely flirted."

"Thank you for agreeing with me."

"Just trying to understand the situation." Nick frowned. "But this was after you cast another spell on Ethan."

"It's not exactly *on* Ethan," Ben protested. "It's more *about* Ethan."

"To-ma-to, to-mah-to."

"The point is, I flirted with her and got no response."

"Maybe she needs to think about it?"

"What's there to think about? We almost kissed."

"But, you didn't."

"No, we didn't." Disappointment filled Ben. Again. "It's okay, though."

"It is?"

"This is all going according to plan." Ben's mood lifted when that realization hit. "No, she didn't respond. But the point was to help her see me as more than a friend over the course of this experiment. That's happening. By tomorrow, Friday at the latest, when Ethan is leaving, Shelly will realize she doesn't want him. Then I make my bold move."

A small cough reminded Ben that the two were out in public. He looked up at the waitress, an older woman with a bouffant hairdo who totally matched the diner's décor.

"Are you young men ready to order?"

"Yes, ma'am," Nick replied and ordered a Rueben sandwich on rye.

"And you?"

Ben ordered his usual pastrami with extra pickles on the side and they handed the waitress their menus. They looked at each other after she left.

Nick smirked. "I'm aware of that plan. Here's another way it goes down. She finds out you've been deliberately sabotaging the intention of the spells and never forgives you."

Ben's mouth went dry.

"You're playing with fire."

Ben fiddled with the napkin in his hands.

"You know what happens with most fires."

"People get burned. I know."

"Tell her the truth."

"What if I lose her friendship?"

"What if you gain her love?"

Ben's lips pulled down and he furrowed his eyebrows, before reminding Nick, "I flirted with her and got no response."

"That's the third time you've told me that. Are you sure you didn't get a response?"

The question stumped him. "She didn't say anything. She didn't kiss me."

"Neither did you."

"Hmm." He rewound the scene in his head and rewatched with an eye toward Shelly's body language. Did she lean into him a little bit? Was he correctly remembering that she closed her eyes? Did she want him to kiss her?

"And?"

"Well, dang. Now I'm not sure." Ben described what he thought he remembered seeing.

"You're so clueless. She wanted you to kiss her."

"You're certain?"

"As certain as I can be without being there to see it."

"That would be creepy."

Nick laughed. "You know what I mean."

"I do."

"What's the plan then?"

"I'm going to tell her how I feel." Mixed emotions swept through Ben at the decisive statement. The expected fear of losing Shelly, of course, but a growing ribbon of hope, too.

A single lifted eyebrow told him all he needed to know about Nick's confidence in his statement.

With renewed determination, Ben withdrew his cellphone and typed out a quick text to Shelly. *Dinner plans?*

Within seconds, her reply. *Wanna come over? Ethan's out tonight.*

See you at 7, he typed, then smiled at the phone when Shelly responded with a series of smiling emojis.

"That seems positive," Nick commented. Ben didn't look up in time to catch him, but wondered if he'd smirked when he said it.

"Dinner tonight at her place."

"You know what to do."

Ben nodded, unable to speak. After years of not knowing, tonight he would find out the truth. Either Shelly had feelings for him, or he was in the Friend Zone for life.

CHAPTER FIFTEEN

SHELLY

If Laura Harkin requested one more additional change, Shelly's moratorium on practicing magic was going to be rescinded. She did every single thing the woman had asked for, down to the minute detail, and here Laura was, criticizing all of it. Again. Shelly plastered a tight smile on her face.

"Anything else, Laura?"

Blue eyes narrowed in response.

Shelly guessed her tone wasn't as conciliatory as she'd hoped. "I want to make sure the coven is satisfied with the work." That, at least, was true. Laura might drive her batty, but her best friend's father was the High Priest and his mother the CFO of the business. Shelly wanted them to like it.

Laura's expression relaxed, ameliorated for the moment. She sighed. "Listen, Shelly, I'm not trying to be difficult."

An eyebrow raised of its own accord.

"I'm not," she insisted. She lifted a hand to get Rebekah's attention. The apothecary manager was acting as the coffee bar cashier today, apparently in addition to her regular duties. Despite the beautiful spring weather, there weren't many tourists here today.

"What can I get you?" the tall, bubbly blond asked when she reached the table.

"Mocha latte, right, Shelly?"

Surprised that Laura had paid attention to her prior order, Shelly simply nodded.

"And I'll take an espresso. Double shot, please."

Rebekah gave them a toothy smile and departed to make the drinks.

Laura moved as though to run a hand through her short red hair, then stopped herself. Probably didn't want to mess up that perfect style. "I know I'm demanding, but it needs to be done right." She lifted a single shoulder.

Shelly held her breath. The next statement better be just to work on this latest round of changes. Otherwise, she was going to be sorely tempted to say screw it to the huge paycheck, that struggling against Laura's increasingly impossible demands wasn't worth it.

"I think we're close."

Shelly's breath whooshed out at the statement.

"Did you know I hired your mother?"

"As a supernatural life coach?" Shelly asked in surprise.

"A little broader than that, but, yes."

"No, I didn't. She doesn't discuss her clients with me."

Laura nodded. "Of course, she wouldn't." A bright smile lit her face. "I love your mother."

"Um, me too?"

"She's been helping me understand myself more, to understand more the person I want to be. And be with."

Shelly had no idea why Laura would be telling her any of that.

"I can tell you're wondering why I'm telling you this."

Shelly's face warmed with a flush. The perils of having zero poker face. "To be honest, yeah."

"Grace and Robert have a love for the ages."

A genuine smile broke open on Shelly's face.

"High-school sweethearts who stayed true to each other, through ups and downs, trials and tribulations," Laura continued, almost like she was talking to herself. "Everyone should have that, you know?"

Shelly nodded, tears suddenly threatening to fill her eyes. "Yes, they should."

"They never gave up on true slove."

Rebekah approached the table with their drinks. Shelly appreciated the break. There was no reason for Laura to be talking like that, except maybe it was Shelly's reminder of what to focus on. Her reactions to Ben this week were unnerving, to say the least, but Ethan was her one true love, and she couldn't give up on it. On him. That was the whole purpose behind the magic spells. She smiled at the memories of fun times with Ethan – visiting museums, hiking, watching movies – before her smile faltered as memories of times with Ben crowded in. Images of him bringing her soup when she had the flu. Calling to see how she did on her final exams. Offering support when she launched her new business.

Was Ethan really just a friend? No. Shelly knew from her parents that you only had one chance at true love, and hers was Ethan. After five years, it had to be.

Rebekah walked away and Shelly lifted her coffee, offering a wobbly grin for her frenemy, Laura. "To true love."

"To true love."

They both took sips, Shelly wincing at the heat from the freshly brewed beverage.

Laura stood. "I expect those changes by tomorrow." She strode off on her kitten heels.

Now that was the Laura that Shelly knew. But this time the demand did nothing to dampen her good spirits. She'd get the changes completed (again) on time because she was a professional. More importantly, she got the universe's hint. You never give up on true love.

Time to head home and see how that morning's spell went. Time for Ethan to regain his lost love. Her.

And, if she was more excited to have dinner with Ben first, well, that was just because he was her best friend. Right?

The universe needed to be clearer.

CHAPTER SIXTEEN

BEN

Boxes filled Shelly and Ethan's apartment, Ben noticed with satisfaction, then felt bad, knowing that hurt Shelly. He tried not to stare at how many of them there were while following her the short distance to the dining table.

Shelly gave him a half-smile. "I know how empty the apartment is looking."

"He's out for dinner?"

"I think he's at the gym?"

It surprised Ben that Shelly didn't know where the love of her life was tonight, but he fully intended to take advantage of the absence. His talk with Nick had clarified things. He'd tell her how he felt. He'd planned it out in his head; once they got through the initial pleasantries of dinner, he was laying it on her. And, hopefully Nick was right that she'd jump into his arms.

Shelly's small kitchen with the older white appliances was tucked off to the side after entering. Along that same wall was the dining area. The apartment designers had extended the linoleum from the kitchen to help designate it, but there were no walls or anything. She'd already set the table with her favorite turquoise tableware, that Ben had bought her when she graduated college.

"I hope you don't mind we're using the smaller forks and spoons," she said, her tone apologetic. The silverware looked designed for children when in his big mitts, but for tiny Shelly, using them was more comfortable.

"You know I don't," he assured her and slid into the seat at the four-top dark brown table, facing the kitchen.

Shelly hurried back toward a couple of pots and pans on the stove.

"What are you making? It smells delicious."

"I thought, for the beautiful spring we're having, that I'd go with something simple and light, so it's a vegetable pasta in a garlic sauce." She turned back to the stove.

Garlic sauce? Hmm.

Shelly lifted one pot and dumped its contents into the other. He watched colorful green, red, and yellow vegetables tumble into the pot of, presumably, strained pasta, probably linguine. Shelly loved linguine.

"Do you want some help?" He suddenly felt weird watching her finish dinner.

Her laugh filled the space. "I've got it." She then transferred the vegetables and pasta into a matching turquoise serving dish before carrying it the few steps to the dining table. She set the dish down on the table. "Let's eat."

They spent the next moments in silence, filling their plates with pasta. She'd also made a spinach salad and uncorked some white wine, which they now served themselves.

Shelly lifted her glass of wine and he mirrored the action. "To gaining clarity in our lives."

His heart stilled at her words. "To gaining clarity in our lives." Now was his moment.

"Shelly, I have something—"

"Wait until you hear—"

They both started and stopped at the same time, chuckling over the simultaneous speech. "Please, ladies first."

Shelly was practically beaming. "Wait until you hear what happened with Laura this afternoon."

"Given your smile, not what I would have guessed."

She shook her head. "Nope, not at all. I mean, yeah, at first it was the typical giving me a hard time nonsense. But, then..." She trailed off, bit her lower lip.

"Don't keep me in suspense," he teased.

"Laura began talking about my parents and true love."

His mouth felt like it was filled with cotton balls.

"My parents had their share of ups and downs, but it was all worth it, because they were high school sweethearts who recognized their one-and-only true love."

He opened his mouth to speak when she paused to take a drink of her wine. Then he closed it; he wanted to see where she was going.

"When Ethan dumped me on Monday, I questioned everything. And, working with you on the spells to win him back, I questioned again, and doubt crept in." Shelly leaned forward, face bright with excitement. "But when Laura started talking about my parents, something that had *nothing* to do with our business talk, I knew."

"Knew what?" Here it was. The moment of truth. She'd declare her feelings, he'd declare his, and they could finally get out of the Friend Zone.

"I knew it was the universe giving me a sign. Ethan is my true love. The doubt I'd felt was misplaced. I was confused—"

Shelly was still talking, but at her words, a roar filled Ben's mind and he couldn't hear her anymore. She'd had doubt. Maybe she was thinking about him differently? His body felt light, like a weight had been lifted. Not all of it, but some. She might be thinking about him differently. "I'm sorry, I missed that," he said when he realized that Shelly was staring at him intently.

"What do you think?"

He bit back the words he wanted to say. Nick would call him a coward later. But if that was what Shelly wanted. "I want whatever you want."

"My conversation with Laura reassured me that my plan to regain Ethan's love is the right one. Like my parents."

Ben nodded, crushed as that just-lifted weight crashed back into his body. His limbs, his stomach, his heart. But he didn't want to ruin her happiness. He guessed he'd read the signals wrong.

"What did you want to tell me?" she asked.

"What? Oh, nothing. Tell me how the rest of the meeting went with Laura," he deflected.

Shelly tilted her head for a nanosecond and he wondered if she'd challenge his non-answer, but she didn't. "I thought it was going horribly, but in the end it was good." She told him the details and he listened, thankful at least to be on another topic.

The front door opened, startling them. Ethan was home.

CHAPTER SEVENTEEN

SHELLY

A frisson of guilt surfaced when Shelly heard the front door opening. Unsure why she'd feel guilty having dinner with her best friend, she tamped it down, pushed back from the table, and hurried over to greet Ethan. And then slammed to a halt when she saw his face. Face flushed. Lips thinned into an angry slash. Eyes narrowed as if awaiting another attack. That didn't look good.

"Everything okay?" she asked.

Ethan brushed past her with a sharp nod aimed in Ben's general direction, and headed toward the guest room to the right.

"Ethan?" Shelly asked his retreating form.

He held up a finger, like he was asking her to wait, before entering the bedroom and closing the door firmly behind him.

She spun to face Ben, her eyes widened in distress. "What do you think happened?"

Ben had already stood at some point during the exchange with Ethan. Now he walked to her side and leaned in to whisper. "Give him a minute."

She nodded, hands flexing opened and closed while she stood there immobile.

Soon enough, the door reopened and Ethan stood in the doorway, his tall frame filling the space.

"Ethan?" Shelly asked again.

He seemed to deflate before their eyes, becoming physically smaller. He sighed and then trudged to the couch, collapsing onto the gray corduroy. His head dropped into his hands.

With a desperate glance at Ben, she moved to sit beside Ethan, wanting to comfort him, though not sitting close enough to touch.

Ethan lifted his head, his reddened eyes met hers. "I don't understand what's happening."

Now guilt filled her, and it was probably earned. "What do you mean?"

"The last few days… since you made me the dinner that sent me to emergency—" His eyes narrowed. "—I feel like I'm under attack."

"You just had an allergic reaction…" She trailed off, sputtering.

"Still. It all started there."

"All *what* started there?"

"Since that dinner, I've spent the night in emergency, had my peripheral vision vanish, and now, it started a few hours ago. The directions to a party I never attended when I was in high school popped into my head. That was weird, but I shrugged it off. Then, my brain began down the path, of all things, of a hiking trail I didn't take because I woke up that morning with the flu."

Ethan paused but nausea roiled Shelly's stomach. She knew what was coming, had figured out what went wrong with the spell this time. Guilt spiked higher and she wondered if this had all been a horrible mistake.

"The weird memories continued with greater speed over the course of that first hour. Do you know what all of them had in common?"

She shook her head.

"In every instance, they were for things I never actually did, for one reason or another. My head has been filled with directions, paths, you name it, for events I *never* did."

Oh, my Goddess, that was their fault. She risked a quick glance at Ben, could see the guilt telegraphed there. Her misfiring magic did that. She tainted Ben's magic with her own, and now Ethan was paying the price. Tears pricked Shelly's eyes.

"Somehow…" Ethan paused. "I don't know how…" He tried again without success. His empty eyes met her tear-filled ones. "All of this started with your dinner. I don't know how that triggered this, but whatever is going on…" Now his gaze took in Ben as well. "Stop it. Please, just stop."

"I don't know what you're talking about." The lie burned as it left her mouth.

Ethan shook his head. "You do. I don't know how."

Because I'm a witch! she shouted in her head. *And I'm a terrible one.*

He took her hand in his, the gesture not sweet. "I'm leaving Friday morning. Whatever started with that dinner needs to end. I'm sorry that it worked out like this, but…" He trailed off again, then released her hand.

Instead of reaching for Ethan to regain the contact, she looked at Ben, saw him standing next to the dining room table, his hands clasped in front of him. Only his expression belied the relaxed stance of his posture. And that broke her heart more. She dragged him into this. He wouldn't have done it for anybody else. She was certain of that. It needed to stop.

Ethan stood, his blue eyes taking in her first and then Ben. "I'm going to bed. Sorry to interrupt whatever was going on here."

Shelly and Ben watched Ethan cross the carpeted floor to the guest bedroom. He closed the door, almost gently this time. Maybe he'd already got his frustrations out. She scurried to her best friend's side, noticing he was still as stricken as she was about what had happened.

"He's right, Shelly."

"What do you mean?"

"It's over."

"It is?" Even though she'd had that thought, too, her irrational worry that she was losing her only chance at true love flared. Her stomach clenched.

Ben sighed. "It is." He embraced Shelly, comforting her as a few tears came loose and tracked down her cheek. That comfort of being in his arms, added to the knowledge that he would always support her, even following her into ill-advised hairbrained schemes, heightened her confusion. But Ben was her best friend. Pulling back, he stared into her eyes for a beat.

"Ben?"

"I'll talk to you tomorrow." With that, he released her and left the apartment before she could formulate a reply.

She returned to the dining room table, sat at her seat, surveyed the meal she'd made and shared with Ben. That brought a ghost of a smile to her face. She drank a large gulp of wine and considered the evening.

Ethan more or less guessed what had been going on – and despite herself, that impressed her – but the universe had given her a sign not to give up on her true love. If she stopped now, she would never know if she gave up too soon. Plus, then she wouldn't get to continue working with Ben on the spells.

A high-pitched bark disrupted her train of thought. Shelly met the fox's gaze and was shocked at the reproach she saw there.

"What?"

Rose barked again, shook her head, and slunk from the room.

Shelly swigged another drink of wine and made her decision. With a smirk and a nod at the Goddess, she declared her intention.

"This is the ultimate test of my loyalty and affection for Ethan. I get it. Tonight was rough, but I get it."

CHAPTER EIGHTEEN

BEN

Ben was glad the morning at the hospital had been quiet. It gave him time to think. He didn't get the chance last night to tell Shelly how he really felt, given Ethan's untimely and mood-killing entrance. Ben groaned. Ethan. It had been so much easier to think of him, even after all these years, as merely an interloper who would be mildly inconvenienced by the spells being cast. Seeing him in pain. Ugh.

First do no harm.

That was basically the primary tenet as both a doctor and a witch. And Ben had followed neither with Ethan. It wasn't as harmless as he'd told himself it was.

"Doctor?" The blond nurse called to him from the bed of their newest guest.

"Yes, Gretchen?"

"He's ready."

With a nod, he headed for the new admit and pulled the privacy curtain.

His phone began vibrating almost immediately. A quick check showed it was Shelly and although his heart sped up at the sight of her name, she'd have to wait until he was finished.

Gretchen and Ben worked seamlessly and quickly, yet someone, presumably Shelly, still texted or called three more times. He waited to confirm it was Shelly until he and Gretchen had finished with the patient and were back at the nurse's station.

"Someone really wants to reach you," the nurse joked as he scrolled through the notifications. Gretchen knew they weren't busy enough for it to be work-related.

He shrugged and offered a half-smile. "What can I say? I'm popular." Ben stepped away to the sound of Gretchen's chuckling. She had been a few years behind him in school, but he seemed to remember her always laughing.

The janitor's closet he'd hidden in before beckoned. A quick glance around the emergency department confirmed he had a few minutes. Shelly's last text had been, *Call me, please.* He assumed nothing bad had happened or she would have been explicit, but she still appeared desperate.

"Ben! Finally. Is emergency that busy?"

"Good morning to you, too, Shelly."

"Of course. Good morning, Ben." He heard the smile in her voice. "You have a minute now?"

"Maybe even two or three minutes."

"Excellent." He heard her take a deep breath. "I did some soul searching after you left last night."

His grip tightened on the phone. "And?"

"I want to try one last time."

"What? Surely I misheard you."

"You heard me just fine."

"Even though the spells have misfired?"

"Yup."

"Even though Ethan asked you to stop." He leaned his head against the closet wall, wanting to bang against it, but not wanting to cause brain damage.

"Yes."

He'd always thought it was only an expression, but he swore his heart fell with that single syllable. "I don't understand."

"I'm so glad you asked."

"I didn't really," he contradicted, but with a smile. Her excitement infectious as always.

"The Goddess sent me a sign with my conversation with Laura, so the spells misfiring and even Ethan's desire for all of this to stop, these are just tests of me. Tests of my belief in our true love."

A knife twisted in his belly at her words. She still thought Ethan was her true love.

"I'll admit last night almost caused me to give up. Look at it this way, Ben, today is the last day. We'll go out with a bang." She chuckled. "That hopefully doesn't blow Ethan up."

His mouth dropped open.

"Close your mouth, Ben. Yes, I know it dropped open."

"How do you do that?"

"You're my best friend," she said softly.

He stood from the upside-down bucket he'd perched on. Was that a hitch he heard on the last word?

"Will you help me with one final, pull-out-all-the-stops spell today? Ethan told me the moving van arrives in the morning. This is the last hurrah."

"Yes, Shelly, I'll help you with one final, pull-out-all-the-stops spell. After all, what are friends for?" He pulled the phone away from his ear at her happy squeal, smiling despite himself. "Lucky for you, this is a short shift this morning. Meet at my place at noon?"

"Let's make it one, I have another meeting with Laura, and it may go awhile."

He laughed. "Good luck."

"Thanks."

The call ended and he sat on the still-overturned bucket on the floor. An idea was formulating in his mind that would allow him to go through the motions of helping

Shelly, but still finally get off his butt and tell her the truth. He knew he wouldn't cast another "Ethan spell". But Shelly didn't need to know that. Yet.

Then again… he couldn't go through all of this to show Shelly he loved her, just to leave town for a new job. He pressed call on his phone.

"Dr. Ben, what can I do for you today?" Dr. Casey Hayes answered without preamble.

"What can I do to prove I'm the right resident to be Chief Resident?"

A low laugh sounded. "Are you turning down Vegas?"

"As soon as I hang up with you."

"Come to the board meeting today and tell them why they should hire you. I'll text you the details."

Ben thanked her for the recommendation and disconnected. That was the right decision. One phone call to Vegas would shut down that option. He was all in, personally and professionally. He hoped he didn't end up unemployed and still single.

CHAPTER NINETEEN

SHELLY

Shelly's meeting with Laura at Wildcrest Wizardry's coffeeshop couldn't have happened fast enough. She actually felt a pinch of anxiety when she sat at her favorite table. That was no good. At least she was a few minutes early, so she could relax with a mocha latte before Laura arrived.

"The usual?"

She turned her head at the sound of Nana's voice reading her mind, then smiled at the purple track suit that matched her grandmother's eyes. She must not have had time to change after her walk that morning with Papaw. At Shelly's nod, Nana hustled to the back to get the drink.

Clacking heels on the floor alerted Shelly to Laura's arrival before she saw her. Red hair slicked back per usual, blue eyes rimmed in dark liner. A cloud of some kind of light citrus fragrance clung to her. She set her bag on the table as she took the seat across from Shelly. "What do you have for me?"

"Hello to you, too," Shelly responded, but still pulled out her laptop. Rather than just mockups, she felt like they were close enough to go ahead and pull the site offline so she could institute the (hopefully!) final round of changes. And to be honest, she also thought if Laura saw them live, it would help her see how good they looked.

Laura frowned. "You already made the changes?"

Shelly bit back a sarcastic retort. "We seemed close to finished—"

"I make that determination, not you."

"Excuse me?"

"I am the client," she overenunciated, "so I make the determination of when we implement changes. Not you."

Speechless, Shelly could only stare at the redhead. A mocha latte appeared. If the look on Nana's face could kill, Laura would be a grease spot in the chair.

"Did you want anything?" Nana asked Laura, the sweetly saccharine tone enough to give everyone in the room cavities.

Laura flashed a not-quite-genuine smile. "Nothing for me. I won't be here long."

A brick formed in the pit of Shelly's stomach. She doubted Laura would fire her at this stage of the website redesign. But anything was possible.

With a curt nod, Nana turned and walked away.

"Show me what you've done."

At her direction, Shelly walked Laura through the implementation of the changes she'd requested yesterday. Laura made notes with every page, but said nothing. When they got to the final page, she made a few more scratches of pen on paper, and then sighed. That did it. Shelly snapped. "Why didn't you push back on hiring me? When Ben's mother suggested it. You don't even like me. This has to be as unpleasant for you as it is for me." She took a large swallow of coffee. That was completely unprofessional. What was the matter?

Laura stared impassively.

What the heck? She'd go for broke. "And speaking of that, why don't you like me?" Shelly pushed harder. "Since high school, you haven't seemed to like me, and I have no idea why." She heard the note of bewilderment in her own voice, and hoped Laura did too.

Laura sighed again, but this time she spoke. "I don't dislike you. Not really. Everything has always come so easy for you," she said, holding up her hand when Shelly opened her mouth to respond. "You asked. Now let me answer. Everything has always come so easy for you," she repeated, "and ...everybody... wants to be with you."

Her word choice baffled Shelly. "Everybody?"

Laura just shook her head.

"And you think everything comes easy for me? Do you know how much my new business is struggling?"

Laura's eyes widened.

"And—" Shelly couldn't believe she was about to admit this to her high school frenemy. "—do you know how much I suck as a witch?"

Laura covered her mouth with a hand.

"Are you laughing at me?"

"I'm not, I swear. I'm laughing at the situation."

Shelly quirked an eyebrow.

"I guess we never know what's going on with others."

"No, we don't."

"How much do you suck as a witch?"

"Is that rhetorical?"

"No." Laura smirked.

"Let's just say that when my magic matured, it didn't know how to manifest the right way," Shelly explained.

Laura looked confused.

"It has a tendency to misfire. Mostly to do the opposite of what I want."

"Can't you just cast spells with opposite intent?"

"It's not even consistent enough for that," Shelly groused.

"I suppose I can stop giving you a hard time," Laura said, her eyes twinkling.

"That would be nice."

"It's just tough."

"Not giving me a hard time is tough?"

Laura guffawed. "Did you know I had a crush on Ben in high school?"

Shelly ignored the whiplash caused by that conversation change. "What? Why didn't you ask him out?"

"He wanted someone else."

"That's news to me."

"Is it?"

Shelly tried to decipher the look on Laura's face and reviewed her years with Ben in high school. "I don't remember him being serious about anyone."

"Maybe he never got up the nerve to say anything."

"You'd think I would have noticed his interest in someone else," Shelly said, more to herself than Laura. This whole conversation was starting to feel deeper than expected.

Laura smiled. "The website looks great. Make it live and I'll let the board know, so they can take a look at it. They may want a few tweaks," she warned, "but probably nothing big."

"You already took care of that for them."

"Indeed." She gathered her papers to leave. "Say hi to Ben for me."

"Wait—" Shelly started to ask her what else she knew, but Laura swept past, clearly done with the conversation.

The comments about Ben perplexed her. Shelly was his best friend. How could she not know who Laura was talking about?

CHAPTER TWENTY

BEN

The employee lounge had only one person in it when Ben made a quick pit stop for some bad coffee before heading home to prepare for Shelly.

"Jason, you coming on or off?"

Dr. Jason Lawson, florescent lights reflecting off his bald head, offered a half smile. "Coming on. You leaving?"

"Yep. Just needed a little juice before I go."

Jason sidled up to Ben, leaned in conspiratorially. "I'm surprised you're leaving. A little birdie told me I should bring my A-game to the board meeting later today."

Ben refilled his travel mug with the swill disguised as coffee. "That meeting's not until 5 o'clock."

"You're the only other person who would be a serious contender for the Chief Resident position."

"I heard they're looking for a chief resident at one of the big hospitals in Vegas."

"Are they now?"

"That's what I heard." Ben took several steps toward the door, before turning back to Jason. "I'll see you later."

His response of, "I knew it," followed Ben into the hallway.

The sound of water greeted Ben when he walked through the front door of his house fifteen minutes later. He wondered what could be the source, before realizing one of his brothers must be home and taking a shower. Ben quickly changed in the bedroom before dumping dirty scrubs in the laundry room and heading into the kitchen. Shelly wasn't due for another half hour. He wondered briefly how her meeting with Laura was going. Better than last time, he hoped. But the break was good. It gave him time to prepare for the board meeting after.

The water from the back-bathroom shower stopped. Ben's plan for today's "spell" had come together nicely in his head. Time to implement. He gathered the spices and honey needed and laid them out across the island.

"Don't tell me you're still going through with your ridiculous plan," his brother, Aaron, said as he came into view from the hallway, his boots solid on the dark laminate wood floor. A shorter, stockier version of the men in their family, he had the same dark brown hair, but startling green eyes. Mischief danced in them right now.

"Did I ask for an opinion?" Ben responded. Aaron's blunt approach brought out Ben's sparring nature.

"I'm just trying to save you from yourself, brother of mine." He opened the refrigerator and pulled out sliced bread and a bunch of vegetables. Aaron's magic was an enhanced ability to communicate with animals; he'd become a vegetarian almost as soon as he could speak. Ben tried not to think about the implications of that.

Ben finished arranging the requirements for the "spell" and noticed Aaron frowning at what he had. "No comments from the peanut gallery, please."

Aaron shrugged and sat across from Ben to eat his veggie sandwich. Where Shelly usually sat. "When is she coming over?" his brother asked.

Ben checked his watch. "About fifteen minutes. She had a meeting with Laura Harkin first."

"Ooh, she's a she-devil, that one."

"She's not that bad. Very opinionated. Like you," Ben pointed out.

Aaron blushed and took a large bite of his sandwich.

"Strike a nerve?"

Aaron shook his head, appearing to concentrate on chewing and swallowing his food, before answering. "Stop being a weasel."

"I'm being a weasel?"

"Tell Shelly the truth."

"Again, not that I asked for an opinion, but I have a plan."

"Right. Noah told me. Help Shelly win back Ethan, and hope she falls in love with you in the meantime. How's that working out for you?" Another chunk of sandwich disappeared into Aaron's mouth.

Now Ben flushed. "That was the original plan. I'm trying something different today."

"Something connected to this hodgepodge you've got going on the counter?"

"I've been considering how to tell her, and I think I have the plan set."

Aaron unexpectedly threw up his hands.

"That was melodramatic."

"I needed to get your attention. You don't need a plan, other than to open your mouth and say the words, I like you, Shelly."

"It's not that simple."

"Good grief, man. Yes, it is. Why are you overcomplicating this?"

"I'm not."

"Uh-huh." Aaron brought his now-empty plate around the island to place in the sink. He gripped Ben's shoulder. "Now is your time. Don't screw it up. We've watched you pine for that girl for literally a decade. Now is your time," he repeated.

A knock on the door saved Ben from a reply. "Come on in," he called out.

Shelly walked through the door, her smile widening when she saw the brothers. "Hey Ben, Aaron."

Aaron and Shelly embraced and she chucked him on the shoulder. "Congrats on getting your realtor license."

"Thank you, Shelly. You let me know when you're ready to get a home of your own and I'll hook you up."

"You got it," she told him.

"I gotta run," he said to them. "You kids have fun. Don't do anything I wouldn't do." He stared into Ben's eyes, his expression serious. "Think about what I said, big brother." Without waiting for a response, he left.

Shelly turned, a question in her hazel eyes.

Ben sighed. "It's nothing. You know my brother has very strong opinions about everything. That he isn't afraid to share." But Ben wondered if his brother was right and he should just open his mouth and say the words.

CHAPTER TWENTY-ONE

SHELLY

Awkward energy floated all around the kitchen, but Shelly ignored it to take her customary seat at the island. She took a quick sip of her not-quite-empty mocha latte. "You ready to do this?"

Ben's mouth twitched. "You bet."

Quite the spread covered this part of the island. He'd laid out dried orange peel, wormwood, elderflower, and acacia, among several others she didn't immediately recognize.

"Gee, do you think you have everything you need?"

The tips of Ben's ears turned red.

"Is there something I should know?"

"How did your meeting with Laura go?" He focused on the ingredients before him, but if she didn't know better, he was randomly moving them around.

Hmm, interesting deflection. Alright, she would bite. Maybe it'd stave off some of the anxiety building in her chest. "It went really well, actually."

"That's wonderful. And a little surprising."

"I know, right?" She laughed. "In fact—" She eyed him shrewdly. "—Laura dropped a rather interesting piece of news. At least it was news to me."

Ben tilted his head. "I'm intrigued…"

"She said you had a crush on someone all through high school that you never revealed."

"Wha—" he stuttered, knocking over the salt. "Shoot." He turned to the counter behind him to grab a rag. If the tips of his ears turned any redder, they'd catch fire.

"You're a great guy. Why didn't you say something to her?"

Ben faced Shelly again, this time making eye contact that caused her to squirm in her seat. "What if she'd said no?"

"What if she'd said yes?"

Ben shook his head.

"Do I know her?" She asked the question lightly, but her heart hammered in her chest.

He opened his mouth to answer, closed it again.

"It's not a trick question." Her mouth had gone dry.

"Yes, you know her," he finally answered.

"Does she still live in Wildcrest?"

"Yes."

Butterflies had taken flight in her belly and she wasn't sure why they'd gone down that rabbit hole. That wasn't what they were there for. Ethan was her destiny. A sick feeling washed over Shelly at that thought, giving her pause. No, that was just the anxiety about missing her chance.

"You just had a whole conversation in your head, didn't you?" Ben asked.

She grinned to suppress that sick feeling, decided to focus on the task at hand. "Indeed." She surveyed the ingredients on the island again, now also recognizing Irish moss and nestle, and frowned. "What spell is this for? It seems… chaotic."

His eyebrows lifted.

"Did you not think I'd notice?"

"Well…"

"Hey," she protested. "My magic might misfire but I know what the spells are supposed to look like. And this doesn't look like anything. Or have you come up with something the world has never seen before?"

"No, you were right the first time. The ingredients aren't anything. There isn't a final spell."

"What do you mean? You couldn't think of one? I had a couple of—"

"No. I mean, I'm not casting any more spells to help Ethan realize he belongs with you."

A strange mix of sadness and elation arose. She pondered how that could be. Did she not want Ethan? Or was something else at play. "I don't understand," she admitted.

"Seeing Ethan last night, his misery." The look of anguish on Ben's face said it all. He'd decided that what they were doing was wrong.

"But I'm running out of time. This is my last chance." Even as the words left her mouth, she realized she was okay with that. That she was okay with losing Ethan. "Wait…"

"What?"

Shelly peered at Ben, saw guilt mixed with the anguish. "If I hadn't recognized this mess of nothing on the counter, would you have pretended to cast a spell?" A horrible thought occurred. "Have you been pretending all along?" Now Ben's entire face flushed bright red and she knew she'd hit home. "But there were consequences to the spells. I'm so confused."

"I wasn't pretending to cast spells." His eyes dropped to his hands gripping the island. "I was sabotaging them."

"Oh." Her stomach lurched and she leaned forward against the side of the island. "Why?"

Ben met Shelly's eyes and the anger there surprised her. "If Ethan can't recognize what he had in his relationship with you, then he doesn't deserve you. It's his loss."

"You lied to me," she said, voice flat despite the anger coursing through her.

"I did," he admitted. "Though not at first. When you asked me to help you, I fully intended on helping you with those spells. How could I ever say no to you?" He offered a half-smile and her expression softened.

"It's me." The words blurted out.

"Who's you?"

"Laura meant me when she said you had a crush on someone in high school." The lift she felt with that realization deepened her confusion. Ben was her best friend. Wasn't he? "I should have known. You're too good of a witch and my misfiring magic isn't strong enough to interfere."

He nodded.

"When did you start sabotaging—" Her eyes widened when she made the connection. "It was with the very first spell! When your hand hesitated over the ingredient. I knew something was off then. I just thought you almost made a mistake. But that was the exact moment you decided to change the spell outcome." If she wasn't already sitting, she would have collapsed. Her entire body felt weak with the realization.

"I'm sorry, Shelly." He started around the island and she bolted to her feet.

"No, don't come near me."

He stopped, dropped his hands to his sides.

"Why didn't you say something to me?"

"I didn't want to lose you," he whispered.

Hot tears filled her eyes and she blinked rapidly to forestall them falling. "That's unfortunate." She grabbed her mocha latte and work bag, clutched them to her chest like a physical barrier between them. "I don't ever want to see you again. Which should be easy, since you're going to Vegas anyway."

"Shelly, please—"

But she shook her head, already turning toward the front door. "No, don't." Her legs threatened to buckle as she made her way to the door that seemed miles away. "I don't know if I can ever trust you again." The door felt heavy in her grasp, but she swung it open. "Goodbye Ben." She slammed it shut. A wave of sadness crashed into her at the thought of never seeing him again.

CHAPTER TWENTY-TWO

BEN

Ben's eyes seemed glued to the front door. That Shelly just stormed through. That just slammed shut behind her. Slammed shut on them.

What had he done?

A noise behind him made him turn. Noah stood at the entry to the kitchen from the hallway, his expression sheepish.

"I didn't know you were home," Ben said.

Noah shrugged. "It seemed awkward to come out."

Ben sighed and sat in the seat vacated by Shelly, still warm from her body. "Yeah."

Noah took the seat next to him, put a brotherly arm

around his shoulder. "When I predicted this would go spectacularly sideways, I'd hoped I was wrong."

"I should have listened to my big brother's advice."

"Well, that's a given."

Ben stood up.

"What are you going to do?"

"I have no idea."

"At least she knows the truth now," Noah said. One corner of his lips lifted in a half-smile. "All of it."

Ben closed his eyes for a moment. "Not exactly how I'd hoped to spill my guts to her."

"No doubt."

Ben drummed his fingers on the counter.

"It's up to her if she can forgive you or not."

"She was pretty mad."

"That she was."

"Not that I blame her."

"That's good."

"You're being far too agreeable."

"No reason to kick a man when he's down," Noah said. "You know you screwed up. You also know it's out of your hands now." He slugged Ben's shoulder. "But, if I were a betting man, I wouldn't bet against you two lovebirds."

Hope flared. "Really?"

"Really."

"I guess there's nothing to be done but wait." Ben's brows furrowed. "What are you doing home in the middle of the day?" His older brother had also gone into medicine, in part because he had healing powers, but also because he liked doing old-fashioned home visits. He spent most days seeing patients in Wildcrest and the surrounding areas.

Noah grimaced. "I thought my healing energy would be enough for someone and it wasn't. A visit to the apothecary was in order. Since I was nearby, I came home to wrap up some chart notes." A wry smile replaced the grimace. "And then you trapped me in my room."

"Headphones before that?"

"Headphones before that," he confirmed.

"Sorry about that."

"No worries, little brother." He clapped Ben on the back. "Give her time. She'll come around."

The hope that flared earlier blossomed. "I hope so. This was why I didn't ever want to tell her," Ben griped.

"Don't even try that."

"What?"

"Are you seriously trying to equate lying to her about casting spells to regain her ex-boyfriend's affections with being honest about your crush on her for over a decade?"

"When you put it that way."

"You lied. She's angry."

"I thought you said you wouldn't bet against us?"

"I wouldn't. That doesn't mean you didn't royally screw up and that she won't need time to process what you did. And untangle her own feelings for you," Noah added.

"You know you're a general practitioner, not a psychiatrist."

"I know people."

"That you do." Ben waved toward the door. "You'd better get that medication to your patient."

With a jaunty salute, Noah headed for the door Shelly had slammed through. Was his brother right? Ben wondered if he needed to just give her time, or if he needed to do something to convince Shelly he was sorry and that they belonged together.

Despite the raging thoughts, Ben centered himself and headed back to the hospital for the board meeting.

* * *

"Welcome back, Dr. Ben," Jason Lawson greeted him with a smirk when he walked up to Jason standing outside the closed meeting room door.

"Thanks, Dr. Jason," he responded.

"Are you gentlemen getting along?"

The doctors turned at the sound of Casey's voice. The Chief of Staff strode toward them, shook their hands.

"I wish you both the best and think Wildcrest will do well with either of you as Chief Resident," Dr. Hayes said.

"Thank you, ma'am," Ben said.

"Ma'am? How many times have I said not to call me ma'am. I'm not that much older than you." Her brown eyes twinkled when she said it.

"Too many to count," he responded. Dr. Hayes looked

good for her age, whatever it was. A little heavy-set, no wrinkles, short curly brown hair cropped close to her scalp.

She entered the meeting room and spoke to them before closing the door behind her. "We'll get you in a moment."

The doctors waited in silence, standing in front of the door, uncertain. After about five minutes, Dr. Hayes brought Jason in, then Ben. The board asked a lot of questions about Ben's magical abilities. He assumed they did the same for Jason; Shelly had previously sensed magic in the other doctor, but neither of them could identify what it was.

Finally, the board asked the doctors in together. Ben and Jason stood side by side at the head of the table, around which the ten members sat. Several of them smiled at Ben, and his cautious optimism increased.

Dr. Hayes stood from her position on the opposite side of the table. "Thank you both for your applications for the Chief Resident position. It was truly a tough decision. You're both incredibly qualified and any hospital would be lucky to have you. However, there can be only one."

Ben swallowed. This was it. This was the moment. He held a breath to quell his jackrabbiting heart.

"Dr. Wright," she began, "we'd like to officially offer you the position of Chief Resident of Wildcrest Hospital."

"Thank you, Dr. Hayes, and board members," Ben said. "I accept the position. Thank you very much." A smile broke out on his face. He was staying in Wildcrest.

A chorus of congratulations came from the board members. Dr. Hayes addressed Jason. "We know you'll do well wherever you go."

"Thank you for that," he responded.

"Dr. Wright," she said to Ben. "Do you have a few minutes?"

"Of course," Ben said.

Jason turned to Ben with an outstretched arm. "Congratulations, man," he said as they pumped hands.

"Thanks. I'm sorry that throwing my hat in the ring last minute derailed you."

"It's all gonna work out for the best." He leaned in. "Looks like I'm moving to Vegas."

Ben boomed a laugh worthy of his father. "That's fantastic. And quick."

"I may have called them when you first mentioned it to me… and maybe followed up while you were interviewing to tell them you were off the market."

Ben's jaw dropped. "Wait, what?"

"I already knew you were getting it," Jason explained with a laugh. "They told me at the end of my interview, so it wouldn't come as a shock when they offered you the position. I asked if I could stay to congratulate you. And to add to the drama," he added with a wink. "When they brought you in for your interview, I figured why not make that call."

Ben shook his head at the audacity as Jason sauntered

away. Of course, Jason was right. The instant the board offered Ben the job, it wasn't even a question whether he'd accept. Except it was bittersweet. He was staying in town for a job he knew he'd love, but his reckless choices cost him Shelly.

CHAPTER TWENTY-THREE

SHELLY

Despite living in a small town, to drive from one end to the other still took twenty minutes, which was what Shelly had just driven from her apartment to her parents' home. They sounded thrilled she'd accepted their standing offer for dinner. She guessed she needed to do that more often.

Robert Newsome answered the door, smile on his face and wide-brimmed blue hiking hat barely covering his wild salt-n-pepper hair. No hair loss for her pop. He gathered his daughter up in a quick hug, then turned away.

"Your mother and I are making another donation. I've been going through my clothing," he called over his shoulder before disappearing around a corner.

"Hi, honey," her mother's voice came from the direction of the kitchen. Shelly's parents had bought their sprawling ranch-style home on the edge of town thirty years ago, when it wasn't the edge of town, but solidly in the desert. Time marched on, however, and the town caught up. It wouldn't get much closer. She believed her parents had purchased the surrounding few acres as well.

Shelly walked across the stone floor toward the kitchen, the smell of curry reaching her before she reached the space. "That smells amazing," she greeted her mother.

Grace Newsome took a few steps forward, dripping spoon in one hand and a cocktail in the other. She wore an apron with *Drinks well with others* emblazoned on it. That had been her apron for as long as Shelly could remember. She'd pulled her red hair into a messy bun and her purple eyes sparkled.

They air-kissed and Shelly sat at the large oak dining table across from where her mother stood at the stove.

"To what do we owe the honor?" Grace asked.

"I can't just have dinner with my parents?"

"Always. But we know you."

"Yeah." Shelly chewed on a cuticle while she delayed.

"Out with it, daughter."

Robert's voice from behind caught Shelly off-guard and she flinched.

He entered the room chuckling. "Not often I can sneak up on someone."

"I'm a little distracted," she admitted.

Her father grabbed a glass of water, patted her mother's bottom (*good grief*), and then sat at the table with Shelly. "What's going on, pumpkin?"

She fidgeted in her seat.

"Out with it," Grace ordered. "Isn't that why you're here?"

"I made a complete mess of things." To her horror, Shelly started to cry. Her mother turned the burner off and Shelly's parents moved to either side of their daughter. She managed to choke out the whole sordid story, right up to the point at which she stormed out of Ben's home.

"Ouch."

"Yep," Shelly agreed with her father.

"I wouldn't say you're the only one who made a mess of things," Grace soothed in her way, "but you definitely played a hand."

A laugh bubbled up. "That's helpful." Shelly bit her lower lip. "Can I save our relationship?"

"Anything is possible," her mother said cheerfully.

"Which relationship?" her father asked simultaneously.

Grace nodded at Robert before rising to bring dinner to the table. "Exactly."

"Which relationship?" Shelly repeated.

"What do you want?" her father tried to clarify.

"I'm conflicted." Shelly's gaze moved between her parents, still in love after all these decades. "I want what you have. True love." She sighed. "When you love someone, that's who you're with. You fight for that." Even as she spoke the words, Ben's image flashed in her mind. "I thought Ethan was my true love."

Her parents' expressions could best be described as stunned.

"What?" Shelly asked.

"Honey, that's a bit of revisionist history," Grace said.

"In what way?" Shelly narrowed her eyes.

"Do you think your mother and I were always together?"

"Well, yes."

They burst out laughing. "I was dating someone else when your mother and I met."

Grace smirked. "And I showed him what he was missing."

Shelly's eyebrows just about leapt off her face. "You broke up their relationship?"

"I wasn't with the right person," Robert defended Grace.

"Plus, we were young. Only in high school."

"Still." Shelly's mind reeled at the revelation. She had this entire love-at-first-sight, never-dated-anyone-else history for her parents, and it was a fantasy.

"Is that why you've been fighting so hard to make it work with Ethan?" Grace asked the question after sitting back at the table.

Both parents began filling their plates with food. Shelly sat like the proverbial bump on a log.

"We've been together for years," she said.

"Do you love him?"

She met her father's eyes. "No, I don't." With a shock, she realized that while she'd always liked Ethan – quite a lot, especially in the beginning – it was never love. She had been so hung up on the fantasy of her parents' story that she'd convinced herself she was in love with Ethan. And that because he was her one true love, she needed to do whatever was necessary to keep him. She wondered how she could have been so blind.

"Then you know what to do," her mother said.

"If you'll both excuse me," Shelly said, already rising from her seat. "I have to go."

If her parents responded, she didn't hear them, as she flew from their house to her car. She almost made a huge mistake. Several, in fact. Trying to win back a man she didn't love. Pushing away a man she—

The engine of Shelly's VW roared to life.

CHAPTER TWENTY-FOUR

BEN

A light knock on his door sounded. Ben wondered who that could be. He wasn't expecting anyone. Unfortunately.

The door swung open to reveal Shelly, cheeks flushed from exertion or excitement, long black hair braided down her back, hazel eyes confident.

Her appearance at his door shocked him. Ben's skin felt taut, nerve endings aflutter. Oh, man, he sounded like a romance novel. He guessed that was anxiety. "Come on in." He heard her footsteps follow, the door closing behind her, and they took their customary seats at the kitchen island. His heart sat lodged in his throat, waiting for her to speak.

Surely she wouldn't have come over to tell him again it was over. That meant—

"Hi Ben," she said softly.

"Hi Shelly. I'm glad you're here."

"Me too."

"Though, to be honest, I'm not sure what you want. You made yourself," he cleared his throat, "pretty explicit that you didn't want to see me."

She nodded. "I did. And in that moment, I definitely did not."

"In that moment?"

A shy smile formed. "That moment passed."

"I'm so glad." He took a deep breath. "Before you go any further, may I say something?"

"Have I ever been able to stop you?"

"That goes both ways, you know?" They chuckled and shared a knowing smile. Some of his uncertainty drained away. He considered what to say. "You're here either to say we're staying in the Friend Zone—"

Shelly snickered.

"—or you're here to say maybe you want to try for something more."

Shelly lifted a hand like she was going to reach out, then replaced it in her lap.

"I am throwing myself on the mercy of the court. You were right to be angry. I don't know what I was thinking." He paused to collect his thoughts. "No, that's not accurate.

I know what I was thinking. But I was in denial that it would end well." He gave her a crooked smile. "I've liked you since high school—"

"I've liked you too," she interrupted.

"Not like I've liked you."

"Oh."

"The timing was never right," he said.

She frowned and he could practically see her thinking through their years as friends.

"When you told me that Ethan broke up with you, my plan was to tell you then how I felt."

"But I ran roughshod all over that plan, didn't I?"

Now he gave her a wry smile. "That you did."

"Why did you agree to help me try to win back Ethan?"

His face flushed. "My initial plan was to help you, and hope it was unsuccessful."

"Gee, thanks."

"Hey, I figured you'd have so much fun with me, you'd realize you didn't want him."

An inscrutable look flashed across her face.

"Then, I decided to be more proactive."

Her lips thinned into a displeased line.

"And you were right to be angry. It occurred to me while casting that first spell that if the spells misfired just enough to be ineffective, it would minimize the possibility that Ethan would see the error of his ways." He quirked an eyebrow. "After all, you're awesome. That was the big flaw in the original plan. Guaranteeing he wouldn't come around."

"You really are a gifted witch," she said, a note of wonder in her voice.

"I don't understand."

"You not only crafted the spells, you altered them just enough to misfire, like my magic normally would, and without causing real damage. That takes skill."

Ben laughed mirthlessly. "Thanks? It feels weird being praised for something deceitful."

"Oh, don't get me wrong," she corrected him. "It was a bad choice. You just executed it very well."

"I figured modifying the spells to be sure they weren't successful would tip the odds in my favor. The rest of the plan was the same... at the end of the week, when Ethan left, I'd finally man up and confess my feelings."

"But I figured it out."

He shook his head. "I should have known you were too smart for me to fool for very long. I should have told you the truth, trusted in my feelings for you."

"That would have been a simpler option."

"I was scared."

"Of what?"

"Of losing you. Of losing your friendship if you didn't want more. I still am," he admitted.

Tears filled her eyes. "Ben."

Here it came. The moment of truth.

CHAPTER TWENTY-FIVE

SHELLY

What could Shelly say to Ben after everything he acknowledged? Her mouth opened and closed so many times, she felt like a fish. The look of expectation on his face broke through her paralysis.

"I remember how much fun we had in high school," she began.

"That's going back a bit."

"That's where it started, right?"

He wordlessly nodded.

"In high school, you were my best friend." She nibbled on her bottom lip. "And, I think you're right. I never thought of the possibility of more than that. As a scared teenager, frustrated with my misfiring magic, and unsure of myself… I probably would have run from you if you said anything."

Ben nodded again, no doubt pleased she confirmed his choice back then.

"College was its own little bubble. Fun, but I knew I wouldn't stay away." A rueful smile rose and fell. "We both know how much Wildcrest draws us."

"That we do."

"Being back, seeing you again." She swallowed against the lump in her throat. "I really liked Ethan, but if I'm honest, I came back to Wildcrest for you, not just for the town and my family."

Shelly sounded almost surprised when she acknowledged that, the truth having been buried so deep for so long. But Ben's intelligence, sweetness, and attractiveness – *how had I missed that?* – had always been there, waiting for her to wake up to them.

"You did?"

"But," she continued, her voice hard. "You almost blew it."

"I did."

"I agree that you didn't trust yourself – or me – enough to be honest. I accept that was a mistake." She half-smiled. "And I understand not wanting to ruin our friendship. When we conspired together to cast spells, it reminded me how much fun we have. Even in just the past few days, I began not caring as much about winning Ethan back. An eye-opening conversation with my parents—"

"Do tell," he said, quirking an eyebrow.

"A story for another day." She chuckled. "That conversation helped me realize my ridiculous inability to let go of Ethan had nothing to do with love. That missing spark wasn't because I was hiding being a witch. It was because it wasn't love. My relationship with Ethan was fun, and lasted longer than it probably needed to. But it was just fun, not love. That's why your betrayal hurt so much."

Ben cringed.

"Though I understand why you did it. And, really, was it so different than my decision to cast spells to win back Ethan?"

"I hadn't thought of it that way. You're as bad as me!"

"I am." They laughed. "We can both be better."

"We can," he agreed, his expression somber.

"And we need to apologize to Ethan," she said, wondering at the irony that she was finally going to tell Ethan the truth about her being a witch when she let him go.

"We will," Ben agreed immediately.

She took his hands, their warmth commingling. "Do you promise to never do anything like that again?"

"I do." His voice had become husky.

"You'll never lie, or otherwise deliberately withhold information from me?"

"Absolutely not."

"I wish you weren't going to Vegas."

An impish grin appeared. "Vegas isn't happening."

Her grip on his hand tightened. "It's not?"

"You're looking at the new Chief Resident of Wildcrest Hospital."

Shelly clapped with delight. "Congratulations! When did that happen?"

"A story for another day," he repeated her words with a smile.

"Would you like to have dinner with me?"

"Absolutely."

As if of one mind, they leaned toward each other, their lips touching lightly, then with more urgency. Energy zinged through them and she knew their magic was finding the other's. Maybe it was finally their time.

EPILOGUE

BEN

They took Shelly's VW bug to Ben's parents' summer barbecue and, as always, he was surprised how well he fit, given his height. On the opposite side of town from Shelly's parents' home, his parents built theirs on fifteen acres, allowing them unobstructed views of both the desert and the mountains. Shelly pulled through the open black wrought iron gates to the winding driveway.

After parking, they didn't enter the sprawling white ranch-style home with the red Spanish-style roof tiles. Instead, they walked around the side to join the others in the backyard. By the sound of it, quite a few people had beat their arrival.

"Happy Midsommer," Nick said, meeting them halfway across the large manicured lawn.

"Happy Midsommer," they echoed back. The celebration of Litha, or the summer solstice, always took place at Ben's parents' country estate, since his father was the High Priest of their coven.

Shelly checked her watch. "The ceremony is only five minutes away. Thank the Goddess we made it."

Nick walked with them toward the decorated folding tables pushed together in the middle of the lawn. Laden with fresh flowers, fruits, and vegetables, everything was in the summer colors of yellow, red, orange, and green.

"I'm so glad members of all the covens could make it out today," Ben said before taking a large bite out of the green apple he'd grabbed from the table.

Shelly pointed. "I'm going to say hello to Nana and Papaw." She took off toward her grandparents.

"Glad to see it's still working out with Shelly," Nick said. It had been a couple of months since their official first date and things continued strong with Shelly. Nick knew that.

"I know, I know. If I had listened to you to begin with." Ben shrugged and Nick laughed.

"There are your parents."

Ben spotted his father's head above a small crowd and moved toward him and his mother. Esther gave Ben a tight hug when he reached them.

"Son!" Elijah's voice boomed out. "You're just in time. We're about to start the ceremony."

With a nod, Ben stepped away from them, scanning the crowd for Shelly.

Elijah, standing next to the already lit candle at the makeshift altar, thanked everyone for being present. They called back their thanks to him for leading the ceremony.

"The sun shines from above, down upon the land and sea, makes plants grow and bloom," he began. All talking ceased when Elijah spoke.

Shelly found Ben, her fingers intertwining with his as they listened.

"Powerful sun, we honor you today, and thank you for the gifts you bestow," he continued.

Shelly's parents stood on the other side of the loose circle surrounding Ben's father. Grace's eyes were closed, Robert's arm wrapped around her shoulder.

"Known by many names, you nourish the crops, warm the earth, and bring life."

Shelly's fingers tightened on Ben's, and when he glanced at her, she gave him a big smile and nodded at something across the circle. He shifted his gaze and immediately understood Shelly's happy expression. Across the circle, Patricia, Shelly's younger sister, stood, feet planted apart, but slightly swaying to Elijah's words. She'd gone away for college, and stayed a little longer, getting some kind of graduate degree. Patty wasn't usually able to come home from Boston for ceremonies. Ben knew how happy her appearance made Shelly.

"The hope that springs eternal, we welcome you and celebrate your light, as we begin the journey once more into the darkness."

Smiles broke out across the faces of everyone in attendance with the last line. Although on the face of it, one would think the ending sad, but Wiccans celebrated the natural world, including moving through all the seasons.

"Hey, middle brother," a voice said.

Shelly hugged Noah the instant he reached them, Aaron only a step behind. "Hey, Wright brothers," she said, and giggled. That had been her running joke since high school.

Aaron's eyes cut to someone to the left behind the group, and Ben turned to see who had drawn his attention. He raised an eyebrow. "Since when does Laura Harkin attend the barbecue?"

Aaron flushed. "It's open to all."

"She's never attended before," Noah said, a small smile playing on his lips.

The three looked at Aaron, acutely aware of his nervousness.

"Okay, fine, I invited her."

"Ooh, you like her," Shelly said.

"No, it's not like that. She just hired me to help her find her own place."

"Uh-huh." Noah waggled his eyebrows at their younger brother.

"You know she and I have been friends since high school," he continued to protest. "I'm going to go say hello." With that, he made a beeline for the tall redhead.

Noah and Ben were talking about Aaron's new job, and who might move out first, when Ben noticed Shelly frown.

"Everything okay?" he asked.

Noah took that moment to excuse himself, and headed back toward the tables of food.

Shelly tilted her head, eyes glued to Aaron and Laura. "There's something about their magic that seems off right now."

Ben and Shelly tried to watch without staring, reading the other couple's body language. Laura stood about a head taller than the shorter, stockier Aaron. But Shelly was right, there was tension in their body language.

"I'm sure if Aaron needs our help, he'll let us know," Ben reasoned.

"You're right. I imagine we'll find out what's going on soon enough." She captured Ben's hand in hers and led him toward the party. "Let's go have some fun."

*Turn the page for Aaron and Laura's road to happily ever after in **Love's Misaligning Magic (Wildcrest Witches, #2)**.*

Love's Misaligning Magic

CHAPTER ONE

LAURA

Laura Harkin wondered if her realtor was showing her houses that didn't meet her criteria so they could spend more time together. Not that she objected, exactly. Aaron Wright was very easy to look at, with his messy brown hair, bright green eyes, and muscles outlined by his fitted blue pinstriped suit. He was too short for her, of course, but then most men were. It was hard for them to be taller when she was six feet tall in kitten heels.

"Is there anything you like about the house, Laura?"

It impressed her that he kept his tone even. The man had the patience of a saint. This was the fifth house that weekend they'd looked at. She wanted out of her rental, and after much hemming and hawing was finally moving forward with the search. Wildcrest, Nevada, being the map-dot-sized town it was, meant there wasn't a ton to choose from. She didn't want to wait for a new build, so it had to be used.

"Laura?"

She turned from the fireplace she was inspecting – *did I need a fireplace?* – and smiled, bright white teeth gleaming next to ruby red lipstick. "Apologies. I was thinking of the answer to your question."

"And?"

"There's quite a bit I like about the house," she admitted. "Single story, three bedrooms, quarter-acre lot."

"But?"

"But it's just not speaking to me." She lifted a shoulder in a shrug.

"I didn't know we needed a talking house."

Laura's laughter mingled with his. Although he was joking, in a town filled with witches, you never knew. Maybe she did want a talking house. "I want turnkey, though," she added.

"Naturally."

She listened for the sarcasm in the single word but didn't hear it. That was good. As a professional, it was important to her that the people she dealt with were also professional. Thus far, Aaron had exceeded those expectations.

If only he could find her the house of her dreams.

They walked together into the kitchen, which she acknowledged was renovated beautifully. "I like the white cabinets," she said, nodding when he made a note of it.

"What do you think of the island?"

Laura wrinkled her nose. It was bigger than she would prefer, and on wheels. She wanted a permanent island in her new kitchen. "Let me show you more of what I'd like to see."

All the witches in town possessed a magical inclination. This magic was an open secret, meaning none of the witches felt they needed to hide their abilities anymore. Not since the Las Vegas City Council officially recognized the existence of supernatural beings. But most still only displayed their powers around other witches.

Laura concentrated on the island and pictured in her head how she wanted it to appear. The top grew hazy, almost like a distant mirage, and then began to darken and change shape. Her magic was the ability to manipulate small amounts of matter. As she imagined the island with a butcher block top, not on wheels, and about half the size, it slowly took on that appearance.

"That's what I'm looking for."

"Very nice," Aaron said, circling the island, snapping a few pictures on his cellphone. He stopped beside her. "What's the most amount of matter you've reshaped?"

"The biggest was a car."

Such an awesome experience. She had wanted a new car when she graduated from college four years ago. They didn't have what she wanted, so she decided to experiment. She purchased a car that looked the closest and then manipulated it to look like what she pictured. Now she owned a bright-red sports car that appeared to be a 1968 Shelby Cobra, her favorite car (which she couldn't afford!)

"Wow, impressive. I've wondered what it would be like to have an active ability." He sounded almost wistful. "You know our family has more passive skills."

She placed her hand on his bicep. "Being so in touch with living beings is an amazing ability." Their eyes met, and she caught her breath when he took her hand in his.

"Thank you, Laura. We're thankful for what we have, too." He grinned and stepped away from her. "Although sometimes the animals can be quite chatty."

"What's it like, hearing what they say?" Laura was genuinely curious. Every witch could communicate in images and feelings with their familiar, or companion animal. That was where it ended for most of them. Aaron, however, could communicate with any animal. She couldn't imagine what that would be like.

Aaron's forehead crinkled. "It's hard to fully describe. It's more than what it sounds like you would hear with your familiar—"

"That's probably a good thing," she interrupted with a laugh. Her familiar was a tabby cat named Edward, the reincarnation of a great- great- great-uncle from the 1920s. He was a raggedy looking cat who preferred to go by Eddie, and missed everything about the Jazz Age.

"No doubt," he agreed. "I can almost understand them like they're speaking. It's like a universal translator in my head." He shrugged. "That's the best I can explain it."

"That sounds so interesting. To be able to communicate, to be that close..." She trailed off and walked out of the kitchen. No reason to consider being close to someone. Those thoughts would be unhelpful right now. Better to focus on the task at hand. "I also like bay windows. You can add that to the list."

"Noted."

"Let's head to the bedroom." Her face flushed at the words, and she hurried forward, the clicking of her heels barely covering the sound of Aaron's snort-laugh.

CHAPTER TWO

AARON

Aaron Wright hoped Laura hadn't heard him laugh. And snort-laughed, at that. He knew what she meant, though, and followed behind her without comment. Her hips swayed under a purple fitted tank dress that looked stunning next to her pale skin.

She turned when she reached the bedroom and he stopped up short, only about a foot from her. Her azure eyes widened theatrically and he stepped back.

"Sorry about that."

"That's okay," she stuttered before striding toward the master bathroom.

He opened his mouth to speak, and smiled instead.

Even though Laura was among the pickiest clients in his new real estate practice, he found that it didn't bother him. And luckily it didn't bother his sponsoring broker, who had a whole cadre of newbie realtors under her.

"I don't believe these renovations occurred at the same time," her voice echoed from the bathroom.

Aaron hurried to join her as she explained why the listing sheet from the seller's agent was inaccurate.

That was why Laura's pickiness didn't bother him. He delighted in spending time with her. She could be snarky, which was entertaining, but mostly he liked her intelligence. They'd spent hours together in the past month and he'd never once felt bored. That had to be a record.

But he wasn't dating her, so maybe just being friends was the difference. "What do you think of the closet size?" he asked.

She cocked a hip and together they stared into the cavernous space. It was huge, relative to the size of the bedroom. "This would do nicely."

"All of your clothes would fit?" He waggled his eyebrows.

"Hah, not hardly," she admitted. "But that's what dressers and guest bedroom closets are for."

Aaron chuckled and wrote, 'Master closet the size of a room.'

Laura stepped close and peered at his note. "I'd think you would have already made a note of that requirement."

"I'm emphasizing the requirement."

"Good, because some of these tiny closets are downright dreadful."

"I don't suppose you could donate some of your clothing."

Her eyebrows jumped. "Did you just criticize your client's wardrobe?"

"Not in the least," he assured her. "Your clothing is fabulous. But," and he waved his hand around the closet, "it's a lot of clothing, is all I'm saying." He smirked. "If this isn't enough for one person's clothing…"

Her smile dropped along with his stomach.

"I'm only teasing," he said, reaching out to touch her elbow. "I don't care how much clothing you own."

"I know you're teasing." She offered a brittle smile and he would have sworn a tear glistened. "It's totally fine."

It most definitely was not totally fine. Aaron could see that. But he was unsure what to say next. He'd apologized for his teasing. As snarky as she was, he couldn't have guessed teasing her about her clothes would elicit such a reaction.

Laura returned to the kitchen and he hastened to follow her.

"I'd better put the island back the way we found it," she said.

"I'd have a hard time explaining that to the owner's agent," he agreed.

"We wouldn't want to get you in trouble."

"No, we wouldn't. Or would you?"

Laura grinned, and it appeared that whatever had struck a nerve with her had blown over. "Nah, what fun would that be?"

He returned her grin, glad to see it reappear. She faced the island and held her hands over it, like before. Aaron took a step backward. She hadn't asked for more space, but it still seemed like a good idea to give her room. He realized he could hear her muttering under her breath. He must have missed that the first time.

The area above the butcher block-topped island grew hazy again and slowly regained its earlier shape and appearance. It raised up as wheels materialized. Butcher block faded and became its original stainless steel. The length grew and the island's handles repositioned themselves.

"That is so incredible."

She turned to him, her face flushed with the exertion.

"Are you okay? Did it take more out of you that time?"

Her smile widened and she shook her head, short red hair not budging. "Not at all. This—" She waved her hand in front of her face. "—is from the adrenaline. It's excitement. Although it does require more energy to transform something twice. It's the same reason why I can't transform large amounts of matter."

"Really?"

She pursed her lips in thought. "I'm not completely sure why, to be honest. And, normally, I don't change things back and forth. The changes are permanent."

"How often do you change things?" The entire process fascinated Aaron.

"Not too often."

"How come?"

"I suppose for the same reason that most witches are careful when using their magic." She sat at the staged glass-topped kitchen table and he quickly joined her, their knees almost touching.

"To maintain the energy balance around us?" he asked.

"Yes. I don't know what would happen if I tried too much or too hard, but I'd not want to risk it. You know?"

"Of course," Aaron said. All witches knew that upsetting the natural order was bad.

Her lips turned down again.

"We'll find you the perfect house," he assured her.

"I have no doubt," she agreed. "But maybe we'll pick this up again tomorrow?"

"I have the list of remaining homes we haven't seen, and I'll do a quick check for any new listings in the morning."

Laura abruptly stood and he hastened to follow. "Thank you so much for putting up with me." She bit her lower lip and then offered a weak smile.

"It's not that difficult." He wondered again about her reaction.

"I'll see you in the morning," she called over her shoulder as she sped toward the front door.

"Looking forward to it," he said into the silence that remained. He'd figure out her unexpected emotional shift tomorrow. An intelligent, beautiful, funny woman shouldn't be sad when house-hunting.

CHAPTER THREE

LAURA

What was wrong with me? Laura sat in her Shelby Cobra lookalike, hands gripping the steering wheel, and stared at her rental home beckoning. Not that it beckoned very well. It was a standard beige stucco house with a red-tiled roof. It looked like most of the rest of Wildcrest – and she'd realized in the house-hunting process that she wanted something different. Something that stood out. Something that matched her personality.

With a sigh, she grabbed her leather bag and headed inside, barely registering the house around her. White walls, stark black and white furniture, not a family photo in sight. She lived in a magazine layout. And normally that didn't bother her. She liked the boldness of it. Now, after a month of hanging out with Aaron – no, spending time with him in a professional capacity – she found herself dissatisfied with her beautifully minimalist home. She couldn't identify why that was, only that she'd been feeling off about something.

Laura reached the kitchen and sighed again, though this time laughter bubbled near the surface. Her familiar, Eddie, lay sprawled in the middle of the dark brown kitchen table. Exactly where he wasn't supposed to be. He didn't care, and truth be told, neither did she. It just seemed logical that a cat shouldn't be on a table where people ate.

Eddie opened a single eye, a remarkably human gesture, then stood and stretched, back arched. He yipped at her.

"Edward," she started, and he growled. "You know you're not supposed to be on the table."

The word *Eddie* floated through her mind. That was how they communicated. He sent her images and feelings that her brain translated into visual words. She never fully understood it, and every witch communicated in a distinct style with their familiar, but they'd never had trouble understanding each other.

Now she belly-laughed. He hated being called Edward. His parents called him that back in the nineteenth century. So, of course, she did it when he did something wrong. And he did something wrong by being on the kitchen table.

He leapt from the table, over the ash-colored engineered hardwood floors, and onto the bay window sill. The tabby cat bathed himself while Laura sat at the table and pulled her laptop from the bag.

"I think I freaked out Aaron," she blurted out, and Eddie focused on her. The tears that had been threatening all afternoon spilled over. She was glad for her waterproof mascara.

"What happened?" Eddie asked.

"He thinks I'm an idiot."

"Why?" Disagreement flooded her and she knew that was from Eddie, too.

"I practically burst into tears when we were talking about closet size." She ran her fingers through her slicked back red hair, heedless of ruining the style. Hair stuck out in all directions after.

Eddie jumped back onto the table and padded over to Laura, pushing his nose against her hand. She began petting him, warmth flooding through her.

"Thanks, Eddie." Laura scratched her familiar behind his ears, enjoying the purring that vibrated his little body. The irony was that her great- great- great-uncle, who died in the 1920s, had been a huge, brawny guy, never caught dead without a stylish pin-striped suit. And now he was a six-pound gray-brown tabby cat with uneven whiskers and tufts of hair.

"Why did a closet make you cry? Was it that small?"

Laura chuckled at the questions. "That's what Aaron joked about." She shook her head. "It was his comment about the closet being enough for one person's clothing. One person."

Eddie rolled over on his back so she could scratch his stomach. She obliged him as she talked through what had happened.

"I've always been fine focusing on my career. That was all I had."

Her familiar swiped at her hand. "Hey! What am I, chopped liver?"

"Of course, sorry Eddie," she said. "I've always had you." The purring grew louder. "After my parents died…" She trailed off, thoughts of her parents triggering waves of sadness and guilt. They'd died in a car accident while she'd been away at college. She hadn't been here. Not that she could have done anything. But, still.

As an only child with no living relatives – except Eddie – and a temperament that seemed to push people away, she'd chosen to focus on becoming successful. Plus, she liked computers and IT. The tradeoff seemed worth it, even without having friends or family. One day, she planned to be CEO of Wildcrest Witches International. "I was happy."

Eddie grunted.

"Fine. I was satisfied."

"And now you're not?"

Aaron's smiling face flashed in her mind. "I don't think so."

"What are you going to do?"

"Do?" She made eye contact with her familiar, her face expressing her confusion.

"To become satisfied again."

"Find my new home," she said.

Eddie grunted again.

"What? What's wrong with that?"

"Nothing. If you think that will satisfy you... or make you happy."

"Having my own house to call home will make me happy," she insisted.

"I have no doubt that will help."

"You're thinking me and Aaron?"

"I didn't say that, but since you're thinking it too..."

"No, I don't think so." Her heart fluttered at the statement.

"Why not?"

"He's my real estate agent."

Eddie jumped to his paws and yipped again.

She didn't respond to his yip, which really was the oddest sounding cat noise she'd ever heard.

"So? You can't be friends with your real estate agent."

"Maybe? Yeah, probably."

"Maybe more?"

"What? No!"

"Why not?" Eddie shook his head and returned to the windowsill.

"Because."

"That's not a reason."

Too much baggage, Laura thought. Although more with the Wright family than with him. Of course, if she eliminated every family in town that she had history with, there'd be nobody left.

She wondered if she was making excuses.

CHAPTER FOUR

AARON

"Maybe she's making excuses?" Ben asked before taking a bite of his pastrami sandwich.

His brother's question caught Aaron off-guard. The two sat on high-backed stools at the quartz-topped island in the kitchen of the house they shared with their older brother, Noah. "What do you mean?"

"Maybe she's pretending not to like what you're showing her."

Aaron's face reddened. "You know, I considered showing Laura houses I knew she wouldn't like."

"Don't be like me," Ben warned. The whole family knew about how his ill-planned idea to deliberately mislead his now-girlfriend, Shelly Newsome, had gone wrong. Even if it did end in a happily ever after.

Aaron laughed. "I'm not, I promise. It was a brief, bad idea." He chewed and swallowed a bite of his veggie sandwich. No pastrami for him; when you can communicate with all animals, you stop eating them. "It turned out not to be necessary, anyway. She's very picky. Do you really think she could be pretending? I just thought she was pickier than I'd imagined."

"Do you want her to be pretending?"

"Maybe…" An image of Laura's ruby red smile flickered through his mind and thoughts of her quick wit brought a grin to his face.

"Take your own advice," Ben said, in a not-so-gentle reminder to Aaron of his own strongly worded suggestion when it concerned Ben and Shelly. "Ask her out." Ben stood and brought his plate to the sink. "I've got to get to the hospital. Don't be like me," he repeated with a rueful chuckle.

"I won't," Aaron said, then carried his half-eaten sandwich to his bedroom. There were three bedrooms in the house; one for each of the brothers. Ben's familiar meowed a greeting as Aaron passed the open door. "Hi Cookie." Aaron reached his bedroom door without seeing or hearing his eldest brother's familiar. That wasn't too surprising, since the familiar was a desert rabbit. Maybe Jimmy was burrowed under some of Noah's clothing.

Aaron sat his plate on the wooden nightstand next to his bed and joined his own feline familiar, Elizabeth, on the black bedspread. He flicked the television on and immediately hit mute. He stared around the sparsely decorated room. Aaron wasn't big on *stuff* and preferred an uncluttered space. His small black bookcase included a handful of recent thrillers, but mostly held real estate textbooks from his recently completed degree. No art hung on the walls, though he did have three framed family photographs on his black dresser. One was of him and his two brothers laughing, covered in mud. Somehow his mother caught that shot – they were maybe 10, 11, and 12 in the picture. Another was of his parents, Elijah and Esther Wright.

His father ran their coven and the coven's business, Wildcrest Witches International. His mother, not actually a witch, though whip-smart and empathic, was the Chief Financial Officer. In the photo, the two were radiant, smiling in front of their (at the time) newly completed home. The final photo was of the entire family, probably taken by a friend at a Wiccan celebration. Several of them squinted in the apparent bright sun, so maybe it was summer. He thought it might be Lammas, which was the next big celebration approaching.

"Do you need to talk?" Elizabeth asked, interrupting his reminiscing. The sleek black panther of a house cat was the reincarnation of a great-something-or-other relative from the 1600s. She refused to answer to Liz or Beth; she was Elizabeth, and she was practically royalty.

"Nope," Aaron responded, though kept the television muted and didn't make a move to grab his remaining sandwich.

"I don't believe that's true."

"I talked it out with Ben. I'm good." Now he grabbed his sandwich and took a large bite.

"Uh-huh."

He chewed and swallowed in the awkward silence that followed. "Do you need to talk?" he asked when his mouth was empty.

"Why would I need to talk?" The reproach Aaron heard in the cat's translated meow was crystal clear.

That was the one disadvantage of his magical inclination to be able to communicate with all animals. His already-enhanced ability to communicate with his familiar reached the heights of human communication. And that meant he heard every bit of reproach, sarcasm, or disapproval of Elizabeth. To be fair, he also heard her pure joy, amusement, and gratitude. It was a good trade-off. Most of the time.

Elizabeth sat on her paws in the classic pancake pose of a contented cat and stared at her witch, green eyes wide. "I'm waiting."

Aaron smiled and scratched his familiar behind her ears. She relaxed and began loudly purring. At the continued scratching, her paws soon made gentle biscuits on the bedspread. Love filled him like an overflowing warmth through his body, and he wondered how non-witches experienced their connections with the animals in their care.

"You're not wrong," he finally said, and she rolled over.

"Of course not."

"But I did talk it out with Ben."

"I believe you."

"But I'm still not sure what to do."

"What is the issue?"

"I think I like Laura."

"Yes."

"And I think I want to ask her out."

"And the problem is?"

"I don't know if she'll say yes."

"It's not guaranteed," the cat agreed.

"What if she says no?"

"What if she says yes?"

The echo of a nearly identical conversation with his brother several months ago regarding Ben asking Shelly out rocked Aaron hard. He couldn't be acting just like his brother.

Aaron didn't overthink things. He was the most decisive of the brothers. The most like their force-of-nature father. He never made things harder for himself. Not in his 26 years of being on the planet. Except this time, he was both overthinking and making things harder than they needed to be.

"What are you going to do?" Elizabeth asked.

Time to man up. "I'm going to ask her out."

"When?"

That was an excellent question. "Soon."

The cat chortled and curled up to go to sleep. "You let me know how that goes."

CHAPTER FIVE

LAURA

"The three houses we're seeing this morning just came on the market. Neither will likely last long," Aaron warned Laura.

"Of course," she said, though her focus was on the nearness of Aaron in the small kitchen.

She already knew this wouldn't be the right house. The energy wasn't right. It felt almost physically discordant, like experiencing the sensation of an unattractive paint color, as opposed to only seeing it. But she'd walk around and appear to consider so that Aaron wouldn't think he'd wasted his time.

"How are you doing this morning?" he asked.

"I'm fine." This was the third time he'd asked her how she was doing since she pulled up in front of the house. Her eyes met his – *were those hazel flecks in his green eyes?* – and heat suffused her. "Is there a reason you keep asking me that?" She half-smiled when asking the question.

Aaron took a step back and coughed. "Oh, um, it's just…" He strode to the other side of the small kitchen, which only put a few feet between them. "Yesterday, you seemed upset by my, um, teasing." His face rapidly became the color of a tomato.

Laura suppressed a small laugh. "I promise your teasing didn't upset me." She squashed the discomfort of the reminder that she was alone.

"That's good." He stepped toward her and opened his mouth to continue speaking, but nothing came out.

Anxiety spiked in Laura and she spun around. She didn't understand why she felt anxious. She enjoyed being with Aaron. They were comfortable together, like friends, yet she needed to put space between them. "Let's take a look at the living room. I'd like to see the crown molding."

"Of course," sounded from behind her.

Her heart thumped in her chest and her heels clicked on the stone floor.

"What do you think of this space?" Aaron stood next to her, and she again felt hyper-aware of his presence.

"It's nice."

It really was, to be fair. For a small space, it appeared

bigger, with a wall of windows, white paint, and light-colored stone flooring.

"How are things with my mother?"

Laura arched an eyebrow at the non sequitur. "Fine?"

Aaron chuckled. "You've talked about how much you like working there."

"True enough." She crossed the living room and opened an accordion door around a half-wall, exposing the washer and dryer. *Hmm, that seems like an odd location for the laundry.* "Things are good," Laura answered his question. "Your mother is very easy to get along with."

He grinned. "Most of the time."

"I mean, she is my boss, so there's that."

"In other words, you'd never say anything bad about her to her son."

Laura held her hands up in mock surrender. "Are you trying to get me in trouble?"

"Do you want to get in trouble?"

The double entendre in his question made Laura's stomach drop. She spoke around the sudden cotton balls filling her mouth. "Let's have a look at the closet." She spun on her heels and hurried away from Aaron and his uncomfortable questions. That the questions pleased her but created discomfort was very confusing. He was clearly teasing her, and that was what friends—

She shrieked when a hand touched her shoulder and then spun to face a wide-eyed Aaron.

"Sorry to startle you," he said in a rush.

She gave a shaky laugh. "I have no idea what's wrong with me today." Embarrassment flooded her, and she hoped she didn't look like a fool.

"Let's see the rest of the house."

Laura appreciated that he didn't continue to ask her what was wrong. Especially since she wasn't sure. She was off her game today, that was certain.

Aaron led the way to the master bedroom (*and didn't that also sound like a come-on!*) and she followed, willing her body to quit betraying her with these weird overreactions.

"This is a lovely room," she said, as she looked around. "I like the tray ceiling." Both of them gazed upward. The tray ceiling added a three-dimensional effect and helped the smallish room seem larger. "It wouldn't be a requirement, but could be a nice extra."

"I'll add that to the nice-to-have list."

"Although my lists are eliminating most of the homes we're seeing."

"They are. That's okay. It just means we haven't found the right one."

"Of course."

"It's the law of averages."

"It is?"

"We live in a small town where not many people leave." He shrugged. "When there aren't a ton of options, most of them probably won't work. Or something like that."

"In other words, I'm never finding a new home." She didn't mean that the way it came out, and laughed.

"Yes, you are."

"Yes, I am. Eventually," she said. "You may be stuck with me for a while."

"That wouldn't be so bad."

"No?"

"No." He lifted a hand as if to touch her and then dropped it. "Let's look at the master bathroom."

"Lead the way," she said before following behind him, enjoying the view. The man wore a suit well, that was clear.

The small bathroom matched the rest of the house. It was all lovely. However, like she'd suspected, the energy didn't work for her. She hoped the next house would be a better fit. Although the thought of the house hunting with Aaron ending led to a swelling of sadness. She didn't want it to end, if she was being honest with herself.

Maybe Eddie was right. Maybe she should ask him out. At that thought, a frisson of anxiety rose again. Something was telling her not to get involved with him. Some part of her didn't think it was a good idea. He was intelligent, sweet, and funny – and hot, truth be told – but he wasn't a good fit for her. She worked for his mother. There was that complication, among others.

Or was she making excuses?

"Earth to Laura."

Aaron's voice jolted Laura out of her ruminations and

she offered a half-smile. "Sorry about that. I was thinking about the next house."

"Ah, so we've eliminated this one, then?"

"I would say so."

He made an elaborate show of pressing delete on his phone. She supposed he was deleting a saved listing sheet and chuckled.

"That was dramatic," she said.

"I try to be entertaining."

"Well done, then."

"Shall we go to the next house?"

"Lead the way, Aaron."

CHAPTER SIX

AARON

Aaron didn't understand why this was so awkward. Ever since he teased her yesterday, their easy conversation seemed stilted and forced. She kept saying everything was fine, though it seemed clear it wasn't. Unless he was reading into things now. He knew he hadn't yesterday, but today was a new day.

He parked his black Jeep Cherokee in front of the next house and watched Laura pull in behind him in her little sports car. She looked radiant as always, this time in black slacks and a purple V-neck wrap shirt. He loved how she kept her short red hair off her face, accenting her flawless skin and sparkling eyes.

Ugh. This had to be a crush. His familiar was right. He needed to ask her out.

But, first, time to work.

Aaron joined Laura at the start of the walkway leading to the house's front door. "First impressions?"

Laura's lips thinned into a line. Not of displeasure. Of deep thought. When she was thinking about something, she really thought about it.

He waited while her gaze flicked around the exterior of the house. It was the typical beige stucco that the vast majority of the homes had, which he knew wasn't her preference. But it also had several large windows, suggesting plentiful natural light inside. Plus, a wide porch ran half the length of the house.

"This is nice," she said, nodding. "It has potential."

"Let's have a look inside."

Aaron followed Laura to the door, watching her eyes taking in everything from the paver pathway and porch to the teal front double doors. When she caught her breath after they walked inside, he had a good feeling about this one.

"What do you think?" he asked.

"This is very nice," she said.

Aaron tried to view the house through her very picky eyes. The open floor plan showcased the vaulted ceilings and dark, wide-beam wood flooring. After entering, a short hallway to the left led to the garage and a guest suite.

Another guest bedroom and a small den were to the right. Further into the house was a grand chef's kitchen and dining area, which led into the living room.

"Look at that view," she gushed. Sliding glass doors at the back of the house showcased an amazing view of the desert and nearby low mountains. "I didn't realize this was right on the edge of town. I don't know how I missed that."

"We've seen a lot of houses."

"Fair enough."

They stood together, gazing out the back of the house at the green of the desert shrubs, contrasting with the brown rocks and red of the distant mountains. It truly was a beautiful view.

"This may be the one," she whispered.

At her words, Aaron's heart stopped. But she didn't mean him. She meant the house.

"The energy is right," she continued, more to herself than to him.

"Do you want to see the rest of the home first?"

Laura turned and unexpectedly hugged him. "Yes, I do. Thank you for finding this."

The feel of her arms around him and the light scent of vanilla lotion tickling his nostrils flooded him with joy. And left him feeling bereft when she withdrew.

Her smile lit up her face.

"Let's look at the rest," he said.

Aaron led her through the other two bedrooms and

bathrooms, then out to the back porch, where she debated herself on whether she needed to screen the porch. She ultimately decided it wasn't necessary. He agreed with her assessment. The smile never left her face the entire time she explored. Unlike in the other houses, she peeked into every nook and cranny this time, clearly indicating this house was different. He'd be shocked if she didn't submit an offer. And while he was thrilled for her, his disappointment at the idea of not seeing her regularly once she bought the home bothered him.

He couldn't account for the awkwardness he'd felt in their conversation. But she said it was okay. And it was going well in this house. Plus, both his brother and his familiar said to go for it.

It wasn't like him to be this wishy-washy. He went for whatever he wanted. And he knew he wanted Laura.

Time to man up.

They'd found their way back to the kitchen. Laura was opening and closing the multiple white cabinets, mumbling about where she would put things.

She'd obviously decided this was the one and she would make it happen. His mother had told him what a go-getter Laura was. That was one thing he liked about her, too. She was like him. Decisive. Well, most of the time.

Aaron stood next to her at the perfectly sized butcher block-topped island with a smile. "Seems like this is the one."

Her eyes shone. "Yes. 100%. Everything about it is perfect. Even the energy feels right." She ran her hand along the top of the island and sighed with apparent happiness.

"I'm so glad we found the one. I'll pull the comps and we can discuss the offer you want to make."

"Perfect. Can we do that today? I don't want to miss out."

"Absolutely. You won't miss out. I'll let the listing agent know we'll be submitting an offer. I can also check if they've received any other recent offers."

Her face clouded at his words. "I'm not losing this house."

He put a hand on her arm. "You won't. I won't let that happen." The words came out before he could stop them. That wasn't a promise he could make, but it was worth it for the blinding smile she offered in return.

"Thank you so much, Aaron. For everything." Her eyes were dilated and if he wasn't mistaken, her voice had taken on a husky tone.

"Would you like to go to dinner with me?" He blurted the question and, at her reaction, wanted to take the invitation back.

She stumbled back a step away from him, her mouth forming a perfect, gorgeous ruby red circle of surprise.

"No."

CHAPTER SEVEN

LAURA

Laura's brain emptied at the unexpected question. Although, if she was honest, it wasn't that unexpected. He obviously felt the same pull she did. But, if that was the case, she had to wonder about her instant negative reaction. Oh, wait, he was apologizing.

"—if I've overstepped. That wasn't my intention. I thought…" he trailed off.

She offered a half-shrug. "There's no reason to apologize. I just don't think we're a good fit." She knew that made no sense, but that was all she had.

Aaron gave a sharp nod.

"I work for your mother and we're business associates."

At that, he cocked an eyebrow. "What?"

"Should you date clients?"

"I'd think that's my choice. Plus, we just found you the perfect house."

Laura's face flushed. She couldn't believe this was the explanation she was giving. There was no way she'd accept that excuse from him if he'd said it. It wasn't like they worked together in an office.

"If I ask you out again in a month after we close, will you say yes then?" His smirk confirmed he was teasing, though it pointed out the ridiculousness of her excuse.

"I'll still be working for your mother after we close, but ask me out again then and we'll see," she said in response, surprising even herself with her flirtatious tone. Her prior crush on his brother would still be in their shared past in a month. It seemed weird to go out with the brother of someone she'd crushed on. And yet, she'd put it out there anyway. Because maybe this was just another excuse.

"I will." His eyes dilated as he promised.

Laura swallowed hard and reached out to touch his arm. "Thank you for understanding."

He covered her hand with his. "Always."

There seemed to be subtext here, and she didn't know what it was. "You said there was a third house?"

He appeared more confused by her question itself than the fact that it was an abrupt non sequitur. "I thought you were submitting an offer on this house?"

"I am. Just trying to be thorough. Maybe the next house will be perfect."

"More perfect than this one?"

Laura groaned inwardly that her attempt to avoid the discomfort by focusing on the house hunting was failing. "We won't know unless we check," she answered his question while striding toward the door. And swore she heard chuckling as he hurried to follow her.

"I'll text you the address."

"Thank you," she called out over her shoulder, avoiding eye contact, before hiding in her car and watching him enter his Jeep and then fiddle with his phone. She wanted to grab herself by the shoulders and give herself a hard shake.

She was acting like a teenager. So what, he asked her out and she said no? It wasn't the end of the world and they could still work together.

Her car roared to life and she plugged the address he'd texted into the navigation app, although she had a general idea of its location. The town wasn't big enough for there to be streets she wasn't familiar with.

Her mind refused to stop swirling over and around her one-word answer to his question.

No.

She wanted to say yes. But she also needed to say no.

There was too much baggage. Between her and his family. Between her and her past.

Or maybe it was all in her head.

Despite beating herself up during the five-minute drive to the new house for how she handled his question, she was composed when she joined him on the sidewalk.

"First impressions?"

"Meh."

"That good, huh?"

She echoed his chuckle. "It doesn't match my energy," she said with a shrug, but he nodded. As a witch, she figured he understood that you never underestimate the power of matching energy. "Since we're here, though, let's go ahead and take a look."

"To be thorough," he said, using her phrase.

"To be thorough."

Aaron stopped short right before reaching the porch, causing Laura to nearly crash into him.

"What is it?" she asked.

He frowned and swiveled his head. "I'm hearing someone."

Laura cocked her head. "I don't hear anything. What does it sound like?"

"It's hard to explain. Like someone mumbling."

"How would you hear that?" she asked out of curiosity and not disbelief.

"That's why it's hard to explain," he said before squinting in concentration. "It's almost like—" he cut off midsentence.

"Aaron?" She was worried now that maybe he was hearing voices that weren't there.

"Don't worry, they're real," he said, as if reading her thoughts. He walked to the side of the stucco house, crossing the artificial turf lawn. He broke into a trot after he rounded the corner. "Hey there."

"Oh!" Laura exclaimed. A small reddish-hued cocker spaniel sat curled against the side of the house. "What did you hear? Was the dog barking? How could I have missed a dog barking?"

Aaron waggled his eyebrows. "Not exactly." He approached the dog, who stood and wagged its tail. "What's your name?"

This time the dog barked.

"It's nice to meet you, Ginger. I'm Aaron and this is Laura."

Laura waved uncertainly at the dog. Ginger, she corrected herself. The dog had a name. That she had told Aaron. Laura was enthralled watching Aaron speak with Ginger. An animal that wasn't a familiar. So cool.

"What are you doing here? This house is for sale." Aaron frowned while Ginger limped around, alternating between silently staring and barking at him. "Slow down. I'm not getting all of that."

"Is Ginger okay?"

"No, but I'm having a hard time teasing apart what she's saying. She's very excitable," he said.

Laura could see that. Ginger continued to move around, barking over and over. "I have an idea." Laura stood tall and cleared her throat. "Sit, Ginger." The dog stopped moving though didn't obey. "Sit, Ginger," Laura repeated. The dog's rump hit the turf. "Good girl." Laura scratched the top of Ginger's head as a reward and turned to Aaron with a grin. "She and I don't understand each other, so there's no need for her to get excited trying to tell me anything. But I hoped she was trained and would recognize the word, sit."

"Sometimes simpler is better," Aaron agreed, matching Laura's grin.

"Now try to find out what's going on with Ginger."

Aaron dropped to Ginger's level and maintained eye contact. "Tell me what we need to know, Ginger. How can we help?"

CHAPTER EIGHT

AARON

Communicating with animals comprised an interesting mix of images and words appearing in Aaron's mind. Not that the animals knew English, of course. It was more that his magical inclination acted like a universal translator for a lot of what they communicated. Not everything, though. And, in those cases, images could flood his mind from the animal trying to convey a message.

Like in this instance.

The senior pup had indeed flooded Aaron's mind, to the point that it made him dizzy. Luckily, Laura's brilliant approach calmed the excited dog and now she waited for the next instructions.

Ginger stared at Aaron, sad whines escaping her throat. Her almond-shaped brown eyes begged him for help.

"Okay, Ginger. How can we help?" Aaron repeated his question.

A face appeared in Aaron's mind. Slight lines around dark brown eyes in a tanned face. Shaggy black hair carelessly brushed off his face. A friendly face. "Who is this, Ginger?"

The cocker spaniel lifted a paw, almost like she was going to shake hands, but then shook her head instead, in a very human gesture.

Instead of an answer, a new face appeared in Aaron's mind. Thinner brown hair framed brown eyes in a more wrinkled face. This face appeared friendly, too, and possibly related to the first image. "Who are these men, Ginger? Is one of them your owner? Do you live here?"

Ginger barked, "Yes."

Aaron realized his mistake. Three questions in a row and a single answer. "Sorry about that, Ginger. Let's take one at a time. Do you live here?" He hoped not, since the house was unoccupied and for sale.

Instead of answering Aaron's question, another whine escaped Ginger's throat. She dropped from sitting to laying on the ground and began panting.

Aaron placed his hands gently on either side of the dog's face, the dog's actions reminding him of the prior limping. "Are you hurt? Where does it hurt?" He realized his error of asking multiple questions again. Ginger whinnied before he could clarify.

"Leg."

"Which leg?" Aaron rocked back on his heels to better view her legs. One of her back legs appeared angled wrong. That fit with the limping they'd seen. "Anything else?"

"Inside," Ginger barked. She rested her head on the artificial turf. Her eyes never left his.

"I don't know what she said, but that high pitch doesn't sound good," Laura whispered from behind Aaron and Ginger.

Aaron had almost forgotten Laura was there. He looked up at her. "No, it doesn't. Let me call my brother."

Laura bit her lower lip while Aaron called Ben, though all she said was, "Okay."

"Ben?" Aaron asked, his hand not holding the phone continuing to stroke Ginger's fur.

Hey little brother sounded in Aaron's ear.

"Laura and I—" Aaron ignored Ben's chuckle into the phone. "—found a hurt dog while house hunting. Can I bring her to you?"

Of course, Ben agreed, all business. *I'm with Mom at the company.*

"We'll be right there. See you soon," Aaron said, and disconnected. "Ben's at Wildcrest Witches International. We're going to bring Ginger there."

If Laura wondered why they were heading to her place

of employment on a weekend to see Ben instead of a veterinarian, she didn't say anything.

"I'm going to pick you up now," Aaron said to Ginger before wrapping the dog in his strong arms and lifting her. He turned to Laura. "Will we fit in your car or can you drive my Jeep?"

"It's probably better to take the Jeep," Laura said after a moment's consideration.

Together they walked to the vehicle and got situated. While Laura drove, careful of any bumps in the road that might hurt the injured Ginger, Aaron continued to speak with the senior in his lap.

"I know it hurts. Can you tell me anything more? Do you know the names of the men you showed me?"

Laura's brow furrowed at his questions, though Aaron didn't answer her unspoken ones. He'd explain when he explained to Ben.

Images of the men, a blue nondescript sedan, and a blacktop road swirled in Aaron's mind. But only one word. "Help."

"Don't worry, Ginger. We're going to help you. And we'll do what we can to help you find your owner." The sweet girl liked that and wagged her tail at Aaron, who scratched her ears and under her chin. Aaron met Laura's concerned eyes. "Ginger's confused, maybe from the pain, and so what I'm getting isn't clear. But, either way, we need to find her owner."

CHAPTER NINE

LAURA

The drive to Wildcrest Witches International passed quickly and soon Laura was parking the Jeep in a spot outside the one-story stucco building that almost resembled a ranch-style home. The coven's company wasn't big, so they didn't need much space. Aaron exited the vehicle, careful not to jostle Ginger. Laura moved ahead to open the front door for them. She used her key card to open the doors and held one open for Aaron to bring the ailing dog through.

"Thanks." Aaron walked through the foyer, straight for the glass double doors that led to the back row of offices. He hooked a left, presumably toward his mother's office.

Aaron hadn't explained why they had taken Ginger to his brother, instead of a veterinarian. When they entered his mother's office and she saw Ben standing beside the empty walnut desk, it hit her. Ben's magical inclination was to know what someone needed when they were sick. She hadn't realized that extended from humans to animals. It made sense; humans were animals, too.

"Mom stepped out but will be right back. Bring the dog to me," Ben instructed his brother. "Hey Laura. Nice to see you."

Laura nodded in greeting, unable to speak. Ben. Her high school crush. Currently dating her high school frenemy Shelly Newsome. He looked great as always, but that was all. She didn't feel the emotions she'd felt years ago. And that made sense. The crush had been years earlier. She didn't still have feelings for him.

So why should that get in the way of seeing Aaron?

The question snuck in and before she could explore it, she refocused her attention on the brothers discussing Ginger.

"Hey sweetheart, I know it hurts," Ben said. He ran his fingers through Ginger's fur, causing her to wriggle her butt. After manipulating her limbs a little and hovering his hands over sections of her body, especially her leg and chest, Ben patted her head a final time.

"What's the word?" Aaron asked.

"Her leg might be broken and a couple of ribs are maybe

bruised. There doesn't seem to be any organ damage. The damage is consistent with blunt force trauma."

"Someone hit her," Laura exclaimed, a hand fluttering to cover her mouth.

Ben nodded. "Or she hit something."

"Like hit by a car?" Aaron asked. When Ben nodded, Aaron directed his next question to Ginger. "What happened?"

Laura watched Aaron, fascinated, as he nodded in response to a series of yips from Ginger. After a few exchanges, Aaron addressed Ben and Laura.

"She keeps showing me a picture of a car, but I can't nail it down more than that. The car and the pictures of two similar-looking men. One of these men could be the owner. Or could be the one who threw her from a car, or hit her with a car. I really can't be more precise."

"That's okay," Laura said, laying a hand on his forearm, not missing the sly smile on Ben's face at the movement. She ignored Aaron's brother. "This gives us a great place to start."

"In the meantime, I'm heading back to the hospital and can drop Ginger at the vet on my way," Ben offered.

"Thanks," Aaron said.

"Perfect. That will give us a chance to do some sleuthing into the men Ginger keeps showing you, Aaron," Laura said.

"What do you suggest?"

"We can use my computer to cross-reference property records with social media—" she answered.

"I can check with the listing agent as well," Aaron added.

"—and between these, we might be able to identify the men and confirm if one of them is the owner."

"Also, if one of them hurt her," Aaron said darkly. He scratched Ginger behind the ears, then carefully ran his hand over the length of her body.

"Hopefully, there's a simpler explanation." Laura refused to believe someone would deliberately hurt Ginger.

"There may be," Ben concurred. "It could have been an accident. Blunt force trauma doesn't have to be an attack or purposeful violence."

A wide smile lit up Aaron's face. "You're both right. I can't imagine someone in Wildcrest doing something harmful like that."

"Exactly," Laura said. The supernatural beings in Wildcrest cared for nature more than most. That didn't mean there couldn't be a sinister witch, but the chances were much lower in their small town.

"I was hoping to see Mom before I left," Ben said, glancing toward the open office door. "But I'm not sure how long her meeting is going to last."

"If it's with someone from book club, it could be another hour," Aaron joked.

Laura joined the brothers in chuckling. Even she knew

about Esther's reading addiction. She loved books and read several every week. At least once a week, Laura popped into Esther's office, only to see her engrossed in a book. 'Just one more chapter' was practically a mantra for Esther.

"We'll let her know you still needed to talk to her," Aaron offered.

"Thanks," Ben said, and leaned over to pick up Ginger from his mother's desk.

A voice from the door interrupted the conversation. "Aaron! So great to see you. Laura, how did the house hunting go?"

Laura turned at the sound of her boss's voice. "Hi Esther. It went well. I think we found the winner."

"That's wonderful." Esther entered her office and then startled when she saw a dog on her desk. "Whose dog is that? She's adorable."

Aaron brought Esther up to speed.

"Oh, Ben, that's wonderful that you can bring Ginger to the vet so Aaron and Laura can go on their lunch date."

"Date?" Laura asked. She and Aaron wore matching expressions of surprise, and Ben tried unsuccessfully to hide a smirk.

"Well, yes." Esther's brow furrowed. "I thought you were going to lunch after looking at houses. Isn't that what you said, Aaron?"

CHAPTER TEN

AARON

"Um," Aaron eloquently responded as his mother crossed her office to her desk. "I didn't say it was a date." When he saw Laura's flushed face, his heart sank. He never should have told his mother that he was asking Laura out. She'd asked him how the house hunting was going, and he'd slipped and confessed.

"Hmm." Esther sat behind her desk and crossed her long legs. "I could have sworn you said it was a date. But perhaps I misunderstood."

"Yeah, Mom, I'm sorry, you did misunderstand," Aaron said in a rush. "I definitely didn't say it was a date. We're work colleagues." His voice stuttered on the last sentence.

Ben and Esther both lifted eyebrows in matching expressions of disbelief. "Work colleagues?" his mother asked.

"Yes. I'm her realtor," he answered, as if that made any sense.

"Sure, of course," Esther said and folded her hands on the desktop.

Aaron wished a hole would open up below him and swallow him whole. That would be preferable to the excruciating embarrassment of having his mother tell the woman he was interested in that he'd talked to her about that interest.

He wondered if Laura could use her ability to manipulate matter to open that hole beneath him. She'd said she could only manipulate small amounts of matter, but she also said she'd changed pieces of an entire car. Perhaps creating a hole in the floor would be easy. Of course, then there was the matter of where he'd go. There was no basement in the building, so she might need to change more matter, perhaps manipulate the concrete base of the building.

Aaron knew that his frenzied thoughts were an obvious effort to avoid remaining in this conversation, or thinking about what his mother said to Laura.

Laura. She was flushed so red she looked like she was having a heart attack or something. No doubt she'd love to make him vanish, too.

Ben chuckled and stood, cradling Ginger to his chest. "On that supremely awkward note," he said with a snort. "I'll take sweet Ginger to the vet."

"Let us know how she's doing," Aaron requested, thrilled with the topic change. He stopped his brother from walking past and scratched Ginger's head. "You're going to be okay. My brother will take good care of you."

Ginger barked. "Feel better."

"Yes, you're going to feel much better," he assured her.

She barked again, and the images of the two men flittered through his mind.

"We'll figure out who those two are," he promised. He held his hand in front of her face and she licked him, then gave a happy sigh.

"Okay, that's enough of that," Ben said. "Let me get her to the vet."

Aaron stepped aside and he, Laura, and Esther watched Ben leave with the cocker spaniel cradled in his arms.

Silence descended on the room. The three stared at each other. Aaron cleared his throat. "How was your meeting, Mom?"

Esther seemed a bit put out by the question and didn't answer.

Aaron wondered if that meant the meeting didn't go well.

"The meeting was fine. Everything is set for the next release," she said.

Laura nodded at the statement. Aaron was confused. He was on the Board of Directors of Wildcrest Witches International, though he rarely interacted unless they needed him for something specific. Whatever the release was, it didn't concern him, apparently.

"Is everything okay, Esther?" Laura asked, approaching the desk.

So, it wasn't just him that noticed his mother seemed… irritated wasn't the right word, but it was close.

His mother closed her brown eyes, then fanned herself with a rolled-up piece of paper. "I'm fine." She set the paper down and frowned. "I don't know."

"Mom? Should I call Ben back to check on you?" If something was wrong with their mother, Ben would be able to tell.

"What?" She appeared startled by that suggestion. "No, that's unnecessary. I got hot for a moment." She stood from the desk. "But maybe I'll head home."

Laura placed a hand on Esther's elbow. "That might not be a bad idea. And since it's the weekend, and you're the CFO, I don't think anyone's going to give you a hard time," she joked.

Esther smiled wanly. "True enough."

Aaron closely watched his mother walk to the office door. Per usual, she looked sharp in a business suit, with her long brown hair held back in a loose bun. Esther appeared fine, steady on her feet and with no evidence of confusion. Maybe she was coming down with something. He frowned. He'd call his brother later anyway, to check in with him about it.

"Have a good lunch that isn't a date," Esther said from the doorway.

Aaron winced at the comment, uncertain whether he was reading a tone in it. Surely not. After all, he couldn't think of a reason his mother would be unhappy that he wasn't going out on a date with Laura. She supported whatever Aaron did; she wasn't an overbearing mother.

"Enjoy your half-day," Laura said before Esther disappeared out of the office.

They listened to his mother's heels on the tile floor until they faded away, and then stared at each other.

"I'm sorry about that. I'm not sure where she got that from," Aaron said lamely, wondering why he didn't just tell her the truth. He was blunt with everyone else.

Laura's cheeks tinted pink again and she waved away his apology and pathetic lack of explanation. "No worries," she assured him. "You did ask me out, so maybe you did say something to her about planning that."

"Yeah, that's true," he admitted, wishing again for that hole to open up. He didn't know why this bothered him so much. He'd asked other women out who had said no. It wasn't that big of a deal. Except this time, it was.

"But we have work to do. We need to find Ginger's owner."

"What should we do first?" Aaron asked, thankful for the distraction and the opportunity to help the cocker spaniel.

"Let's head to my office and start researching. We can order food."

CHAPTER ELEVEN

LAURA

The walk to Laura's room took but a minute, though felt much longer. The awkwardness in Esther Wright's office reverberated around them as they crossed the building from there to Laura's.

"Are you ready to find Ginger's owner?" Laura asked, taking a seat at her walnut desk. All the executive offices contained the same furniture. No particular reason for that, she assumed, other than expediency. Artwork and knickknacks provided touches of personality and color. In her case, photographs of the surrounding mountains covered her walls.

"Is that one new?" Aaron asked instead, peering at a

vivid image of snow-capped mountain peaks.

"Yes," she answered, joining him before the latest image. "I took that this past winter."

"It's gorgeous."

"Thank you. It doesn't do it justice." Laura was keenly aware of how close they stood to each other while admiring her handiwork. She cleared her throat and moved away from his heat to sit again behind her desk. "What do you want me to order for lunch? I can see if *Magic Eats* doesn't have a wait."

"Perfect. I'll take a grilled cheese sandwich with fries."

Laura checked online. The 1950s-style diner was popular in town, but it looked like they weren't busy today. That was a lucky break. She stuck with a veggie sandwich for herself; Aaron was a vegetarian, and even though she knew he didn't mind if those around him ate meat, she chose not to.

She finished the order and smiled at Aaron. "You ready?"

"Yes, ma'am," he joked with a salute, then took the brown leather chair opposite her and whipped out his cellphone. "I'll call the listing agent on the house where we found Ginger and get the name of the owner."

Laura was already clicking keys on her keyboard. "I'll check the county for the official property owner to confirm." She clicked through to the property assessor's website, and with a few more clicks, entered the address in the search bar for the records.

Meanwhile, Aaron located the listing agent's number and called her. "Hi Lisa, it's Aaron."

Laura tuned his conversation out while scrolling to the exact address of the home. She jotted down the name listed for the property owner just as Aaron concluded his call.

"Jack Panner?" she asked.

"Jack Panner," he confirmed.

"Did you get a phone number for Mr. Panner?"

"I did."

"Let's give Mr. Panner a call and find out if he's Ginger's owner." Excitement rose in Laura that they might solve their mystery so quickly.

Aaron typed the number into his cellphone, then held it up to his ear. After a moment, he gave a quick shake of his head. "Voicemail," he told her, then, "Good afternoon Mr. Panner. This is Aaron Wright. I'm a real estate agent. Your agent Lisa gave me your number. If you could, please call me when you have a chance." Aaron ended the message with his phone number.

"Now we wait," he said.

"Not quite," Laura disagreed. She began typing again, talking to him as she did. "Now that we have a name, we can look him up on social media to see if his picture matches what Ginger showed you." She scrolled through profile names. "Okay, there are several Jack Panners, but only one here in Wildcrest. If he's kept his location updated, this could be him!" She waved Aaron over. "Do you want to see his picture?"

Aaron came around the desk to stand beside Laura in her chair. He leaned over to look at the photograph. It was of a man hiking in the desert. "Can you make it bigger?"

"Yep," she answered, double-clicking on the picture. Aaron's light musk wafted over her and she barely stopped herself from inhaling deeply. That would have been awkward. When his arm bumped hers, the physical contact gave her goosebumps.

"That's him," he said. "That's one of the images Ginger showed me. He has to be her owner."

Laura stood and impulsively threw her arms around Aaron. He stiffened a moment and then they melded together, warmth flowing over them as they reveled in their success and enjoyed the closeness. Although she wondered about the fact that she'd now hugged him twice in one day. That was most definitely not like her. At all. And yet.

"Good job," Aaron whispered.

"You too."

Aaron's cellphone rang, and he released Laura before pulling the phone from his pocket. "It's him," he said before answering. "Hello, this is Aaron Wright." He listened to a voice on the other end, his smile growing wider. "Yes, I'm calling about your house for sale, but not for the reason you're probably thinking." Aaron explained about finding Ginger and asked if he was her owner.

When Aaron's smile fell, Laura flattened her palms against the desk and bit her lower lip. That didn't look good.

"Do you know anybody who may have lost a cocker spaniel? Her name is Ginger." He listened to the response. "No? That's too bad. If you think—"

Aaron stopped mid-sentence and Laura perked up. "Does he have an idea?" she whispered.

"Okay, thank you," Aaron said. "That's a great help." He ended the call and retook his seat. "Give me a sec to type out some names."

"Of course," Laura said, but he was already typing. Her phone dinged. "The food is here. I'll go grab it."

She hurried through the house and collected the meals from Billy the delivery driver. When she returned to her office, Aaron had finished and was waiting to explain what he'd learned. She spread out the food and they ate while they talked.

"Jack said he'd listed his house *For Sale by Owner* for a day or so before giving the listing to an agent yesterday, since he unexpectedly would be heading out of town for a couple of weeks. He says he remembered showing the house to a guy who had a cocker spaniel. He couldn't be sure which guy it was, so he gave me three names of people he showed the house to before he decided to go with a realtor."

"Give me the names," Laura said and he slid his

cellphone across the desk. She typed the first into the search bar.

"Do you have a picture for me to see?"

Laura shook her head while she answered, "There's a picture, but this guy is bald, so I doubt he's the other one Ginger showed you."

"Ah, okay. Try lucky number two."

"Hmm, this one is a maybe. Let me open another browser window and get a picture of the third man, and then you can compare them." A few more keystrokes and she spun the laptop around to face him. "Um, no need for you to get up again."

"Sure," he said, though she thought she saw disappointment flare.

Because he wouldn't be able to stand near her again? Or maybe that was wishful thinking on her part.

He focused on the photographs blown up on the screen. "This one," he crowed, pointing. "Definitely this one. The one on the left," he clarified as she turned the laptop back toward herself.

"Marvin Kelm," Laura read from the screen. "Hmm." She frowned. "He hasn't posted anything in days."

"Maybe he's not active on social media?"

She scrolled further down the page. "No, before that, he posted every day. Including pictures of Ginger!"

Aaron held up his hands and they shared a congratulatory high-five.

"Now we need to find him." Laura typed some more. "I've got a number." She entered the number and mouthed *voicemail* when Marvin Kelm's voicemail greeting started. "Good afternoon, Mr. Kelm. My name is Laura Harkin and I believe my… friend… and I found your dog, Ginger. Please call me at your earliest convenience. We'd love to return her to you." She concluded the call and frowned at Aaron.

"What's wrong? Ginger's being treated right now anyway, so it's not a big deal that we didn't reach him right away."

"I know, but what if something happened to him? To Marvin Kelm?" She nibbled her lower lip. "I know it's only social media, but he hasn't posted anything. Not even looking for his lost dog."

Now Aaron's frown matched hers. "Do you think he's been hurt? Or worse?"

Laura's eyes widened. "I hope not. Maybe you can check with your brother to see if he's been admitted to the hospital."

"That's a great idea. I'll text him the name and picture, and ask."

Laura watched Aaron while he did just that, admiring his strong jaw and how he stuck his tongue out like his brother did when he was thinking. Must be a family trait.

Aaron looked up and caught her staring. She flushed and he waggled his eyebrows. "Like what you see?"

Her mouth dropped open at the flirtation, and she changed the subject. "Should we head to the hospital now? Just in case?"

He seemed to smother a smile at her not-very-smooth topic change. "Sure, why not? Maybe Ben will have an answer for us by the time we arrive."

CHAPTER TWELVE

AARON

"After we reunite Ginger with her owner, I have a couple more homes to show you," Aaron said as they sat in his Jeep at the one stoplight between Wildcrest Witches International and Wildcrest Hospital.

Laura laughed. "Oh, no, I'm finished. I'm ready to put in an offer on the house from earlier. The one before the one where we found the dog."

He'd remembered she'd said that, but secretly hoped she wasn't ready. Although, her other words came back to him, too. "Ah, because once you buy the house, I can ask you out." His eyes cut to her as he accelerated through the intersection.

"Oh. Right. I said that, didn't I?"

"You did." His heart pounded while he waited for the next sentence to come out of her mouth. He didn't have to wait long.

"I guess we'll see what happens," she said in a playful tone.

He didn't have a snappy comeback for that, and the silence stretched for the final few minutes of the drive. After he parked and turned off the car, Aaron faced her.

"Wait," he said, reaching for her arm before she could open her door.

"Yes?"

Aaron didn't speak. He opened his mouth, closed it. "I'm glad we're on this adventure together," he finally said.

"Me too." Her hand reached across the center console.

He held his breath. Her fingers grazed his cheek. They leaned toward each other. And just when Aaron thought their lips would meet, she jerked backward.

"We should finish this adventure," she said, the unspoken *first* floating between them.

"Okay," he whispered.

Aaron barely noticed crossing the parking lot. She almost kissed him. Or he almost kissed her. Whichever it was, he felt phantom lips on his. An arriving text brought him back to the moment.

Laura looked at him. "Ben?"

"Yep." He scanned the text. "Nobody by that name, but

there is a John Doe who resembles the photo. He gave me a room number to meet him in, in about ten minutes."

"Okay, sounds good," Laura said, and then tripped over a pothole near the sidewalk.

Aaron caught her by the arm and pulled him to her to prevent her fall. "Are you okay?"

She breathed into his ear – she was so tall! – and shakily replied yes.

"They really should fix that," he mumbled, more to himself than to Laura.

"I can," she said, and stood over the break in the blacktop.

"You what?"

"I can fix it."

"You can fix—" he started, then stopped. "Right, of course." He stepped back to watch the literal magic.

Laura concentrated on the hole and, like when she'd manipulated the kitchen island at the house for sale, the area above the hole grew hazy. It darkened and the blacktop appeared to move of its own volition.

Aaron bit back a snort. The movement reminded him of the movie *The Blob*.

"Wait." Laura frowned. A bead of sweat broke out on her forehead.

As Aaron watched, the center of the new blacktop crumbled and collapsed in on itself, leaving the hole bigger than it was before.

"I don't understand." She concentrated harder. The haze reappeared and the process repeated.

Including the part where it fell apart. Now the hole was twice the size it had been before Laura attempted her magic.

"I don't understand," she repeated.

Before she could try a third time, Aaron stopped her. "I don't know what's happening either, but maybe we should just let the hospital know they have a pothole that could cause an accident." He said the words gently, and still her eyes shined with tears when she looked at him.

"That's never happened before."

"Let's check in with Ben. Maybe he can see if there's something on the fritz with you." His attempt at a jovial tone worked and she cracked a slight smile.

"Maybe I'm tired," she said. "But I'll let Ben look me over, anyway."

CHAPTER THIRTEEN

LAURA

I'll let Ben look me over. Laura couldn't believe how that sounded, but Aaron didn't react, so maybe it was all in her head.

"Let's find the room Ben texted," Aaron said after they entered the hospital's sliding glass doors. He beelined for the elevator.

Laura was slower to follow, her mind stuck on her magic not working.

"You coming?" He held the door open with one arm and beckoned her with the other.

"Yes, sorry." She stepped into the elevator and stood beside him, very aware of his closeness. "I was thinking."

Aaron touched her hand. "It's going to be okay."

Of course, he knew what she'd been thinking about. A witch without magic. Well, that was like missing a part of yourself.

The elevator doors opened and Laura snickered. Tall Ben towered over short Shelly where they stood outside a room at the far end of the hall. Not that long ago, Shelly had had an issue with not feeling like a witch, because of her own misfiring magic. Laura now had a small sense of her former frenemy's frustration.

Ben and Shelly waved as Laura and Aaron approached.

Before she could lose her nerve from the risk of embarrassment, Laura blurted out her request. "Ben, I'd rather not discuss the specifics, but can you tell me if anything seems off? Anything medically?"

Although Ben quirked an eyebrow, he didn't question. "Of course." He eyed her up and down, in a clinical way, though she still felt her throat tighten.

Thankfully, it didn't appear that he needed to go hands-on with checking. Laura thought she'd have a stroke if that was necessary. And it didn't even occur to her to ask first.

Ben smiled. "Everything checks out."

Laura felt both relief and disappointment at the pronouncement.

"Isn't that good news?" Shelly asked.

"Of course." Laura needed to focus on something else. "Guys, do you mind if I borrow Shelly for a moment?"

"Sure," Aaron said, his eyes questioning.

"Just girls' stuff," she explained.

Laura strode away from the men, assuming Shelly would follow. Hearing footfalls on the linoleum, she was right. They stopped near a window back toward the elevator. This section of the hallway was deserted. Laura poked her head into the nearest room and, seeing it empty, pulled Shelly inside.

"I need to talk to you," Laura said. She inhaled deeply. And didn't say anything.

Shelly quirked an eyebrow. "You need to actually speak for this to work. Is it about what you asked Ben to check for?"

"No, it's not." Laura wasn't ready to talk about her magical issues yet, but she had another issue that Shelly was uniquely qualified to weigh in on. "You know Aaron and I have been looking for a house. For me," she added when she realized how that sounded.

"Yes."

Laura stared over Shelly's shoulder. "I realized today that I've been delaying choosing one."

"Not because you couldn't find the one you like?"

"Yes and no."

Shelly laughed. "That's not really an answer."

"I mean, no, I didn't find one that I liked. But." Laura bit her lower lip. "I kept changing what I told Aaron I was looking for."

"You didn't!"

"Well, that's not accurate. I kept increasing what I wanted. Yeah. That's more accurate."

"That seems logical, to be honest. The more homes you see, the more you realize what you want."

Laura glanced out the window on the far side of the room. "True."

"Except that it's more than that," Shelly guessed.

"He asked me on a date," Laura blurted out, then averted her gaze.

"You said no?"

"I work for his mother and we're work colleagues."

Shelly shook her head. "Those aren't reasons. It's a small town; everybody works for or with someone's family. And he's only finding you a house. *He's* not your boss."

"What about if it's because I liked Ben before? That's weird, right?"

"Yes, it's weird that you're using that as an excuse. Because, no, it's not at all weird to like one person years ago and someone else now," Shelly said. "Besides, I thought you moved on from high school." Shelly added this with a knowing look, and Laura flushed at having her own words tossed back at her.

"It's not weird that I liked Ben before and now I find Aaron attractive?"

"Not at all," Shelly repeated.

Relief swept over Laura. Intellectually, she knew that

there was nothing wrong with liking one brother years before liking the other. But, emotionally… She needed to hear someone else say that it was no big deal.

"Besides, I took Ben off the market, remember?"

"Indeed," Laura said and impulsively threw her arms around the smaller woman. "Thank you."

"You're welcome."

"Sorry if that was awkward," Laura said. Although that made three hugs in one day. She was acting all out of sorts today.

"No need to apologize. It's nice to see this—" Shelly paused. "—softer side of you. Human."

"Oh." Laura didn't know what to say to that. She never really had friends before. Maybe this was what that felt like.

"Don't worry, I won't make it more awkward," Shelly assured her with a laugh.

"Thanks." Laura glanced at the room's exit. "Let's join the men and find out if this John Doe is our missing owner."

CHAPTER FOURTEEN

AARON

"What do you think they're talking about?" Aaron asked nervously, wishing he could be a fly on that wall.

"Relax, little brother." Ben glanced down the empty hall in the direction the women had gone. "I don't hear yelling, so I don't think they're fighting or anything." He grinned. "Or are you worried they're talking about you?"

Aaron's eyes widened. "Why would I think they're talking about me?"

"Oh, I don't know. There's some wicked chemistry between you two."

"There is?" Aaron swallowed. "Yeah, there is. Except I asked her out and she said no."

Ben pursed his lips. "Give her time. She'll come around."

"I hope so."

"That's not what you came here for."

"No, it's not. Is this the John Doe's room? And he looks like the photo I sent you?" Aaron asked, indicating the closed door behind Ben.

"Yes, to the first question. And a strong maybe to the second."

"What happened to him? I know you're not supposed to talk about his medical condition with me, but maybe it'll help us identify him."

"Oh, yeah, I wouldn't be doing this if not for the fact that we're making zero headway with him."

"What do you mean?"

"A concerned citizen found him wandering a few blocks from here."

"Near the house that's for sale."

"Um, not too far off from that. The town's not that big, though, so that could be said about almost anything."

Aaron laughed. "Touché."

"He has some facial contusions suggesting a fight or accident."

"What did he say when you asked him?"

"We didn't. By the time he arrived here, he was delirious. We started treatment immediately, of course, and now we're just waiting for him to wake up." Ben lifted the chart from its holder next to the door and scanned the top.

"What's his prognosis?"

"Pretty good. I expect him to wake up sometime today. His vitals show he's responding well to the treatment."

"I guess that means the police haven't found his family yet."

"No, I assume not—"

"I need to give this name to the police," Aaron interrupted. "His family must be worried sick."

"Maybe see if you agree that he looks like the same guy," Ben cautioned, "before you notify the police and give a potentially worried family false hope."

"I see what you mean." Aaron brightened. "There's another option."

"There is?"

"Ginger can tell us."

Ben was well-aware of his brother's magical inclination, so didn't bat an eye at Aaron's idea. "If she's not in surgery, yeah, she probably could. Regardless of his facial bruising, she'd recognize his smell."

Aaron saw the women approaching in his peripheral vision.

"What have you been talking about?" Shelly asked, all wide-eyed innocence.

Ben smothered a laugh, and both Aaron and Laura turned beet-red.

"We were just about to go in and see John Doe," Aaron said into the awkwardness.

"That's a great idea," Laura said with more enthusiasm than the situation warranted. She opened the door and walked between the others to stand by John Doe's bed.

Aaron, Shelly, and Ben were a moment behind her. Aaron took his phone from his pocket and opened the photograph of Marvin Kelm.

The bruises, wires, and oxygen mask complicated their review, but in the end, they were confident it was him. His legs stretched to the bottom of the bed, so he was tall. His shaggy black hair fell in lank pieces around a face with slight wrinkles. He appeared to be the same late 30s or early 40s that Marvin did in his profile photo. The fall of the sheet suggested he was a little plump, maybe like an athlete gone soft.

"Is he going to be okay?" Laura asked, her heart breaking for the likely Marvin and Ginger.

Ben walked the women through the background and prognosis he'd provided to Aaron.

"Since we think it's him, what do we do next?" Shelly asked.

Ben and Aaron exchanged a look.

"I had an idea." Aaron explained the plan to bring Ginger to the hospital, sneak her into this room, and then she could identify whether the man in the bed was her owner.

"That's brilliant," Laura said, and Aaron warmed at the compliment.

"Is Ginger okay to be picked up?" Shelly asked.

"I was about to check." Ben typed into his phone and within a minute, a response arrived. He winked. "The vet okayed her to travel. She didn't need surgery after all."

Aaron grabbed Laura's hand without thinking. She curled her fingers around his. "You ready to go get our dog?"

CHAPTER FIFTEEN

LAURA

Go get our dog. Warmth flooded Laura at Aaron's choice of words and the fact of his fingers entwined with hers. They were in this together. On an adventure to help someone. She'd missed this feeling of closeness with someone else. *Not since my parents—*

Thankfully, they reached Aaron's Jeep before she could follow that thought. This time he drove the short distance to the veterinary office. As they parked, a text dinged on Aaron's phone.

"It's my mom," he explained. "She wants to know how Ginger is doing."

Laura grinned. Esther really had a big heart.

Aaron typed a response, then frowned at the reply.

"What?" Laura asked.

"She's asking how our lunch went." His ears turned red as he typed. "I'm explaining we ate at your desk while we found Ginger's owner."

Laura didn't know what to think, so she nodded and waited for him to finish.

Aaron put his phone in a pocket and then they headed for the vet. He held the door open for her and they entered the foyer.

"Hey Aaron," the receptionist greeted him when they entered.

"Hi Shannon," he said. "We're here to pick up Ginger. I believe my brother called?"

"Yep." Shannon picked up the phone. "Can you bring Ginger up?" She flashed a smile at them then hung the phone up. "It'll just be a minute. By the way, she has a microchip. When we scanned it, it didn't have current information. The person we called said they gave her to a rescue. They didn't remember which one. And she hasn't been a patient in this office before."

"Okay, thanks, Shannon. That's helpful."

Laura hung back, watching the easy conversation between Aaron and Shannon. He was so personable. She doubted he had any frenemies. Laura almost laughed at the rambling nature of her thoughts, but stopped short when another technician appeared, leading Ginger out on a leash.

The cute cocker spaniel had a bright orange wrap on her leg and a small shaved spot, where maybe they had to give her fluids. She seemed happy to see them, wagging her tail and offering quick little barks.

Aaron chuckled. "Yes, Ginger, we're here to bring you to your owner." He kneeled before her. "Is his name Marvin?"

Ginger barked.

Laura had no idea if it was a confirmation until Aaron said, "Yes."

"We're going to bring you to him to confirm, okay?" Aaron asked the cocker spaniel.

Ginger barked again and both the receptionist and technician looked on as if this were the most natural thing in the world. As if every day, someone spoke Dog in their office.

Of course, this was Wildcrest. Maybe they did see this more often.

Aaron scratched Ginger behind the ears again, and her wagging tail wiggled her entire body. He stood and accepted the leash from the technician. "Thanks."

With that, the three of them returned to the Jeep. Aaron secured Ginger in the backseat. Laura giggled when he pulled the seatbelt over her. It was necessary, but she wondered if the dog would stay put. Then Aaron explained to Ginger that she needed to stay put, and Laura understood.

"That's handy," she said.

"What is?"

"Being able to tell an animal what you want them to do."

Aaron slid into the driver's seat and smiled at Laura. "It's not always that easy, but when I can share a simple picture of her in the seat with the word *Stay*, that has a higher likelihood of success."

"I love it," Laura said.

"Me too."

They stared at each other, the air heavy with promise. Laura licked her lips and Aaron's eyes dilated.

"We'd better get Ginger to the hospital," Laura said shakily. She couldn't remember the last time she'd kissed a man, and the thought saddened her.

Aaron gripped the steering wheel. "Of course."

The short drive back to the hospital remained expectant. Laura wondered what it would have been like to kiss Aaron at that moment. Butterflies took flight at the thought and she concentrated on settling them.

He parked the Jeep without comment, and let Ginger out of the backseat.

"She moves well with that flexible cast," Laura commented.

"It was just a hairline fracture. Shouldn't take too long to heal," he said. "Ben told me," he added, at her questioning look.

The trio walked to the side of the main entrance and considered their plan.

"Ben obviously knows we're doing this," Aaron said.

"But the hospital doesn't allow dogs?" Laura asked.

"No. What do you think?"

"Are therapy dogs allowed?"

"Maybe," Aaron answered. "There's only one way to find out."

They shared a conspiratorial grin, then waltzed into the hospital.

"May I help you?" a woman at the front desk asked, staring back and forth between them and Ginger.

"We're here to visit Marvin Kelm," Aaron explained.

"This is Ginger, our therapy dog," Laura added, with an air of complete confidence.

"Oh, okay. Do you know where you're going?"

"Yep. Dr. Benjamin Wright provided the room number," Aaron said.

The receptionist visibly relaxed at the chief resident's name, and Laura wondered if that might get him in trouble later. She hoped not.

"I hope the patient enjoys the visit," the receptionist called out as they headed toward the elevator.

"That was fun," Laura admitted while they rode the elevator up to the third floor.

Aaron nudged her with his shoulder. "Rebel."

"You know it."

The elevator doors opened and the trio walked down the hallway to the closed door of Marvin's room.

"Let me text Ben that we're here and headed in."

While he did, Laura crouched at Ginger's level and scratched her behind the ears, rubbing the velvet softness. The dog rewarded her with a lick on the cheek.

"She likes you," Aaron said.

"What's not to like?" Laura quipped.

"Indeed."

Laura reached for the doorknob. "Moment of truth," she said.

It was obvious they had the right man the instant they entered Marvin Kelm's room. Ginger began dancing around, offering quick, happy barks. She swiveled her head back and forth between Aaron and Marvin, the latter sleeping in the bed.

"I'll wake him up," Aaron assured the excited dog. "Hold on."

Ginger sat on her back haunches at Aaron's words.

"Mr. Kelm? Marvin?" Aaron approached the bed. "We have someone here who'd like to see you."

Marvin didn't respond. Aaron continued to speak softly to Marvin and then switched focus. "Ginger?" The cocker spaniel cocked her head in response. "I need you to bark, but as quietly as possible. Can you do that?"

Before Laura could voice her question, Aaron answered. "She understands what I'm telling her, I promise."

Laura chuckled. "I believe you." She watched with rapt attention.

Ginger padded closer to Marvin's bed. When her rump hit the floor, she emitted a tiny yip.

Marvin's eyes fluttered open. "Hello?" He rasped the question. His eyes focused on Aaron and he licked his lips. "Hello?" he repeated.

"I'm Aaron. You're in the hospital. We found someone who belongs to you." He leaned down and picked up the wiggling dog.

"Ginger!" Marvin tried to sit up further but floundered among the wires.

"You might want to use the bed controller," Laura suggested, hiding a smile at the obvious delight of both Marvin and Ginger at being reunited.

Once Marvin adjusted the bed to be seated upright, Aaron carefully set Ginger in his lap. They showered each other with kisses while Aaron and Laura watched.

"Thank you," Marvin said to them, tears of gratitude in his eyes.

"You're welcome," Laura and Aaron responded together, eliciting a chuckle from all three.

"What happened?" Laura asked.

Marvin explained he hadn't been feeling well a couple of days ago, and had run out of supplies to check his sugar levels. Stupid, he knew. So, he tried to manage it without checking. He realized that wasn't working and so tried to drive himself to the hospital. He was so unaware that he hadn't even noticed Ginger jump into the back seat before he closed the car door. Unfortunately, he must have blacked out, because he drove into a tree. What happened next was a bit of a blur, he said. He remembered fragments of walking on the street, then getting into someone's car and being brought there.

"I was so worried about Ginger, but couldn't find my words to express it." He sipped at the water by his bed. "I can't thank you both enough for bringing her back to me." He glanced at a meal tray. "If only I had orange Jell-O instead of green," he joked with a tired smile.

Aaron laughed dutifully at the attempt at levity, though Laura beamed.

"I might be able to do something about that," she said with a wink.

"You can?"

Laura grabbed the Jell-O off the tray. "Be right back."

Aaron followed her out of the room. "Are you doing what I think you're doing?"

"Yep." Standing outside of the room, with Aaron shielding her from the view of interested eyes – although the hallway was empty – she held the container in her hands and concentrated.

Laura imagined the green dessert as orange. She tasted the flavor of sun-ripened oranges in her mouth, pictured the bright orange of a tangy gelatin. The air above the container grew hazy and the color fluctuated. She could do this. There was nothing wrong with her magic.

The fruity concoction resembled a rainbow, a chaotic mix of green, orange, blue, and red. She frowned. That wasn't supposed to happen.

"Is everything okay?"

Laura heard Aaron's voice as if from a distance. She concentrated harder, but it was like before with the parking lot blacktop. The air grew hazy a second time and the colors swirled. Until they stopped.

"It's not supposed to be brown, is it?" Aaron asked.

"No, it's not." Laura stared at yet another failure of her magic. She couldn't imagine what was happening. Nothing had changed—

The moments with Aaron. She'd almost kissed him twice. Right before each instance of her magic going haywire. There couldn't be a connection.

Could there?

CHAPTER SIXTEEN

AARON

Aaron kept wanting to say something to Laura, but the thought of saying the wrong thing stopped him each time. They were on their way to Laura's house. Ben had agreed to keep Ginger in his office until Marvin was discharged; as Chief Resident, nobody would enter his office uninvited.

Aaron pulled up in front of her current house. "We solved the mystery," he said, and she offered him a slight smile in response.

"We did. What should we do next?" she asked.

"Since Marvin's awake, he can let his family know he's okay. I guess I'll work on the offer you want to put on the earlier house. Sound good?"

She stood outside the Jeep, leaning against the frame. "That sounds good. Let me know what you recommend for an offer."

"I'll have a draft this afternoon. Talk soon." That last was said to her back. She'd closed the car door already. She gave a half-wave over her shoulder and walked to her front door. He waited until she'd gone inside before pulling away.

During his drive home, his mind remained occupied with thoughts of Laura and her magic not working. Those thoughts still crowded his mind as he opened the door to the home he shared with his brothers. Although he figured Ben wouldn't be with them too much longer. Aaron couldn't imagine Ben and Shelly wouldn't have moved in together by the end of the year.

Aaron crossed through the open floor plan living area toward the three bedrooms in the back, pleased as always by how well their remodel of the home had gone. The real estate agent in him loved to highlight in his mind what he would put into a listing. *Quartz-topped kitchen island. Dark laminate wood flooring throughout.* He shook his head. They weren't looking to sell yet, that was certain.

His familiar, Elizabeth, stretched out on his black bedspread, barely visible with her sleek black fur. Until she opened her bright green eyes when she sensed him in the bedroom.

"What's wrong?" she asked.

He should have known his reincarnated great-something-or-other ancestor would know he was mulling an issue. As much as he could understand other animals, the connection to his familiar surpassed that communication and understanding by leaps and bounds.

Aaron sat beside her on the bed, stroking her fur. "I don't know what to do," he admitted. He summarized asking Laura out, her refusal, their almost kisses, and her magical fiascos. "I thought I just needed to wait out her resistance. She clearly has feelings for me. Then it hit me in the car driving home that her wacky magic happened after we had our moments." His voice softened. "Surely our feelings for each other aren't affecting her magic. Right?"

Elizabeth rolled over to sit in a perfect pancake pose, paws under her chin. "I wasn't there," she meowed, "so I couldn't say with complete certainty. But."

"What?" Aaron dreaded what his familiar might say next.

"If intimate moments—"

"They weren't intimate," he interrupted.

If a cat could roll her eyes, she probably would have. "You know what I meant. If emotional moments between the two of you preceded her magic not working properly, it may very well be that your magic isn't aligned with hers." Elizabeth licked her paws.

"We have misaligned magic?" His question dripped with dismay.

She stopped licking her paws. "It's possible."

"Can we fix it?"

"Not if it's truly misaligned. No."

Aaron laid back on the bed and stared at the ceiling. "If we get together, it may cost Laura her magic."

"It's possible."

"I can't do that to her. I can't hold her back like that." Aaron laced his fingers behind his head. What he liked to call his thinking position.

He considered that Elizabeth couldn't say for certain that his and Laura's magic were incompatible. Something else was possibly going on. It could have been a coincidence that her magic messed up after they almost kissed. But if they were misaligned? Aaron knew he couldn't be the cause of Laura not being able to use her magic. They'd joked about him asking her out again after she bought her house. That would never happen.

There was no way he could pursue her now.

CHAPTER SEVENTEEN

LAURA

The awkwardness topped the scale. Laura couldn't believe Shelly Newsome was sitting across from her in her own kitchen. It had been a tough call to make, but Laura knew she needed guidance.

"Walk me through what happened," Shelly instructed.

Laura did, explaining how her magic didn't work right after the two near-kisses with Aaron. "It can't be that, can it?" Laura pursed her ruby red lips.

"I've not heard of magic interacting like that," Shelly said, then frowned.

"What?"

"There was something…" Shelly's sentence trailed off.

Laura's stomach clenched. "What? What is it?"

"At the barbecue."

"When? Oh, right, the barbecue." Laura and Aaron had gone together to celebrate Litha. She rarely attended those events, but that was at the start of her home search and he'd encouraged her to go. "Wait. What happened at the barbecue?"

"I remember there being something off there."

"What did you notice? What was off?" Laura asked.

Shelly's brow furrowed. "The magic floating around was off."

"Whose magic?"

"I'm not sure," Shelly admitted, "but something was wrong."

"You could already sense our magic was incompatible?" Laura's heart broke. Shelly's magical inclination was an ability to see the order in chaos, and this extended to sensing the magic of others. If Shelly said their magic was incompatible, then that confirmed it. Laura should have known not to develop feelings for Aaron. So stupid.

Shelly reached for Laura across the dark brown kitchen table, thought better of it, and placed her hand between them on the wood. "Don't overthink it. That's not what I said."

"Then what are you saying?" Laura demanded.

"What I said," she responded lightly. "There was something off. Something about the magic seemed chaotic." Shelly offered a lopsided grin. "But remember, there are two caveats to that."

Hope bubbled up. "There are?"

"One is that you know my magic has a history of misfiring."

"I thought that had settled down once you identified your magic."

"Not quite," Shelly said. "I understand it more, for sure. But it still isn't always accurate."

"Oh, wow." That blew Laura away. She hadn't realized that Shelly's misfiring magic still misfired. "And you're okay with it?"

Shelly lifted a shoulder in a blasé shrug. "It is what it is. Would I rather it not misfire? Sure. But, it's not the end of the world. At least I know it better now. Plus, sometimes it's great."

Laura's mind swirled with that idea. Even if her magic was incompatible with Aaron's, maybe that would be okay.

"The second caveat is that there were dozens of people at the barbecue," Shelly continued. "Just because I sensed something off when I was focused on you and Aaron—"

Laura flushed at the idea of the two of them as somebody's focus.

"—doesn't mean it wasn't somebody else near you."

"And there were a lot of people near us," Laura finished the thought.

"Precisely."

"Ask him out," came a voice from the bay windowsill.

Laura and Shelly swiveled their heads toward Laura's familiar sitting in the sun. "The peanut gallery speaks," Laura said.

"What did Eddie have to say?" Shelly asked. Of course, she only heard the meow, not the words and images that came through for Laura.

"He said to ask Aaron out."

"Pretty good advice," Shelly said.

"Yes, it is," Eddie agreed, licking his front paw. "As always, you're overcomplicating things. Ask him out."

Laura laughed.

"What?" Shelly asked.

"He's agreeing with you." Laura considered the advice of both her familiar and her no-longer-a-frenemy. They were probably right. Her chemistry with Aaron was undeniable. His asking her out already made it clear he wanted to go out.

All she had to do was call him and ask.

"You're overthinking it," Eddie said.

Laura rolled her eyes and translated the meow for Shelly, who nodded in agreement with the tabby.

"Is there something else?" Shelly asked.

The uncertainty in the question hit Laura hard. She wasn't sure how to respond; while they were no longer frenemies, they weren't friends. But why weren't they? Because Laura had crushed on Ben in high school when all he wanted was Shelly? Because Laura had thought everything came so easily to Shelly?

"You're definitely overthinking things," Shelly echoed Laura's familiar.

"There is something else," Laura answered Shelly's question.

Shelly waited for Laura to decide whether or not to share with her.

"It's more than just possibly losing my magic. Although that would be huge."

"It would."

Laura swallowed past her dry throat. "I don't know if I can risk it again."

"Risk what?"

"Loss," Laura whispered, the single word barely audible, but sounding loud in the silence that followed.

Understanding dawned on Shelly's face. "Your parents?"

Pain flooded Laura. She had never known her grandparents; they'd died before she was born. But, her parents...

"You don't have to talk about it."

"I know." Laura's eyes burned hot with unshed tears and she blinked them away. "I thought they would always be there. I didn't think it would matter if I went away to college."

Now Shelly took Laura's hand across the table.

"They died."

"I remember when that happened." Shelly squeezed Laura's hand. "I'm so sorry."

"I left. And they died." It had been a thunderstorm during Nevada's monsoon season. An unexpected flash flood had wiped their car from the road, and them from Laura's life. "I don't think I could take another loss."

A tear slid down Shelly's cheek.

Laura yanked her hand from Shelly's and wiped at her own dry cheek. "People leave." There was no point in rehashing the memory.

"They do," Shelly agreed. "That's inevitable, to some degree."

A hysterical laugh broke through. "That's not making me feel better."

Shelly chuckled softly in response. "It's true, though. Part of the risk of opening yourself up to another is recognizing that they will eventually leave. Or you'll leave them."

"Why do it then?" The raw need in her voice startled Laura.

"Because life is empty without it."

Laura sat with Shelly's pronouncement. Her life was pretty good. She had a great job that she loved. Coworkers she liked. A familiar she loved. Even a rental she liked well enough.

But.

Having Shelly here, like a genuine friend. Experiencing a true connection like she'd felt with Aaron. She'd missed having those in her life.

Maybe Shelly and Eddie were right. Maybe she was overthinking this. Nobody could predict the future. Her magic might be just fine with Aaron's. And maybe they'd be soul mates, destined for decades together. A smile flitted across her face.

"You've decided."

"I have."

Shelly smiled. "Then my work here is done."

Laura walked to the kitchen island to retrieve her phone, then sent a text to Aaron.

Come over when you have the draft offer ready.

CHAPTER EIGHTEEN

AARON

Aaron smiled at the text. Laura didn't ask as most people would have. She stated what she wanted and expected him to agree or explain why he didn't. He appreciated her blunt style, so similar to his own. Disappointment rose at the thought they could only be friends, and he stamped it down. She was a great person. He'd count himself lucky to be her friend.

Laura's timing was perfect. Putting together the draft offer on the house had been easy enough. And he knew they would accept it. He'd recommend offering less than asking, since she was paying cash, and that was the true magic word with house buying. Aaron had been about to email the draft offer to her. Instead, he printed it out to bring with him.

The short drive to her current rental gave him time to steel himself for seeing her. He was resolute that he wouldn't be responsible for her losing the magical side of herself. If they couldn't be together, then he'd have to watch for and avoid opportunities to flirt.

How disappointing. Flirting with her had been so much fun. Maybe they could? No, he shut that line of thinking down. No matter how much fun she was; how much he enjoyed being challenged by her; or how beautiful, smart, and capable she was, he could never ask her to risk losing what it meant to be a witch. If she couldn't even make Jell-O a different color. No, his feelings weren't more important than the essence of who she was.

He almost threw all of his mental effort away when she opened her front door. Her short red hair, a little disheveled, which was unlike her, framed her beautiful pale face. And those lips. He didn't know the name of that color red, but it sure made her lips kissable.

Ugh. That was exactly what Aaron wasn't supposed to be focusing on.

Her smile becoming uncertain clued him into how long he'd been standing silently in her doorway.

He gave a quick shake of his head. "Sorry about that. I was thinking." He thrust the papers at her before she could ask him what he was thinking about. "Here's the offer."

Laura's azure eyes sparkled and she took the paperwork. "Wonderful. We can review in the kitchen."

Aaron considered the black furniture and stark white walls with no photographs. It made his fairly minimal furnishings appear downright decadent. Somehow, though, it worked for her. Sleek, sophisticated. More expected in a bustling city, maybe, than in a small town, that type of classy.

They entered the kitchen and Laura gestured to a tiny cat sitting on top of the dark brown kitchen table. "That would be Edward. Eddie. He's not supposed to be up there." Though she crossed her arms, her half-smile gave her away. This was clearly a game they played.

"Hi Eddie," Aaron said and the cat's uneven whiskers twitched in response. Aaron sat opposite Laura at the table. "Go ahead and read the offer, and we can go from there."

"Of course." Laura began reading the first page.

Aaron watched her read, wondering why it was taking her so long to finish the first page.

She placed her hand flat on the page and stared at him.

"Is something wrong?" His stomach flip-flopped the longer she looked at him. "Take a picture. It lasts longer," he quipped.

She snorted at the terrible joke, but that broke the tension. "Thank you for bringing the offer. I'll read it. However, first," she started. Laura stood from the table.

Aaron pushed back his chair to join her. "Laura?"

"I've given this a lot of thought, and I overreacted when you asked me out before. You were right that saying I couldn't date you because work connected us made no sense. So, I'd like to correct that." She paused her rush of words and offered a hesitant smile. "Would you like to have dinner with me?"

Yes! his brain shouted.

"No," his mouth said instead.

Laura appeared confused and her shoulders hunched for a moment. Then she straightened up to her full height, so that in her heels she was looking down at him. "My apologies for misunderstanding. Thank you for—"

"Don't you want an explanation?" Aaron asked, his traitorous brain trying to find a way to salvage the situation.

"You don't need to explain," Laura said. Then she crossed her arms again, before dropping them to her sides. "Actually, if you have one, that would be great."

"I do," he said, eager to explain. "It's not that I don't want to go out with you."

"I don't understand."

"It's that I don't think we're a good fit." He dropped his head back for a moment. "That came out wrong. When your magic didn't work right before, what did those events have in common?"

She walked to lean against the kitchen island, her back to him. "We almost kissed."

"We almost kissed," he repeated. Laura turned and Aaron was startled to see tears glistening.

"Do you think our magic doesn't go together?" she asked in a flat voice that made his heart hurt.

"I don't know," he admitted, "but Elizabeth thinks it's possible."

"Your familiar?" she asked, and he nodded.

"Elizabeth thinks there's something wrong. She wasn't certain, but she said we may have misaligning magic." He struggled to finish. "And that if we get together, you might lose the entire essence of your magic."

CHAPTER NINETEEN

LAURA

"Shelly said the same thing," Laura gasped. She escaped the closeness of Aaron to return to her seat at the kitchen table. *This can't be happening.*

"She did?" he asked.

"She didn't call it misaligning, just said something seemed off about us when we were together at the barbecue."

"At the barbecue? Oh, the celebration."

"Yes." She told Aaron what Shelly had said about the magic seeming off, instead of the typical orderly magic she felt. "She couldn't state it with certainty though because other people were around. So, I thought it was worth the risk. But now?" If her feelings were visible, they'd be ricocheting all around the kitchen, like the chaotic magic Shelly described.

All that potential hope that might have become love crashed into the despair and disappointment of having Shelly's words echoed by Aaron's familiar.

Aaron pulled a chair closer to her and took her hands in his. "But now?" he repeated.

His touch sent shivers of pleasure down her spine. She reveled in the feeling, and didn't know how they could ignore this connection when they were together.

When she didn't continue, he did. "I couldn't forgive myself if I caused you to lose your magical essence." His thumb rubbed circles in her palm.

"I know," she whispered. There had to be a way. "Maybe it's worth taking a chance. After all, neither was certain."

Aaron released her hands and sat back, almost as if he needed the physical distance between them to say what he'd say next. "You're right that they weren't certain. Elizabeth definitely said it was only one possibility."

"And Shelly said it could have been someone around us at the barbecue," Laura continued the line of reasoning eagerly. They could work this out, she just knew it. "Who was around us at the barbecue?"

He tilted his head in thought. "Members of my family and our friends were the closest, most of the time."

The unspoken *and none of yours* bounced around in her head, though she knew he didn't mean it that way.

"Except that nobody else was around in the parking lot when you made the pothole bigger," he said.

She flinched at his words, despite their neutral tone. He was only working through the hypothesis that she had proposed.

"And nobody except Marvin Kelm was around us when you tried to turn the Jell-O orange. I don't see how somebody else at the barbecue could be the cause." He opened his arms wide in helplessness.

Laura felt like she was trying to breathe underwater. He was right, of course. Nobody at the barbecue had been around them when her magic failed. She had been so sure they'd find a solution, some other explanation. It couldn't be that they had misaligning magic. The Goddess wouldn't be so cruel as to bring him into her life just so she had to choose between him and her magic.

"Tell me what you're thinking," Aaron said.

She hesitated.

"Please." He batted his eyelashes at her.

"You're such a dork," she said. But it worked and she smiled, albeit wistfully. "You're right."

"That doesn't happen every day," he quipped, still trying to break the mounting tension.

"It's going to be okay," she said, not sure if that was directed at him or herself. "I wouldn't want you to feel responsible for me losing my magic, either. That wouldn't be fair to either of us."

"I wish it was different," he whispered.

"Me too." Laura stood. "I'm sure the paperwork is great. I'll review it this afternoon." She started to leave the kitchen, Aaron jumping up to follow.

"Good. It's a great house. You'll look great in it." He flushed.

"Thanks," she said, her thoughts stuck on the idea that there had to be a solution or explanation that would allow her to be with Aaron.

"Ben asked if I could take Marvin and Ginger home from the hospital today," Aaron said as they stood in Laura's front entrance.

"I'm so happy they're going to be okay. That's nice of you to bring them home."

"What can I say? I'm a nice guy," Aaron said with an impish grin.

Laura grinned in return. "Yes, you are."

Aaron gave her a side-hug. "I'll see you later."

"Yes, you will," she whispered. Her resolution grew stronger.

This wouldn't be another confirmation of people leaving her. There had to be an explanation for why their magic appeared to be misaligning. She'd find it. Then she and Aaron could be together.

CHAPTER TWENTY

AARON

Aaron drove his Jeep too fast through town, finally exhaling when he reached the hospital. He needed the distraction of bringing Marvin and Ginger home.

Laura had asked him out. And he'd said no. Knowing she wanted him as much as he wanted her broke his heart. They'd just realized they both felt the same way. Including that a relationship wasn't worth losing a part of herself for. If only they'd found another explanation.

Aaron texted his brother. *Do you want to bring Ginger to Marvin's room? Or do you want us to pick her up on our way out?*

I'll bring her to you.

Aaron trudged to the elevator, still not able to leave his conversation with Laura behind. His spirits rose along with the elevator. It would be nice to help a man and his dog get back to their home.

Thus, a smile brightened his face as he reached the doorway to Marvin's room.

"Are you my ride?" The tall man sat on his bed, shaggy black hair sticking out in all directions.

"Yes, sir, I am." Aaron scanned the hospital room. "Do you need help with anything?"

"Nope," Marvin answered. "They gave me this fabulous outfit. Mine had some, um, stains on it."

Aaron considered Marvin's oversized t-shirt with the yellow smiling emoji and baggy jeans a few inches too short. "I suppose that's preferable to a stained outfit. Barely."

Marvin belly laughed, the skin at the corner of his eyes crinkling.

Commotion at the door drew both men's attention.

"Ginger!" Marvin practically lunged for his dog, who gave him sloppy kisses in return.

"Thanks for bringing her up," Aaron said to his brother.

"Just glad I could help." Ben glanced at his watch. "Perfect timing. I gotta go."

"A Chief's work is never done?" Aaron asked.

"Something like that." Ben handed the paperwork to Marvin. "Since you're following up with a private physician, I went ahead and completed your checkout. You're free to go."

"Thank you, Doctor," Marvin said solemnly.

"You're most welcome." And with that, Ben disappeared into the hallway.

"Are you two ready?" Aaron asked.

"Yes," Marvin and Ginger responded.

Aaron led them to the elevator.

"What am I taking you away from to be my taxi?" Marvin asked, Ginger trotting beside him.

An image of Laura flashed in his mind. "Nothing important." The words burned even as they left his mouth.

Marvin's dark brown eyes flashed with something like merriment. "I don't believe that for a moment."

Aaron's face flushed as the three of them entered the elevator. "Why not?" He tried deflection instead of answering.

"Are you asking why I don't believe you?"

"Yeah." Aaron stared at the elevator doors, willing the car to reach the ground floor.

"Because you're a terrible liar."

"Gee, thanks." Aaron cut his eyes at Marvin. "You know, I don't have to take you home."

"I know." The elevator doors opened and Marvin and Ginger stepped off first, with Marvin holding his arm out to let Aaron off, too. "But I also know you won't do that."

Aaron sighed. "No, I won't."

"I'm just playing, anyhow."

The trio crossed the foyer and soon were blinking in the bright afternoon sun. Aaron led them to his Jeep and got them situated before he spoke again.

"I know you're teasing," Aaron said with a smirk. "You're also not wrong. About any of that. Address?" He typed the address as Marvin recited it.

Once the Irish-accented voice on the GPS began, Marvin picked the conversation back up. "Sometimes talking to a stranger is easier."

"Sometimes there are things you can't discuss," Aaron responded.

"Is it related to how you can speak to and understand my dog?"

Aaron jerked the car over to the side of the road and hit his hazards. "What do you mean?"

"When you and the lovely lady brought Ginger to me, you communicated with Ginger. For-real communicated, not just empathetic-but-still-human guesses. I'm assuming the issue you don't want to discuss is something supernatural."

The statement was matter-of-fact, but Aaron probed the man's face for apprehension, disgust, or some other judgment. He saw nothing. "It is."

"Maybe related to the young lady, too?" Marvin asked in a sing-song voice.

"You're good," Aaron said with a laugh.

"It wasn't hard to see that the two of you have feelings for each other." Marvin lifted one hand from where it rested on his legs to point at Aaron.

"Alright. You've convinced me." Aaron pulled back on the road and drove exactly the speed limit as he spilled forth his tale of woe about misaligning magic.

Marvin remained silent when Aaron finished.

"What do you think?" Aaron asked.

"I'm collecting my thoughts."

After Aaron turned onto the next street, Marvin pointed out his house and Aaron coasted to a stop in front of it. Aaron shifted in his seat.

Marvin similarly shifted so the men faced each other. "It's a doozy, for sure. And unfortunately, unless you can find another reason for the misaligning magic, I think you're making the right decision to not pursue her."

Aaron's face must have reflected his misery on hearing Marvin's conclusion.

"Sometimes the best thing we can do for someone is to let them live their life," Marvin said, patting Aaron's knee. "Good luck. Thank you again for getting us home."

"Of course," Aaron responded, then helped Marvin and Ginger into their home, essentially on auto-pilot.

Everyone seemed in agreement. He and Laura likely had misaligned magic. And, without another explanation, letting her go was the best thing he could do.

But if that was so, why couldn't he accept it?

CHAPTER TWENTY-ONE

LAURA

The thought that she could find an answer to the mystery of her magic misaligning with Aaron's buoyed Laura's energy. She'd considered calling Shelly to meet her at Wildcrest Wizardry for an afternoon coffee, but she ran into an even better possibility before she could do so.

"Hi Laura. It's good to see you," Grace Newsome greeted Laura when they crossed paths in the checkout line. The supernatural life coach stood next to her youngest daughter, Patricia, who went by Patty. The older Newsome wore her typical long flowing skirt, and the younger wore jeans and a concert t-shirt.

"Hi Grace. It's good to—" Laura started to reply then

stopped. Seeing Patty, who Laura thought was away at graduate school, gave her an idea.

Grace quirked an eyebrow. "It's good to what? I think you're missing part of your sentence there." She stepped up to the counter before Laura could respond. "Hey Mom."

"Hey Nana," Patty added.

Laura watched tiny Grace stand on her tiptoes to hug her equally short mother on the other side of the counter. Grace's parents had owned the apothecary and coffee shop for years. Laura stared at the back of Grace and Patty's heads as they placed their orders. When the two turned and stepped aside to allow Laura to order, she reached out a hand to stop them.

"Do you have a few minutes?" she asked.

Grace squinted her purple eyes. "I do. I can see you need help."

Since Laura was a recent client of Grace's life coaching, she knew the comment wasn't malicious. "Thank you."

"Mom, I can catch up with you later," Patty said.

"Actually, would you mind staying too?" Laura asked.

Patty's hazel eyes widened at the question. "Um, sure."

Laura placed an order for a double shot espresso, her usual, and the three women sat at one of the handcrafted wooden tables.

"How can Patty and I help?" Grace asked.

"How come you're in town?" Laura asked Patty instead of answering Grace.

"I'm on a break from grad school. And you're deflecting," Patty said.

Laura reddened. "Guilty." She picked nonexistent lint from her dress, then laid her hands flat on the table. "How can you help? I'm not sure. Grace, your insightful thoughts are always helpful. But, Patty, you're the one I think I need more." She took a deep breath and then shared all the recent back and forth she'd had with Aaron. Patty was nodding by the time she finished.

"I can see why you wanted my help," Patty said.

"Sorry to interrupt, ladies, here are your coffees," said a voice over Laura's shoulder, before she could reply to Patty. Rebekah, the tall, bubbly, blond manager of the store, leaned over to distribute their beverages.

They murmured their thanks and Rebekah withdrew.

"Do you think you can?" Laura asked eagerly. She knew that Patty's magical inclination was like the other women in her family: she was in touch with the magical energy of others. Specifically, Patty read the magical energy of witches as if they were auras. She could see if there was anything wonky going on. If anyone could alleviate Laura's concerns, it was Patty.

"I can tell you that nothing stood out about you or Aaron's magical auras at the barbecue," Patty said.

"Thank the Goddess," Laura said in a rush.

"But," Patty continued, "I get what my sister said. Even though I didn't notice anything off about your magical auras, there was some funny energy floating around that day."

"Was anyone else's magical aura off?" Grace asked her daughter.

Patty sipped her coffee. "I thought maybe I saw something, except when I looked closer, it wasn't what I thought."

"That was clear as mud," Grace said, laughing her deep-throated husky laugh.

"Whose magical aura was it?" Laura asked.

"I can't answer that," Patty answered.

"But what if that person is related to mine and Aaron's misaligning magic?" Laura heard the desperation in her voice and she didn't care. This was too important.

Patty placed her hand over Laura's on the table between them. "I understand you want answers. And I wish I could give them to you. But I don't know for certain what I saw. Plus, either way, it wouldn't be my information to give."

Intellectually, Laura understood. Emotionally, she hated that Patty wouldn't tell her.

The younger woman smiled sympathetically. "You said there wasn't anybody around you either time your magic didn't work correctly, except Aaron. The likelihood that this other person I saw at the barbecue being involved is therefore pretty small." She patted Laura's hand. "If it makes you feel any better, right now when I look at your magical aura, it looks clean and bright. No issues. Believe it or not, it could have been a coincidence that your magic didn't work in those two instances."

Relief flooded Laura. Of course. Coincidence. How did the saying go? Once is a chance. Twice is a coincidence. Three is a pattern. Maybe they just needed to test the theory. Her face flushed at the thought of almost kissing Aaron again.

"I can see you liked that news," Grace said drily.

"It does make me feel better," Laura admitted. The thought that she and Aaron could have a chance thrilled her.

"For what it's worth, I don't think your magical alignment is a problem. Even if it is..." Patty shrugged. "It could be temporary. It could be permanent. I still say if you like him, go for it."

"Really?" Laura looked at Grace, who nodded in agreement with her daughter. "I'll think about it."

And the next time I see Aaron, we'll test the theory that it was a coincidence, Laura thought to herself, biting back a grin.

CHAPTER TWENTY-TWO

AARON

"Hey, Mom, yeah, I'm waiting for Laura now," Aaron said to his mother, who'd called him right as he'd unlocked the front door. With a glance around the house, he decided to wait for Laura at the desk staged in the front den. That way, he'd be close to the door when she arrived. He smiled at the thought of seeing her.

"Does that mean you're finally going on a date?" his mother asked.

Aaron sat on the edge of the desk. "No, it doesn't," he said. His mother sighing in response didn't make him feel any better.

"That's a shame," Esther said.

"I know, but you know what the issue is."

"There has to be a way around it."

"I appreciate your enthusiasm, Mom, but I really don't think there is." Saying the words out loud made them seem more real. His throat tightened and he coughed to clear his throat.

"I love you, son." Her voice sounded thick with emotion.

His eyebrows lifted. Although he knew she felt that way, his mother wasn't the touchy-feely type to express it randomly like that. "Love you, too, Mom."

The doorbell rang. His heart rate galloped like a wild horse.

Aaron hopped off the desk and rushed to open the door. "Gotta go, Mom. Laura's here." He ended the call before opening the door.

Laura stood in the doorway, appearing uncertain, though still commanding with her height and demeanor. Her personality filled every space she was in, but he saw her softer side, too.

"Thank you for asking the listing agent about my seeing the house one more time before putting in the offer," Laura said.

"Of course," he responded. The sunlight glinting off her red hair mesmerized him. Ugh, he knew he shouldn't think like that. "Is there something specific you wanted to see?" Despite his internal emotional wrestling, he was a professional and could focus on that. He stepped aside so Laura could enter.

"No, nothing specific," she said, strolling around the main open floor space.

"Really?"

"That surprises you." She giggled as she continued to walk, almost aimlessly, but wound up in the kitchen.

His mouth dropped open, and he snapped it shut before she could see – right now, she was staring down at the kitchen's quartz countertops – and that's when it hit him. She seemed happy, yet nervous. It was an unusual combination. Almost like first date nerves. Which this wasn't.

"Um, yeah, I guess it does," he said. "I'm used to you being pragmatic." He leaned against the counter. "Wanting to come here without a specific purpose seems out of character."

Her eyes met his, her expression sober. "Is that a bad thing?"

"Not being pragmatic?" Aaron found the entire conversation bizarre. There had to be subtext he was missing.

"Being out of character," she clarified.

"I like your character." Aaron couldn't believe he'd said that. His palms felt sweaty. Now he was the one acting like this was a first date. That he was failing miserably. Of course, they weren't on a date. They'd decided to just be friends. If only his heart would accept what his brain had decided. In truth, what he and Laura had decided together.

"You do?" she asked.

The coquettish tone in her voice threw him and he went bold. "You know I do. I asked you out," he reminded her with a smirk.

"True. Except then you said no when I asked you out." She stepped closer to him.

Aaron fought the desire to cross his arms as a physical barrier between them. She was confusing him. He'd thought they'd decided to just be friends. To protect her magic.

Laura took another step closer. A kaleidoscope of emotions crossed her face and she sighed, almost imperceptibly.

"What?" he asked. The naked fear on her face shocked him. If only he knew the cause.

She shook her head. "Maybe later," she mumbled before offering a wide smile that didn't quite reach her eyes. "I don't really need another tour. Let's discuss the offer we want to make on the house." She pulled the paperwork he'd brought her out of her leather bag.

The whiplash change of topic hurt his brain, but she obviously was working through something. He suspected it involved him and he wanted desperately to ask.

But their misaligned magic had thrown her, so he withstood the barrage of his own emotions to give her space to work out her own. He knew she'd tell him when she was ready.

Based on her ping-ponging emotions, he figured he didn't have long to wait.

CHAPTER TWENTY-THREE

LAURA

Laura saw that their conversation was confusing Aaron. That made sense since her own mind was a whirlwind of thoughts and emotions. It was time to present her plan. Except Aaron had accepted her topic change and was talking.

"Of course, we can skip the tour and discuss your offer. Their listing agent said they're expecting another offer on the house, given the limited availability in Wildcrest."

Laura frowned. The home was perfect. She would do whatever it took to get it.

"I wouldn't worry about it, though. Your all-cash offer will be hard to beat, even coming in below list."

"Are you sure?" She bit her lower lip.

"I can't guarantee it, of course," he said with a grin, "but cash is king, as they say."

Her ability to present an all-cash offer was bittersweet. Yes, she'd saved a lot while working. That was easy to do when you did little outside of work. But, she had more than was typical for someone her age because of the deaths of her parents. Between the life insurance and the sale of her parents' home, she had a full bank account.

A wave of sadness crashed over her. She'd give all of it back in an instant if she could have her parents alive and well.

She offered a shaky smile and ignored the concerned look on Aaron's face. "That's wonderful. I'd like to make this offer," she said, indicating the paperwork, and then put it back in her bag.

Aaron checked his watch. "I'll text the listing agent she'll get our offer tonight. She'll most likely present it to the owners in the morning. I suspect they'll accept or counter by the end of the day."

Hope flared. "But not a rejection?"

"I'd be shocked if that happened." Aaron quirked an eyebrow. "Then everything will turn over to the title company and I'll be out of your hair."

Her heart lurched at the thought. "Maybe not," she blurted out.

"No?" he asked.

Laura couldn't read his neutral face or the inflectionless word. *Time to go for it.* "I have an idea."

"You do?"

She paced to the living room's sliding glass doors, hearing Aaron's footsteps on the hardwood floor as he followed. The view of the desert and low mountains beyond calmed her. Laura faced him.

Aaron had stopped by the staged beige couch. He'd remained on the far side of it. To give her space?

"It's possible that our magic isn't misaligned."

A cautious smile surfaced. "It is?"

Laura nodded. "It is. It may have been a horrible coincidence that after we shared, um, emotional closeness, my magic didn't work the way it's supposed to." She swallowed past the lump in her throat.

He gripped the back of the couch. "What makes you think that? That would be great if it's true."

Laura explained what Patty had said about her magical aura looking clean. "So I'm proposing a test."

"What kind of test?"

"We recreate an emotional moment, and then I try to use my magic. We see what happens." Her effort to maintain an objective tone failed.

Aaron's eyes dilated. "And what would this emotional moment look like?"

Her face flushed and she waved in the couch's direction. "Let's have a seat."

They sat, not touching, though with their knees only inches apart. "Now what?"

She reached a hand toward his face. "I'm not sure," she admitted.

His hand captured hers. "This seems like it's going well."

Laura exhaled and tightened her grip. She was hyperaware of the softness of the couch's fabric under her other hand, the mild musk of his aftershave, and the sound of the wall clock in the kitchen ticking off the seconds.

He leaned in to kiss her.

She jolted back.

"What?" he asked and released her hand.

"Sorry about that. We've never kissed before." Oh, but she wanted to!

He grinned. "There's always a first time."

"That wouldn't fit the parameters of our experiment."

Aaron chuckled. "Fair enough."

"I think I should try to use my magic now." Fear coursed through her. *What if it fails?*

"You can do it," he encouraged her.

"Thanks," she responded shakily.

"What do you want to change?"

Laura glanced around the room, feeling relief as the intensity of their closeness faded to tolerable levels. That had to have been enough emotional closeness for the experiment.

Her gaze landed on a staged flower on the coffee table. A beautiful yellow rose. Signifying friendship. "I'm going to change that yellow rose to red," she told Aaron.

"Go for it," he said, then shifted slightly away from her, again presumably to give her space.

She sat up straight, keeping the yellow rose in her vision and creating a representation of it in her mind. She concentrated on changing the yellow rose in her mind to red. It began to shift from yellow, the familiar haze appearing above and around the physical rose.

The haze shimmered. Splotches of pink appeared on the rose. Almost like it was being tie-dyed. The pink spread and darkened. Happiness filled Laura as the rose became redder, almost matching the richly red rose in Laura's mind. It was working.

Pink reappeared. The haze wavered. Soon the physical rose resumed its tie-dyed look. And there it stayed.

"No," Laura whispered, devastated by the failure of her magic and what that meant. Three failures were a pattern. She looked up to meet Aaron's face. His expression of dejection no doubt matched her own. "That's it," she stated.

"I don't know what to say," Aaron responded, reaching for her hand again, before dropping it onto the couch.

"What is there to say?" Laura asked sadly. "We tested the coincidence theory. And we proved the theory false."

"That's it," he echoed her.

Laura choked back a sob. "I'm just not ready to accept that I won't be able to have functioning magic anymore."

"I understand." He half-smiled. "I couldn't ask you to do that, either. But I suppose I'm glad we tested the theory."

"No questions left unanswered," she said.

"Exactly. No regrets," he added.

Laura couldn't agree with him. She had plenty of regrets. Or to be more accurate, she wondered if this would become a regret.

CHAPTER TWENTY-FOUR

AARON

Aaron sat slumped on their shared gray couch in the living room when Ben walked in, though Aaron didn't acknowledge his brother.

"Earth to my little brother," Ben said and flicked the back of Aaron's head. It had been the brothers' greeting since they were kids. It was done with love, and not enough force to actually hurt.

But it got Aaron's attention and he stood up. "Hey big brother. How's the hospital?"

"Fine. How did it go with Laura today?"

Aaron snorted. "You've been talking to Mom."

"I have," Ben admitted with a shrug. "Since you didn't

say anything about Marvin, I assumed you got him and Ginger home safely."

"I did. Sorry, I forgot to text."

"No worries." Ben smirked. "That leaves seeing Laura. Do you need a glass of wine to talk about it?"

"Sure, why not?" Aaron agreed and followed his brother into the kitchen.

"Mom didn't seem thrilled," Ben said, grabbing glasses and a bottle of red wine.

"No, she didn't." Aaron perched on one of the high stools at the center island. "I know she's always advocated for Laura, but her interest in this seems weird." He accepted a glass from Ben. "Thanks."

"Of course," Ben replied, and they both sipped their wine. "Ah, that's good. As for Mom, yeah, I don't know. She definitely likes Laura. Maybe she sees something you two crazy kids can't see." Ben's eyes twinkled.

"Don't start. You know that's not the issue."

"I know." His expression softened. "What happened?"

Aaron brought Ben up to speed on Laura's hypothesis, and how it bombed.

Ben appeared thoughtful. "Interesting."

"Not really," Aaron disagreed. "Her magic failed again after we..." he trailed off.

Ben waved that away. "I realize that. This time seemed different."

"What do you mean?" Aaron cupped his wine glass.

"You don't see it?"

"Obviously not."

"What was different that time compared to the first two times?"

"I'm not one of your medical students," Aaron warned. "Don't Socratic Method me."

"Mea culpa," Ben said with a laugh. "The third time, it almost worked."

Aaron ran through the three events in his head. Ben was correct. "It backfired at the very end. What do you think it means?"

Now Ben shrugged. "That I don't know. But I suspect it's not as clear-cut as you and Laura are treating it. Patty could be right about it not being permanent. Maybe it's already adjusting," he suggested.

"Hmm, that *is* interesting. I hadn't thought about it that way." A light appeared at the end of the tunnel. "I wonder if I can convince Laura to see it that way."

"It's not about convincing her of anything," Ben cautioned.

"Oh, I know. Bad choice of words. Besides," he said and smiled wickedly, "I don't believe anybody has ever convinced Laura to do something she doesn't want to do."

Aaron needed to show her that she wanted to be with him, and that she wasn't risking her magic. He picked up his phone and texted her.

"I'm going to need the room," he told his brother.

"Good luck." Ben topped off his wine glass. "I'll leave the rest of this for you."

Aaron hoped he'd need it to celebrate and not to drown his sorrows.

His phone dinged an incoming text.

I'll be right there.

CHAPTER TWENTY-FIVE

LAURA

The turquoise front door shined in the waning light of the early evening. It was gorgeous. Aaron was gorgeous. Laura bit back a laugh at how quickly her thoughts had gone there. It confirmed the decision she had made. She pressed the doorbell, listened to the short chimes inside the home.

"Thank you for meeting me here," Aaron greeted her.

Laura smiled at his disheveled hair and untucked shirt. He really unwound at home. "Of course, you beat me to it. I was about to text you."

"You were?"

He appeared so hopeful that she knew she was doing the right thing. Following her gut. "I was." She smiled shyly.

"Please come in. Would you like some wine?"

"Definitely," she answered while they walked through his beautiful home.

"Please have a seat," he said, gesturing to the stools lining the island.

She almost smiled at the formality. *Is he nervous?*

"I'd like to discuss something with you."

"Can we talk?"

They asked their questions simultaneously and laughed.

Aaron handed her a glass. "I hope red is okay. And, please, ladies first."

Laura accepted the wine, gulped a large swallow, and organized her thoughts. "I like you. As more than friends," she added.

If her bold opening startled him, he didn't let on.

"And the fact that we both asked each other out confirmed mutual interest." She didn't know why she was acting so formal.

She rolled her shoulders back and breathed deeply. "I don't like that we have misaligned magic. And, maybe the others are right, that it's not misaligned. Or that maybe it is, but it won't be permanent."

Aaron sipped his wine, his eyes never leaving hers.

"Regardless, I don't care."

He almost spat out his wine. She laughed as he brought a hand up to his lips to make sure he didn't dribble any.

"I'll figure that out as we go. We only live once. And I

can't speak for you, but it's not every day that I have such a connection with someone."

"It's not every day for me either."

Laura stood from the stool and walked around the island to Aaron. "So, if you haven't been put off by this craziness, and you're not worried that our misalignment will affect your magic—" She took his hands in hers. "—I'd like to ask you out again."

"Before I answer…"

Worry spiked through her and she tightened her grip. "No, I must insist you answer the question first."

His eyes crinkled with a smile. "Technically, you didn't ask a question."

"You should have been a lawyer," she said, though she relaxed her grip. "Would you like to go out with me?"

"Yes, I would," he said.

Her heart fluttered with happiness and she leaned toward him. Their lips met. *Who knew such a blunt, fast-talker would kiss so sweetly?* The feelings of closeness and connection filled her heart. She knew she sounded like a romance novel, and that was okay. This was why people read them. Whatever was happening with her magic, they'd work it out together. This. This was what mattered.

He pulled back with a smirk. "But I do want to say something."

"After a kiss like that, you can say anything," she whispered.

Aaron told her about his conversation with Ben, pointing out what she had also missed about the difference with their magic test.

"He's right," Laura gasped. "How could I have missed that? That truly does suggest some other factor at work, or the temporary nature of the misalignment."

"It does."

"I'm so glad," she said with a sigh of relief.

"Either way, we'll go through it together," he said, almost verbatim echoing her thoughts.

Laura knew for certain at that moment. They had their happily ever after.

EPILOGUE

AARON

Laura's hand entwined with his brought Aaron so much pleasure. They had arrived in the backyard of his parents' home to celebrate Lammas, the first day of the grain harvest. The coven enjoyed celebrating the seasonal sabbats, and since the focus was on grain, various baked goods covered the folding tables set out around the spacious backyard for the afternoon's celebration. Everything was decorated in red, orange, brown, and yellow, and Aaron saw goblets for wine and apple cider.

"So glad you could make it," Ben greeted the couple.

"Sorry we're late," Laura responded. "It's my fault. Aaron was helping me move furniture."

Aaron squeezed her hand. She'd been so happy when she closed on her new home. And to be there at every step had thrilled him.

"No need to apologize. I like having excuses to tease my brother." Ben nudged him with his shoulder.

"Whatever, old man."

"How're things going?" Ben asked, his tone serious.

Aaron knew what he was asking, and deferred to Laura for how she wanted to handle it.

"It's been mixed," she admitted. "Sometimes my magic does what I want it to do. Sometimes it fails. And sometimes it does something unintended."

"That sounds like my magic," Shelly said, hooking an arm into one of Ben's. "Mine misfires all the time."

Laura smiled ruefully. "I'm focusing on the good over the bad, and hoping that one day it'll work itself out."

"That's a positive approach," Shelly said. "Uh-oh, we're about to have all three brothers together."

"That's outstanding," Noah said, joining the two couples. "We're like Superman, Batman, and Spiderman."

"Hey, wait, let me guess, I'm the kid," Aaron objected.

"I think it's more like the three musketeers," Laura said.

"At least then they're all for one and one for all," another voice chimed in. The group turned to see Patty Newsome, in a flowered shift dress, her short dark hair held in place with a flowered headband. She joined the group and Aaron couldn't help but notice how she and Noah snuck glances at each other from the corners of their eyes. *Hmm, maybe there would be another Wright-Newsome union one day.*

"There's Mom and Dad," Ben said, interrupting Aaron's musings. "It must be time for the ritual."

The group made their way into the center circle, offering greetings to the other members of the coven encircling Elijah and Esther Wright. Aaron, as always, was struck by how downright regal his father was. He made a great coven High Priest.

"Welcome to our home, everyone," Elijah's deep voice rolled over the participants. "For Lammas, the first grain harvest of the year, we celebrate the fertile soil, remain thankful for the food on our tables, and we ask the Goddess for continued abundance, so that none may go without.

"Stalks of wheat, pieces of bread, and a small section of corn on the cob should be making their way around to you." He started the procession by handing those to Esther and saying, "I pass this gift of the first harvest to you." Elijah waited while voices rose and fell with the passing of the wheat, bread, and corn until everyone had them.

"As you consider the wheat you hold in your hands, consider the power of the planet we call home. Allow pieces of the stalk to fall to the ground as an offering, and remember that the power of the harvest is within each of us. The smallest seed can become the largest bloom. We each will send our roots to bloom and flourish.

"Now, consider the bread remaining in your hand. We are blessed to have this bounty."

Aaron repeated the phrase, the expected call-and-response of the ritual, before the group ate the bread pieces.

"Now consider your ear of corn."

Aaron smelled the richness of the barbecued surface of corn, his mouth salivating at the prospect.

"This corn represents the fruition of your intentions. See your intentions as part of a cornfield full of ripening corn. As you bite into your corn, remember what you offer for yourself, the coven, and the wider world."

Aaron watched Laura nibble at her corn, but he took a huge bite. The corn's juices flowed over his lips and he considered where he was today. The seeds he had planted professionally, within his family, and romantically, and how they'd come to successful fruition.

"May the love of friends, family, and the Goddess stay with you always." Elijah led them through closing the elemental gates and releasing the circle.

"And now we drink," he concluded, and the group laughed.

"Oh my," Patty whispered.

Aaron turned to her, as did Shelly, who stood on her other side.

"What?" Shelly asked.

"It can't be," Patty murmured to herself.

"Sis, talk to us," Shelly said.

Patty's gaze swung between her sister, Aaron, and finally came to rest on Laura, who narrowed her eyes at the scrutiny.

"I have a theory." Patty spun around and strode away from the larger group of coven members. Aaron, Laura, Shelly, Ben, and Noah followed, exchanging confused glances. Once Patty was beyond earshot of the group, she stopped. Her eyes shone. "I have a theory," she repeated. "About Laura's magic."

"Wait, what?" Laura asked.

"You do?" Aaron asked, flabbergasted that they might, at last, understand the misaligning magic.

Patty glanced around at them. "Remember what I'd said about the barbecue?"

Aaron knew Noah would be the only one who hadn't heard that. "I'll catch you up later," he whispered to his oldest brother.

"I didn't want to say anything because it had happened so fast, I wasn't sure of what I saw. Then, I didn't want to say anything, because I didn't feel like it was my story to tell if what I saw was true."

Laura grabbed Aaron's hand, and he hoped for her sake she was about to get some answers. Shelly looked like she wanted to shake her sister to get her to get to the point.

"But," Patty said. "Based on what I'm seeing now, I think it's okay to tell you because I think we may need to work together."

"On what? What are you talking about?" Shelly asked.

"I don't think you have misaligned magic." This Patty directed at Laura and Aaron, who both sighed in relief. "This will come as a shock. I think Esther is causing the magical malfunctions."

Dead silence for a moment, and then overlapping comments and questions came fast and furious. Aaron couldn't keep track of who said what.

"How do you know that?"

"How can Esther be the cause?"

"Esther doesn't have magic."

Patty shook her head.

The group quieted in anticipation. Aaron couldn't believe what Patty had said. His *mother* caused his and Laura's misaligning magic.

"At the barbecue, I saw an aura around Esther."

Shelly gasped, but it took Aaron a minute to understand.

"She shouldn't have a magical aura?" he asked, and Patty nodded.

"It flashed on and off so quickly, I thought maybe I'd hallucinated it. Even though that had never happened before," she said, with a glance at Noah, who dropped his gaze.

"What did it look like?" Ben asked, and Aaron almost laughed. Of course, Ben would be more interested in analyzing the *why* and *how* of it all.

"Chaotic," Patty said with a frown. "But again, it was gone so fast, I couldn't be sure. Until today." She stared across the backyard to where Elijah and Esther were chatting with other coven members. "While Elijah conducted the ritual, colors appeared around Esther. A magical aura."

"Oh, my Goddess," Shelly whispered.

"Exactly," Patty said, nodding sagely.

"But my mother doesn't have magic," Noah said.

"Except that can't be true," Patty argued. "Not if she has a magical aura."

"You must be mis-seeing or misreading, or something," Noah insisted. "She's middle-aged. Magic always appears at puberty."

Patty lifted a single shoulder. "I don't know what to tell you. She has magic. Whether she's always had it, or it's recently manifested, I have no idea."

"What does that have to do with my magic?" Laura asked.

"Esther's magical aura is chaotic. There's a very good chance it could affect the magic around her. You work with her almost every day."

"It doesn't seem to be affecting anybody else," Noah pointed out.

"As far as we know," she corrected, and he dropped his chin in a brief show of deference. "As I said, it's a theory. And something we should definitely talk to her about."

"Mom would be horrified at the thought of this happening," Aaron said. "I doubt she even knows she *has* magic, let alone chaotic magic."

"That makes sense," Ben agreed.

Noah nodded at Patty. "You're right. We need to talk to her about it."

Aaron looked around the group as they echoed Noah's sentiment. This had been an eventful Lammas. His mother apparently had chaotic magic now. And Noah and Patty clearly had some kind of *something* happening between them.

The year was shaping up in quite interesting ways.

Turn the page for Noah and Patty's road to happily ever after in **Love's Misbehaving Magic (Wildcrest Witches, #3).**

Love's Misbehaving Magic

CHAPTER ONE

PATTY

Patricia Newsome hoped that once she walked through the teal double doors before her, she would find her personal, magical path. That lofty expectation explained the butterflies swarming inside her. Time for action. She raised her hand to rap on the door with her knuckles. Except the door swung open, and a body came barreling out.

"Oof, excuse me," Patricia mumbled into the shoulder of the person who had just crashed into her. The tall, well-built someone who smelled amazing, with a clean, bright herbal scent. "I was about to knock," she explained as she lifted her gaze and saw longish brown hair framing dark brown eyes. "Noah! What are you doing here?"

The skin around Noah Wright's eyes crinkled with a smile. "Hi Patty, sorry about that. I didn't see you there."

She laughed and lifted one shoulder in a shrug. "Wouldn't be the first time, given that I'm, ahem, height-challenged." Unlike Noah, who was the very definition of a tall drink of water.

Noah stepped through the front door of his parents' home and held it open for her. "I was just leaving. Are you here to see my mother or my father?"

"Your father, if he's available."

"I believe he's out back. Do you want me to get him for you?"

"Nah, that's not necessary. I'll head around the side." She stepped away from the open door, and Noah followed. Curious. And a bit intriguing.

"How's school?" he asked, shifting his green backpack from one shoulder to the other.

"Great. I can't believe I'm graduating with my master's degree in only one more semester." She shook her head.

"In Theology, right?"

"You remembered."

Noah winked. "My excellent tutoring clearly helped you get there."

"No doubt, my improved algebra skills made all the difference when studying alternative religions," Patty responded deadpan.

"No doubt," he agreed with a solemn nod.

They stood in silence for a beat, and she wondered if she was imagining the spark she felt between them. Patty had always found him attractive. Especially in high school, when he was her older tutor – high school senior to her freshman. But she hadn't seen him until this summer when she'd made her discovery about his mother.

"How's your mother?" she asked, and his face grew troubled. All the witches in Wildcrest, Nevada had a magical inclination, and Noah's was healing abilities. He might look like the stereotype of a cowboy in his flannel shirts, jeans, and brown boots. But, no, he was Wildcrest's only family doctor who made house calls.

He ran a hand through his longish brown hair. "The same," he answered in a lowered voice. "Ben tried to read her, to find what might be wrong with her. He couldn't tell, so I tried a general healing spell. It didn't seem to do anything."

"Have you spoken to Esther about it?"

Noah flushed.

"That would be a no, then," she teased.

"We've seen the impact of whatever is going on with Mom," Noah said. "But since you're the only one who has actually seen something wrong with her, we're not sure how to approach it. My brothers and your sister have said we need to meet to discuss what to do, but we don't."

"Avoiding?"

Noah nodded.

"Is that a good idea?" Patty scanned his face, took in the worry lines and troubled expression marring the chiseled cheekbones. She knew she'd upended the family during their last Wiccan celebration when she had been shocked to witness Esther Wright's magical aura.

All witches had magical energy radiating from them like an aura. Patty's gift was to see and interpret those magical auras. Except that for as long as she had known Esther Wright, though the woman might be a brilliant and beautiful person, she was not a witch. Esther never had a magical aura. Only apparently, now she did and therefore she was a witch. There was no other explanation for why Esther would have a magical aura. And her developing magic was interfering with other witches' magic. It was a bizarre scenario none of them had encountered before. Patty had researched it when she returned to school after the celebration, but found no recorded instances of a person developing magical abilities outside of puberty.

"How do you tell your mother she's not only a witch, but possibly a broken one?" Noah crossed and uncrossed his arms. "Have you seen anything else?"

"No, I haven't. Maybe we should have a meeting with her?" Patty suggested.

Noah looked uncomfortable, though gave a curt nod.

"How's work?" Patty asked instead, hoping it would be a safer topic, though she made a mental note to speak to his brothers.

Noah's relieved expression reinforced Patty's decision to change the topic. "It's great. This morning, I healed a small femur fracture that happened when a goat tripped and fell on its owner."

"A goat? No!" Patty exclaimed.

"Yep."

"Is the goat okay?"

"Yes," he responded, and they shared another smile.

A moment before the silence grew uncomfortable, a booming voice sounded from the back of the home.

"Who's at the door, son?"

"It's Patty," Noah called over his shoulder to his father, his eyes never leaving Patty's.

She grew warm under the scrutiny. "I'd like to talk to you about a job after graduation," she hollered from the front doorway to Elijah Wright, the coven's high priest, who likely was in the kitchen on the other end of the large home.

She couldn't miss the bright flare of Noah's typically muted pink aura to a brighter, richer pink, with her explanation of why she was on his parents' doorstep. The flare threw her for a moment.

To respect other witches' emotional privacy, she tried not to read their auras without their permission; except sometimes when their emotions sparked, their auras were unavoidable.

Noah's bright, rich pink aura suggested attraction. She'd thought she'd seen a hint of it at the celebration earlier in the summer, and again when he opened the door. But it definitely flared brighter just now. And if he could read magical auras, hers no doubt would match.

CHAPTER TWO

NOAH

The rush of pleasure when Patty stated her intention with his father surprised Noah. Because that meant she wanted to move back to town after graduation? That wasn't surprising. Most witches returned to Wildcrest. After all, who wouldn't want to live relatively openly among other supernatural beings, chiefly witches, if they had the opportunity to do so? His father's continued speech stopped Noah's rush of thoughts.

"A job?" Elijah hollered, his booming voice easily traveling from the kitchen to the front door where Noah and Patty still stood.

"Yes, sir," Patty hollered back and then winked at Noah.

He caught himself before he winked back. That wasn't an appropriate response, he didn't think. She was staring at him, waiting for him to… oh right. "I guess you don't need to go around the side of the house," Noah said, stepping back through the doorway into the foyer.

"Kitchen?" she asked him, pointing as if they both didn't know the way by heart. They'd spent hours in the kitchen together when he tutored her.

"Kitchen," he answered, and then closed the door behind her. She wore jeans, a t-shirt, and turquoise Converse, which he swore she wore almost exclusively during high school. "Nice Chucks."

She glanced at him over her shoulder and gave him a coquettish wave. Then she kicked up one foot, but didn't say anything.

Noah laughed and continued to follow the tiny woman through the foyer, her shoes silent on the terracotta tile flooring, in contrast to the clacking of his boots.

He stopped in the doorway to the kitchen. Patty was embracing his parents.

"Elijah," she said, wrapping her arms around the burly man, her head not reaching his shoulders.

"It's great to see you," Elijah said. "I'm sorry we didn't get a chance to chat much at the celebration."

Patty waved away the apology, disentangled herself from his father's hug, and hugged his mother. "How are you doing, Esther?"

Noah understood the subtext to that question, but he doubted his parents did. And, judging from his mother's response, she definitely didn't pick up on anything other than a social nicety in the greeting.

"I'm great, Patty. I'll echo my husband. It's great to see you." Esther sat at the white oak table, gesturing for Patty and the men to do the same. "Did I hear right? Are you here about a job?"

Patty glanced around the table at Elijah, Esther, and Noah, then bit her lower lip.

"Hadn't planned on a whole crowd, had you?" Noah teased and she gave a bobble-headed nod. "We can leave."

"Oh," Esther said, "of course. You're like family. It never even occurred to me." She lifted her hand like she wanted to run it through her hair, but forgot she had done her French braid.

"Let's go, Mom," Noah said to Esther, before mouthing *good luck* to Patty. She mouthed *thank you* and visibly relaxed.

Patty and Noah stood. "I can't wait to catch up after we're finished," Patty offered, as Noah led his mother back out of the kitchen and onto the deck.

The two sat on wooden deck chairs situated to overlook the Nevada desert beyond the property. It was still early afternoon, so the sun blazed in a cloudless blue sky. Its rays warmed the brown and green scrub brush surrounding the home.

Noah sank his tall frame into the chair and breathed in the fresh air.

"Do you know what job Patty's asking your father about?" Esther whispered the words, though Noah doubted that Patty or Elijah could hear inside the house.

Nevertheless, he matched her tone and volume. He even leaned closer. "I don't. Her degree is in theology, so it might have something to do with Dad as the high priest of the coven." He cocked his head. "Is that Richard?"

Esther and Noah peered at the scrub brush off to the side of the deck. A gray wolf appeared and sauntered over to them, stopping between their two deck chairs.

Noah scratched the wolf behind the ears and was rewarded with a tail thump of pleasure. "How are you doing, Richard?"

The wolf's tongue lolled out in response and Esther chuckled. "Elijah is inside," she said to her husband's familiar.

Noah didn't think the wolf fully understood his mother, but the wolf certainly understood his father's name. Richard – a Wright warrior ancestor from several hundred years ago – settled between the chairs and rested his head on outstretched paws.

"Did I sense something between you and Patty?" Esther asked her son.

Noah's eyebrows practically jumped off his forehead before he recovered. But not fast enough.

"I did," she answered her own question.

"She's like my little sister," he blurted out in response, his face flushing. His reaction to Patty continued to *not* feel like family-member feelings.

"Uh-huh." His mother leaned back in the chair, eyes closed, lifting her face to the sun.

Noah mimicked her, enjoying the gentle breeze on his skin, and wondered about his mixed reactions to Patty. He'd always thought she was cute, but in a platonic way. Like a little sister. Except, that rush of pleasure when she'd said she was asking his father about a job… that wasn't like the pleasure of reuniting with a family member. Not at all. The thought of seeing her every day, or spending time with her… he never felt like that when he thought about seeing his brothers, that was certain.

He found himself wondering if she'd experienced something similar.

CHAPTER THREE

PATTY

Patty hadn't realized how much the clashing auras in the kitchen upset her magical balance until Esther and Noah left the room. It hadn't just been Noah's aura, suggesting an interest in her. Esther's aura continued to swirl a chaotic mix of colors, and for the first time, worry appeared in Elijah's aura. Patty sighed in relief with their exit.

"Is that sigh about me?" Elijah teased.

Her face reddened and she sat across from him at the kitchen table. "Not at all," she said, though that wasn't entirely accurate.

Did he sense something with Esther, or was it unrelated? She wasn't comfortable asking him, since he wasn't aware his aura was flashing like this, so she cleared her throat and focused on her reason for the visit.

"As you know," she began, her hands rubbing the smooth oak top before she caught herself, "I'm graduating with my Master of Arts in Theological Studies at the end of the upcoming semester."

"Congratulations in advance," he interrupted her.

"Thank you," she accepted with a grin. "The next step in my career is to secure employment." She breathed deeply, the scent of the Wright's coffee calming her. "And I'd like that job to be with Wildcrest Witches International."

"Tell me what role you'd like to fill," Elijah said. "We don't have any openings."

Butterflies returned at the comment, but she wasn't surprised. "I can appreciate that," she said with a nod. The coven's business was a small one, and she'd need to make the case for herself. "I have an idea for a new role, one that would combine my Wiccan knowledge with business acumen."

"I'm listening," he said, leaning back in the chair, his arms resting on the white oak table, brown eyes reflecting curiosity.

Patty paused before launching into a summary of her ideas. She recommended creating an online version of their coven. That would allow the company to grow beyond the local activities they currently focused on, without sacrificing their in-person activities. "We could even have retreats for witches who want to experience in-person celebrations."

Elijah frowned.

Worry spiked that he wouldn't accept her ideas. "It would never be at the expense of our town members, of course," she rushed to reassure him. "But it would offer solitary practitioners in the supernatural world the support they might not otherwise get." His nod emboldened her. "It would also allow me the opportunity to learn from you and…" She swallowed as she mentally tripped at admitting her true ambition aloud.

"And?"

"Become the high priestess myself one day." Her eyes widened as she waited for his reaction.

Elijah tilted his head, taking her in.

She tried not to fidget under his gaze. This was a big plan for the future and he was the first person she'd shared it with. What if he hated her aspiration? Her breath caught in her throat.

"That's intriguing," he finally said.

She whooshed out the breath she was holding.

He chuckled. "Diversifying sources of income, growing the company without sacrificing our local witches," he processed what she'd offered. "And become the high priestess when I retire. Intriguing indeed."

Patty had considered her pitch a lot. She didn't believe any of the Wright sons were interested in becoming the high priest, and although it wouldn't be soon, Elijah would eventually step down. She believed in her heart that she would be a great coven leader. Her natural empathy for others combined with her magical inclination and the information she was learning in graduate school seemed like the perfect trifecta. At least to her.

"Let me think about it," Elijah said, holding out his hand, which she took. "I'll let you know." Elijah's magenta aura pulsed brighter, unavoidable, but the powerful color, consistent with his strong-willed originality, suggested the idea indeed intrigued him.

Patty relaxed further at the unexpected sight. "Thank you." She stood from the chair. "I appreciate the consideration."

Elijah walked her out, and her heart jumped when she saw Noah sitting in his truck in the driveway. His head down indicated he was reviewing a patient chart or was on his phone. She crossed the stone paver driveway to knock on his window.

He startled, then relaxed when he saw it was her. The window lowered.

Although unable to explain why the Wrights' auras seemed conspicuous today, Noah's bright pink shining aura of happiness in seeing her bolstered her nerves and she boldly opened with, "Hey good-looking."

CHAPTER FOUR

NOAH

Did she just greet me with hey good-looking? Noah stammered something unintelligible in response and waited for her follow-up, while he berated himself for missing an opportunity. Wait, did that mean he wanted to flirt?

Her expression fell, and a frisson of guilt surfaced. She surely was joking around, and he took it too seriously, and maybe hurt her feelings.

"How did it go with my dad?" he asked, choosing the path of ignoring the discomfort.

Patty accepted the side-stepping. "It went well. I offered my ideas for a job and he said it was intriguing."

He wondered about specifics, but figured she'd share when she was ready. "You staying in town is definitely intriguing," he said, echoing his father's response. Again, a flash of pleasure surged through him at the idea of her staying in Wildcrest after graduation. That needed to stop. They were just friends.

"Thank you." Patty frowned and bit her lower lip. "I'm still concerned about Esther."

At Patty's expression of concern, Noah's worry about his mother heightened. "Did you see something new today?"

She hesitated. "Not new, exactly, but there appeared to be an increase in the intensity of the chaos in your mother's magical aura."

"An aura that she shouldn't even have."

"That we wouldn't expect her to have," Patty gently corrected. "Shouldn't is a strong word."

"Touché," he said, inclining his head.

"Certainly, since as far as we knew, she never had any magic, the presence of a magical aura is unexpected." She placed her hands on her hips.

He smothered a smile. She'd adopted that superhero stance as a kid and used it whenever she was thinking. Noah wondered if she was aware of that.

"The intensity increase within her new aura concerns me, though. Especially since we don't understand what any of this means."

"It might be a good thing?"

"An increase in chaos is rarely a good thing, but, honestly, I just don't know." Patty nibbled on her lower lip again, and heat suffused his face. He hoped she missed it.

Noah closed his eyes for a moment. Patty's comment from earlier was accurate. They needed to call a family meeting to discuss his mother's… condition? He didn't know what to call it.

"Noah?"

His eyes popped back open. "Apologies. I was considering our options."

"And?"

"You're right—"

"Of course," she interrupted with a wink.

He chuckled, then sobered. "We need to meet as a family to discuss what this might mean."

Patty reached up to place one hand on his arm where he leaned out his open window. "I think you should include your parents."

The feel of her fingers against his skin distracted him.

"It's about Esther, so she should be there," she added in a stronger tone.

Patty's tone broke the spell of her distraction. "I'm not disagreeing with you."

"Oh, when you stayed quiet…"

"I was distracted." Both their gazes landed on his arm, where her hand still lingered.

She snatched it back. "Ah, I see."

He wished she'd put her hand back on his arm.

"You know," Patty said, her voice taking on an unfamiliar slinky sound. "We could go out sometime."

"Like on a date?" he stammered. "I don't know."

"I'm only here until the end of the month," she backtracked.

"So not a date?"

She shook her head, appearing confused. "I'm not a big label person. But we could call it a summer fling." She hooked a come-hither finger at him. "I hear those are popular."

He opened and closed his mouth like a fish, unable to find his voice.

"It's not a trick question," she teased, leaning against the truck.

A scent of vanilla wafted around him. That had been her signature scent since high school. Right then, it made him hungry. "I'm not interested in you," he said instead.

"Your aura would suggest otherwise."

"That's unfair," he grumbled, though her observing his aura uninvited surprised him. A smidge of irritation bubbled. That wasn't like her to read auras without permission.

"Life isn't fair," she responded cheerfully, and he couldn't help but laugh. "And just so you know, I'm not trying to see your aura. Your family is very... visible today."

"Thanks for explaining." He broke eye contact, now feeling bad about his unwarranted irritation. Of course, she wouldn't purposefully read his aura without permission. "I'm still not having a fling with you."

"You're so caught up in labels," she joked, though he thought he heard the disappointment underneath.

Or was he confusing her tone with his own disappointment that all she wanted was a fling?

CHAPTER FIVE

PATTY

With Noah's reaction, Patty wanted to eat her words. She was so convinced he'd say yes – his aura told her that he found her attractive – it hadn't occurred to her that he wouldn't. She tamped down the surge of disappointment and backpedaled.

"No worries," she sang out with false bravado. "It was just an impulsive question."

"I hope you know it isn't—"

"Personal? Of course, I know that," she interrupted and waved off his explanation. Her hurt feelings could be dealt with later. This would only get more and more awkward if she didn't cut it off. Now. She made a show of glancing at his watch, as if they both had more important places to be. "It was great seeing you, as always." She turned to walk away, then stopped. "Though if you'd like me to come to the family meeting about Esther." She bit her lower lip. "I'm not family—"

This time, he cut her off. "You're family," he disagreed.

Her pressured thoughts to flee the uncomfortable conversation settled at the finality with which he made the statement. "Thanks," she whispered. "My job suggestion to your father was to assist him with his high priest duties, so that I can be the high priestess one day."

Noah's jaw dropped open at the blurted statement.

But, she found this time she didn't regret the impromptu detail. The comfort she'd felt in the conversation led her to believe he would support the idea. Support *her*, if she was honest with herself.

"That's a wonderful idea," he said. "You'd make a great high priestess when my father steps down."

A shy smile played at her lips. She'd hoped for his support, but actually receiving it – and immediately, no less – flooded her with warmth. "Thank you, Noah."

"Of course," he said, and they shared a heated glance. "As for Mom, I'll let you know what we schedule." This time, he glanced at his watch. "I really do have to go, though."

"Have a good day," she said with a half-wave, glad the awkwardness had abated somewhat. Albeit not fully.

She walked to her vehicle, the sound of his truck starting and pulling away a mixed soundtrack to her walk of shame.

Patty mentally smacked herself. It wasn't a walk of shame. No need to exaggerate. She asked him out and he said no. They were both adults. It could disappoint her without embarrassing her.

Driving back to her parents' house in her bright red hatchback, she kept the windows lowered to enjoy the late summer breezes and sang along to the radio. She gave her brain time to process what she'd said, done, and learned that morning at the Wright house.

An idea percolated to the top as she pulled into her parents' driveway.

A deep bark greeted her when she opened the door to the sprawling ranch-style home. She entered the foyer and kneeled down to love on the Great Dane before her.

"Hey Max," she said, running her fingers along his black face and down his tan body. He wiggled his butt in appreciation, before heading back the way he'd probably come. Maximillian, better known as Max, was her father's familiar. Max was reticent about where in the family tree he resided, and Patty assumed it would remain one of life's great mysteries.

Sort of like her own familiar, she thought, as she headed toward her childhood bedroom. Like all the women in her family, she too had a less common familiar. No cats or dogs for any of them. "Hi Aveline," she greeted the sandy brown desert owl whose ancestor spirit was so ancient the source seemed lost to time.

"Welcome back," Aveline hooted. The shy owl rarely left Patty's room during the day, though enjoyed touring the desert surrounding Wildcrest at night.

"Let me run something by you," Patty said to the owl before laying back on the yellow bedspread of the unmade bed.

"Proceed," Aveline hooted.

Patty caught her familiar up on the proposal to Elijah Wright and the continued chaotic magic in Esther's aura. She swallowed, reminded herself that there was no reason to be embarrassed, and then shared how Noah shot down her invitation.

"A summer fling?"

"Is that disdain in your voice, Ave?"

"That's not really like you, and it's definitely not like Noah."

A flush crept up Patty's neck. "What was I thinking?"

"You weren't."

Patty chuckled. "Isn't that the truth?"

"What are you going to do?"

"I don't know," Patty admitted, staring at the ceiling, waiting for inspiration. Her prior idea continued percolating. She considered the connections between the personal and professional issues with her and the members of the Wright family. Perhaps she could kill two birds with one stone.

Ugh, that's a horrible saying. Patty shot a glance at her owl, glad the familiar couldn't read her mind.

She bolted up. "I think I have a plan."

"This isn't anything harebrained like your sister's plan was?"

Patty's older sister, Shelly, had played with magic to convince an ex-boyfriend to reunite with her, with the expected disastrous results. Although, in the end, Shelly figured out where her heart was, and she'd gotten her happily ever after.

Noah's face flashed in her mind, and Patty startled. She was interested in Noah, sure, but he wasn't her happily ever after.

Was he? They both prioritized family, valued professionalism, and enjoyed what life offered. Plus, they had a healthy dose of attraction between them.

Why couldn't he be her happily ever after?

Oh, yeah, because that's not what he wanted.

"Patty? Your plan?" The owl interrupted Patty's rapid thoughts.

"Yes. My plan!" She inhaled. "There are several overlapping areas in my life right now," she said both to Aveline and herself as she worked this out in her mind. "I want Noah to look at me like more than a little sister – and act on it," she clarified. Relief surged that she could acknowledge to herself that she did, in fact, want him.

She frowned. "I want to help Esther in whatever way I can, to help her understand and develop whatever type of magic she now has."

"Finally, I want Elijah to agree to my proposal to expand the online footprint of Wildcrest Witches International, with a long-term goal of me becoming the high priestess."

"Excellent summary," Aveline hooted and Patty swore she saw laughter in the owl's yellow eyes.

"Thank you," Patty said, accepting the praise at face value. She leapt from the bed and spun to face the owl, who perched on a large tree in the room's corner.

"So, this is my plan. I'll offer to help Esther, which will hopefully actually help her. That help will show Elijah what I'd bring to the coven in an official capacity. Last but not least," she said with a grin, "I'll use the proximity to Noah to convince him we should at least go out on a date."

Aveline's hooting response was unmistakably laughter this time, though the owl offered her support. "If anyone can do it, you can."

"All before I leave for my last semester of school at the end of the month. Easy peasy." She nibbled on her lower lip. "First step. Figure out what the heck is going on with Esther and her unexpected magic."

CHAPTER SIX

NOAH

Wildcrest Wizardry was one of his favorite places in town. Between the delectable scents from the coffee shop side of the business and the incredible array of herbs on the apothecary side, he loved that it represented the notion of helping. Each aisle of the apothecary focused on a different area of magic. Right now, he needed additional herbs to supplement his magical healing for his next house call.

"Can I help you find anything, Noah?" Rebekah, the tall, blonde manager of the store, asked him. "Probably not," she answered herself, "but I figured there's no harm in asking. I suspect you know even better than I do where everything is."

He joined in her easy laughter. "I'm good, thank you."

"Tell me if you change your mind," she said and then hurried to the front station to check out a customer.

Noah frowned as he considered his options. He needed peppermint, ginger, and stinging nettle to address Bobby's damaged lungs.

The scent of vanilla reached him before he heard her voice.

"Let's turn that frown upside down," Patty said in an unusual, lilting cadence.

He placed the last of his selected herbs in the handheld cart and offered her a smirk. "How do you plan to do that?"

"Depends on the source of the frown."

"It's for a patient."

"Ah, a little natural magic booster."

"Precisely." Although his magical inclination was to heal others, it wasn't that cut and dried. With some illnesses and injuries, the healing was like a movie. He'd hover his hands over the problematic body part, and they'd get better.

His younger brother, Ben, had asked him about the process when Ben's ability to recognize what a sick person needed, whether physical or magical, first developed. Their parents had said that it wasn't uncommon for siblings to develop similar magical abilities like that.

Noah had explained that when he healed someone, his fingertips tingled. With practice, he'd learned that when those tingles turned painful, that was the Goddess telling him that his magic alone wasn't sufficient to heal the person's illness or injury.

When his magic wasn't sufficient, he turned to other magical enhancement, whether crystals, herbs, or intentional spell work. Except in the most advanced cases, between his own magic and the magical enhancements, he succeeded. In only a year, he had built up a thriving house call service. He enjoyed helping individuals who wouldn't otherwise be able or willing to seek help outside their homes.

Patty knew all of that, too. They'd had many conversations about his medical intentions during their tutoring sessions. He remembered her, as always, so supportive of his plans.

"Do you expect it to be enough?" she asked now, and he understood she was curious, not questioning his abilities.

"I believe so," he replied. The patient's illness had progressed further than Noah would have liked. He wished Bobby had contacted him sooner. But Noah had healed similar issues before, so he remained optimistic.

She placed her hands on her hips.

"What?" he asked, an unfamiliar emotion fluttering through him, feeling heavy in his chest. He wondered about its origins, before focusing on Patty instead. "Lay it on me."

"Can I come with you?"

His eyebrows rose. "To see my patient?"

"Yes."

He couldn't imagine a reason she'd want to. "For what reason?"

"I have an idea to help your mother, and it'll give us the ride out to the house to discuss it."

The explanation, and shift from his patient to his mother, startled him. "How do you know the drive will be long enough?"

"Educated guess. I don't believe many of your clients are close to town."

"You're not wrong," he agreed, a thrill surging that she'd thought about his practice. "Is there a reason you can't explain the idea to me now?" He asked for curiosity's sake, since he'd already decided to say yes.

She scuffed sandals on the floor, not meeting his eyes.

That confirmed she had an ulterior motive.

"I don't want to hold you up," she explained.

A perfectly reasonable explanation. And yet. He knew her. There was something more. Could it have something to do with her asking him out before? He'd already told her no, so surely she wouldn't ask again. He ignored that as a possible explanation.

She watched him consider her request; he hoped his aura wasn't flashing again.

"I'll text the patient, and if he's not okay with you coming inside, you'll have to wait in the car," he warned her, his already baritone voice deepening.

"Understood."

He pulled his phone from the front pocket of his jeans to text Bobby. Noah emphasized that Patty needed to talk to Noah during the drive, and could wait in the truck at the house. He read the response and then lifted his gaze, his brown eyes finding her hazel ones.

"It must be your lucky day. He said it's too hot for you to wait in the car, regardless of the existence of air conditioning."

"Aw, that's sweet." She touched his arm. "But I don't want to be an imposition, or to make him feel uncomfortable."

He enjoyed the touch of her hand on his elbow for the briefest of moments before responding. "Believe me, if he didn't want you there, he would have said no. This is not someone who has a hard time speaking his mind."

"As long as you're sure."

"I am. Let's do it." He'd just try to figure out her ulterior motive while they drove.

CHAPTER SEVEN

PATTY

The mapping software informed her she had twenty minutes to lay out her plan before they reached Noah's patient's home. That would be plenty of time.

"While we don't understand the *why* or *how* of what's happening with your mother, the existence of a magical aura tells me she has magic. Period," Patty bluntly began.

"Agreed."

"So, I envision a multi-step plan."

Noah chuckled. "You do, huh?"

She gave him the side-eye, which only made him laugh harder. "I do."

"Please enlighten me." His fingers on the steering wheel tapped along with the radio playing softly in the background.

"Step one is to talk to your mother." Patty remained shocked the Wright men hadn't broached the topic. That needed to be rectified as soon as possible.

"How would you recommend we approach her?"

"Matter of fact. With me present, ideally."

"Ideally?"

"Yes. Probably Laura too."

Noah nodded as he took the highway entrance ramp. "That makes sense."

"I can explain that I see a magical aura, and Laura can explain how Esther's proximity to her has made her magic wonky."

"Wonky?"

"To use the technical term," Patty explained with a wink.

"Please continue," Noah said with a theatrical wave.

"Your mother is smart—"

"Thanks," he interrupted.

"—and I think that will be enough for her to accept that something is happening. Plus, then we can ask—" Patty side-eyed Noah again. "—your mother how she's been feeling. There's a very good chance that she can tell something is happening."

Noah's eyebrows rose. "Do you think she knows she's got magic?"

"I don't know." Patty lifted a single shoulder. "But I find it highly unlikely that she has enough magic for me to see a magic aura AND for it to interfere with Laura's magic, without Esther feeling something."

"Makes sense," Noah said again. He exited the highway and hung a sharp right onto a dirt road. "Step two?"

"Step two," Patty began, "is to help your mother learn to manipulate the magical energy she has."

"How exactly are you going to do that?"

She fiddled with the A/C vent, angling it toward her and then off her face again. "That's the tricky part," she admitted.

"No doubt," he said as he pulled up to a small, squat, but well-kept beige stucco house.

"Once we have a better understanding of how the magic feels to Esther, then we can work with her. I can watch how the chaos in her aura responds to anything that we do. My assumption is that as she learns how to control her magic, the chaos in her aura will decrease."

Noah turned the truck off and twisted in his seat. Patty read the uncertainty on his face.

"Trust me," she urged him. "It'll work."

"I don't know," he said and turned away to exit the car. Patty scrambled to do the same, anxiety spiking that her plan might be finished before it even started. When she met him at the front of the truck, she grabbed his elbow.

"What's the worst that can happen?"

His gaze dropped to her hand on his arm, but this time, his expression remained unreadable.

She spread her arms wide. "It's our best bet right now. Do you have a better idea?"

"No, I don't. But." He sighed. "I'm just not comfortable experimenting on my mother."

Before Patty could argue with him that her plan wasn't experimenting, the door to the home opened and an older man stood in the doorway.

"I'll check with my brothers after the visit, but the answer will probably be no," Noah said with finality. He strode away from her, hand extended. "Bobby."

"Hey, doc," the older man responded in a raspy voice. "This is your friend?" Bobby asked as he peered beyond Noah at Patty, who'd remained a few feet back.

At the question, she also strode forward, hand extended. "Hi, Bobby, I'm Patty," she said, startled by his weak handshake. "Thank you for allowing me to accompany Noah." She gazed up at Bobby's wrinkled face surrounded by wispy, gray hair, and he offered a lop-sided smile. Stained teeth combined with his raspy voice suggested a probable source of his illness.

"Nice to meet you," Bobby said, before indicating the two should follow him inside.

The faint scent of tobacco confirmed Patty's guesses about his illness; lung cancer or emphysema, she wondered.

Bobby hitched up the pants falling off his narrow hipbones and collapsed onto the faded corduroy couch.

When Noah took the spot next to him, Patty scooted over to a blue rocking chair and perched on the edge.

"How are you feeling today?" Noah asked Bobby.

The older man knelt over as a coughing fit overwhelmed him. Patty's heart broke to see the suffering, and she hoped Noah's abilities weren't overstated. She recognized it was silly superstition, but she crossed her fingers behind her bag in a quick wish to the Goddess.

"Sorry 'bout that," Bobby said when the fit subsided. "Emphysema," he explained to Patty, and she nodded. "Quit smoking, but, eh, the damage's been done."

"Are you ready?" Noah asked, and Bobby nodded.

Patty realized with a start that they were jumping right into the healing. Noah had obviously already done a preliminary visit. Despite their shared history, she'd never seen him heal someone.

Noah placed a ceramic mortar on the glass top of the coffee table before them and filled it with the herbs he'd bought at the apothecary earlier.

Patty and Bobby remained quiet, absorbed in Noah's process.

Noah crushed the peppermint, ginger, and stinging nettle with the ceramic pestle, muttering under his breath.

Patty strained to hear the words, but they stayed unintelligible; however, she couldn't miss his aura. It blazed with shades of green, blue, and a light teal. All the colors associated with healing.

"This part will be quick," Noah assured Bobby, before lighting the mixture on fire.

The sweet scents of peppermint and ginger filled the small space. This was why Noah had left Bobby's front door open, Patty realized. With a final few words of the incantation, Noah blew out the flame. Embers continued to glow. Noah faced Bobby, who closed his eyes without being instructed to do so.

Patty sat transfixed while Noah's hands roamed maybe an inch or two over the older man's body. Noah's hands slowed and halted over Bobby's chest. She caught her breath when an aura sputtered around Bobby. Noah's healthy aura grew darker as Bobby's strengthened, then both auras mixed, before separating and brightening. Noah's returned to a healing light blue and green, and Bobby's settled at a warm orange. That social and thoughtful color fit with Bobby inviting her to stay for his healing.

Bobby inhaled deeply and a wide grin broke out over his weathered face. "I haven't been able to do that in… I don't know how long," he admitted.

"We'll get you in for some testing to confirm, but I believe you're good to go," Noah said, his voice bearing a hint of exhaustion to Patty's ears. He provided detailed follow-up information, and the two exchanged their goodbyes.

Watching Noah heal Bobby had been exhilarating for Patty. All magic was amazing, a gift from the Goddess. But, something about Noah's healing moved her in a way other witch's magic hadn't. Could that be connected to her attraction to him?

Patty rose to her feet when the men did, caught by surprise, as she was still reviewing in her mind what she'd witnessed. Noah's healing abilities impressed her tremendously. His medical background combined with his magical abilities made a potent combination. His ability to work directly with a witch's aura to aid their healing was nothing short of miraculous.

Now that she understood more about how those abilities worked, she had an idea to convince him to partner with her to help his mother.

CHAPTER EIGHT

NOAH

Gratification and exhaustion coexisted in Noah after the healing. He understood he had a gift, and he received immense pleasure in helping his fellow witches. It was also tremendously exhausting work. A trickle of unease filtered in, wondering what Patty thought of what she'd witnessed.

"What did you think?" Noah asked Patty once they were seated back in his truck for the return to town. For obvious reasons, other than family members of his patients, he'd never had someone watch him work like that before. The small surge of anxiety suggested he wanted her to be impressed. That seemed odd to him.

"That was amazing," she gushed, and pride washed over Noah. "I've never seen anything like that before."

"I imagine you don't follow doctors around much," he joked.

"True," she said with a laugh, "but that's not what I meant."

He glanced at her. "What do you mean?" She met his gaze for a moment before his eyes returned to the road.

"I could see you heal him."

"Well, yes, you were right there as I combined my abilities with the spell." He heard the confusion in his tone.

"No, I mean, I saw his aura change as you healed him," she explained.

"Oh." His mind swirled with that knowledge. "What did that look like?"

Patty walked him through what she'd seen, and his mind continued to swirl in the background as she did so.

"Bobby's magic really suffered during his illness," Noah said when she finished.

She nodded. "I wondered. The way it sputtered, but then grew in strength." Now she shook her head. "That was just so amazing," she repeated.

"I'd never realized my magic mixed with theirs so specifically," he admitted. "Knowing his magic seems to have recovered along with his physical self, right there during treatment..." Noah trailed off. "We make a good team."

"Yes, we do," she agreed. She placed her hand on his, resting on the stick shift. The softness of her skin and the naturalness of the movement caught him. He wanted more of it. More of Patty. "And I think I know how to help your mother."

He opened his mouth to remind her he was going to speak to his brothers, but she removed her hand from his and barreled forward.

"If we partner on this, we'll be that much more effective."

Noah remained quiet; his mind had taken him down a similar road. He wondered if they'd ended up at the same conclusion.

"The way your aura mixed with Bobby's suggests perhaps the same would happen with Esther. You can use your healing powers – and the interaction of your aura – to help stabilize hers, while I guide her verbally." Patty spoke as if working through the plan while she uttered the words. She spun in her seat to face him. "What do you think?"

He cut his eyes to hers before returning them to the road. "I think you've convinced me," he admitted.

"You don't need to run it by Ben and Aaron?" she teased.

"No, I don't." He smiled. "Though, of course, it'll be my mom's call."

"Naturally. I'd never try to work magic on someone without their knowledge."

She sounded so indignant he couldn't help but probe. "Unlike our siblings?" His brother and her sister had made some poor choices together earlier in the year, though everything ended well.

"Exactly," she agreed.

Her silence after the emphatic agreement surprised him, and he glanced at her again. She wore an odd expression; when she caught him looking, it changed into something lighthearted, but slyer. A chuckle threatened to erupt; he loved how she brought out such joy in him with her exuberance and playful scheming. She leaned closer, her vanilla scent brushed against him, tantalizing.

"Yes?" he asked.

"Since we make such a great team—"

"Are you sure you want to go there?" he interrupted her, clearing his throat to cover the sudden dryness.

"You'll go out with me then?" she continued as if he hadn't interrupted.

"I'm not dating my brother's girlfriend's baby sister," he blurted out.

"Exactly."

"Huh?" he responded not-so-eloquently to her unexpected rejoinder.

"You wouldn't be dating your brother's girlfriend's baby sister," she agreed with him.

Noah laughed. "Now I'm just confused. Are you asking me out again or not?"

"Yes, I am."

He cut his eyes at her again. "Explain."

"I'm not a girl." She rolled her eyes.

That strange dryness found his throat again. "No, you're not." She was certainly all woman, nothing like the girl he knew when they were teenagers.

"And it's not dating."

His heart fell, though a hitch in her voice suggested less surety than she presented. "I'm not interested in a summer fling," he reminded her as the truck coasted to a stop in front of Wildcrest Wizardry.

They faced each other in their seats. Patty opened her mouth and closed it. Noah waited for her next words, his eyes probing her face for which direction she was leaning. Could he dare hope she was interested in more?

When the silence entered uncomfortable territory, Noah broke it. "Meet me at my parents' house in the morning? I'll confirm a time with them and let you know."

Was it his imagination, or did a flash of disappointment cross her face? It was gone now, if it was ever there.

"Sounds good," she said as she broke eye contact and exited the truck. "See you tomorrow," she called over her shoulder before striding toward Wildcrest Wizardry.

He waited for her to turn back and wave goodbye. She didn't. Frustration blossomed, became another episode of tightness in his chest. He wished he understood what subtext he'd missed in their conversation.

CHAPTER NINE

PATTY

Patty wanted so much to look back at Noah as she walked to the apothecary's door, but she didn't, and she wasn't sure why. Because he'd turned her down again? She wasn't imagining the attraction between them. She knew that.

"Earth to Patty," came a familiar voice, and Patty focused in time to not crash into her older sister, Shelly.

"Hey, sis." Patty grinned at Shelly, who gave her a quick hug.

"Did you just get out of Noah Wright's truck?" Shelly asked, an indecipherable glint in her hazel eyes.

"I did," Patty said. "I went with him to visit one of his patients."

"You don't have to explain anything to me." Shelly opened the store's door, but not before Patty glimpsed her expression.

The merriment was unmistakable. "I'm not explaining anything," Patty disagreed. "I'm…" She stopped herself, unable to find the right word.

"Explaining?" Shelly suggested with a laugh.

Patty half-tackled her sister from behind, Shelly's long black hair tickling Patty's nose. "Whatever. It doesn't mean anything."

At the comment, Shelly pulled from her sister's grasp and faced her. "What does that mean?"

"Do you want a coffee?" Patty asked instead, not meeting her sister's eyes.

"I'll regret it when I try to go to sleep later," Shelly said, "but, of course."

The sisters walked through the apothecary to the coffee shop side of the business, offering a quick wave to the store manager behind the main register. Patty collapsed into one of the wooden chairs, running her hands over the top, hand carved by their Papaw. She'd never tire of seeing his amazing handiwork.

"Hi, girls," Nana greeted them. "Lattes?"

They nodded and watched their grandmother retreat to create the delectable drinks. Nana moved like the former runner she was, her short, wiry frame topped by black, almost spiky hair.

"What's going on?" Shelly asked Patty when their grandmother was out of earshot.

"Why would something be going on?"

"Seriously."

"What?"

"It's been years since I've seen you alone with Noah."

"Wait? What does—"

"And neither of you are teenagers anymore."

Patty's mouth dropped open. "What are you talking about?"

"There's no denying there's something between you."

"I…"

"Everyone could see it at the last festival," Shelly commented offhand.

"Everyone?" Patty squeaked.

"Have you asked him out?"

"Sort of."

Shelly rolled her eyes. "That sounds like the kind of answer I would have given earlier this year."

Patty scrunched up her nose at the thought she was engaging in the same silliness her sister had.

"Either you did or you didn't."

The silence stretched out long enough for Nana to return with their lattes. Her purple eyes narrowed. "Is everything okay?"

"Yes, Nana," they responded in unison, and all three women chuckled.

"Enjoy the coffee."

"We will," the sisters said in unison again.

Shelly inhaled deeply before bringing the piping-hot liquid to her lips.

"Careful," Patty warned.

"It's worth it," her sister said after taking the tiniest of sips.

Patty sipped at her own, the smooth liquid with a hint of chocolate sliding down her throat. She sighed.

"Exactly," Shelly agreed. "Now out with it."

Patty didn't bother to deny or avoid, and laid out the recent encounters with Noah. "What do you think?"

"We'll definitely revisit your idea about Esther," Shelly said, "but let's focus on Noah first." Her voice dropped with the second half of her sentence.

Patty appreciated the effort at discretion, but in a small town, eh, it would be all over Wildcrest by dinnertime that she was hanging out with Noah. "You're not wrong. There's an attraction between us."

"Did he acknowledge that?"

"Not immediately, no."

"What does that mean?"

"I read his aura," Patty admitted.

"Without his permission," Shelly said, the shock clear in her voice.

Patty defended herself. "It flashed so bright the first time, it was impossible to miss." She smirked.

"Okay, fair enough. But be careful," Shelly cautioned her baby sister, before sipping her coffee.

"I am, I promise."

"Then what happened?"

"He said no when I asked him out."

"Really?" Shelly narrowed her eyes. "What aren't you telling me?"

Patty became very interested in the cup of coffee before her on the table. She wrapped her hands around her mug, brought the delectable drink to her lips.

"Patty." The warning tone in Shelly's voice was one only a big sister could use.

"I may have suggested I only wanted a summer fling."

"Ah." Shelly sipped her coffee. "And do you?"

"Want only a summer fling?" Patty drummed her fingers on the wooden top. "I thought so. That made sense. He's hot. I'm cute—"

"If you do say so yourself," Shelly interrupted.

"—but I'm going back to school soon and I just asked his father for a job."

"Wait, what?" Shelly interrupted. "A job?"

"Oh, yeah, I didn't tell you," Patty said. She quickly brought her sister up to speed.

"That sounds amazing. Congrats, sis."

"Elijah hasn't offered me the job yet."

"The one you created?" Shelly scoffed. "He will, you're fantastic."

Patty flushed with pleasure. "Thanks. You can see, right, that in the moment, it seemed too complicated to add a relationship."

"And now?"

"He's not just hot." Patty's eyes took on a faraway look. "He's compassionate, funny, and sweet."

Shelly snorted.

"What?" Patty asked, the spell she'd put herself under broken.

"You surely already knew those things."

"There's a difference between knowing something in the abstract, and seeing it play out in front of you." Patty pursed her lips, remembering her sister's shenanigans from earlier that year. "You, of all people, should understand that." She sipped her coffee, giving her sister a knowing look over the top of the cup.

"True." Shelly blushed. "Now what?"

"Now what, what?"

"Now that you've realized that you want more than a fling, what are you going to do?" Shelly pointed at her sister. "Do I have to spell it out?"

Patty laughed at the unintended pun, and after a moment, Shelly joined her.

"I have a plan," Patty answered her sister.

"Uh-oh." Shelly shook her head. "You know where my planning got me."

"You got the guy!"

"Not for lack of trying to screw that up."

"Do you want to hear my plan or not?" Patty asked.

"Of course."

Patty laid out the idea she'd shared with Noah for helping his mother and impressing his father. "Naturally, the result will also be that Noah will see me as more than just the youngest Newsome—"

"I doubt that's all he sees you as," Shelly interjected.

"—and we can go out on a real date, and maybe have something more after I graduate."

Shelly reached across the table to take her sister's hands in hers. "I think that sounds like a brilliant plan."

"You do?" Patty asked, a shock of surprise hitting her.

"It's much better than my plan had been."

"Any plan is better than your plan was," Patty pointed out.

"Touché." Shelly checked her watch. "I need to pick Ben up. Do you need a ride?"

"I do, thanks."

The women waved goodbye to Nana and headed to Shelly's bright orange VW bug. Patty's mind swirled with the possibilities. It would work. She would help Esther understand and control her magic. That would impress Elijah enough to hire her upon graduation. And, Noah would see what an amazing team they made, not just as friends, but as more.

Tomorrow morning would begin Phase I.

CHAPTER TEN

NOAH

Noah, Ben, and Aaron sat at the kitchen table opposite their parents, who stared at them with curious anticipation.

"You boys called this meeting," Elijah said, his deep baritone rolling around the room. "It looks like something serious. Perhaps you should just say it."

Ben and Aaron glanced at Noah, and he gave a slight nod. "Mom, Dad, we have some… news."

"What is it?" Esther asked, placing her hand over his.

Noah's heart lurched. His gut told him this would ultimately be good news, but it was such a bombshell that he wasn't sure how to introduce the topic. Perhaps his father was right and he should just jump in with it. Or he could work his way toward it. That seemed safer.

"How have you been feeling, Mom?" he asked, covering her hand with his free hand.

She squeezed his hand beneath hers. "I'm fine. Why do you ask?"

Noah exchanged another look with his brothers. "Has anything been different? Felt different recently?"

The skin around his mother's mouth tightened, but she demurred. "Of course not."

When Elijah grimaced, Noah brought in the big guns. "Dad, is that correct?"

Esther rewarded Noah with an irritated sigh. "You don't need to ask your father how I'm doing," she snapped, but appeared contrite. "Sorry about that." Esther pulled her hand from her son and fanned herself. "Maybe I haven't been myself."

"We promise we have a reason for asking," Ben encouraged her.

"We do," Aaron chimed in.

The three men smiled at their mother; her chuckle reduced the tension in the room. "Your father is right. Why don't you just tell us what's going on?" Although her tone remained light-hearted, the flash of worry on her face told Noah that she knew something was awry.

Noah's lips thinned into a line and he blurted out, "You've developed magic."

Elijah's mouth dropped open and Esther belly laughed. "I don't think so," she disagreed.

The doorbell interrupted Noah's intended reply to his mother. "Perfect timing," he said instead.

"Perfect timing?" his mother echoed. "Are you expecting someone?"

"I'll get it," Aaron offered.

Noah thanked his younger brother and stood, preparing to greet their guest. "Patty Newsome is here, and she can explain it much better than I can."

Esther quirked an eyebrow. "Patty can explain what? That I have magic?" She shook her head, her French braid not budging. But her eyes narrowed. She knew Patty's magical inclination.

"Hello Wrights," Patty sang out when she joined them in the kitchen, Aaron a step behind, though he quickly retook his seat at the table. She stopped next to Noah and looked up at him, seeming to search his face for something.

"Hey Patty," he said softly and her grin lifted his spirits. "Are you ready to explain to my mother?" If he wasn't mistaken, her face paled a little at his question.

"You haven't told her?" she hissed, trying to keep the comment between them. "Laura couldn't make it?"

"I was getting there," he said, breaking eye contact. "And, no, she couldn't."

"You know I can hear you both, right?" Esther's fingers tapped on the tabletop. "I'm not even ten feet away."

"Sorry, Mom."

"Sorry, Esther."

Their simultaneous apologies resulted in a shared conspiratorial look. Patty took the seat Noah had vacated. "You're right. We should not have a conversation about you. We should have this conversation with you."

"You know what Noah meant when he said I have magic." A statement, not a question.

Patty nodded. "I do." She brought Esther through the story of seeing Esther's chaotic magical aura at the Lammas celebration; her theory of the magic interfering with Laura's magical abilities; and her offer to help Esther tame the chaos by combining her own magical ability to read auras with Noah's healing. Both Noah's parents' mouths hung open at the end of the tale.

"That does explain a few things," Elijah said, more to himself than anyone in the room, though Esther responded.

"What does it explain?"

Elijah wrapped a hand around his wife's shoulders. "Lately, I can feel a strange pull related to my memory magic. Memories randomly floating to the surface. Other people's memories popping into my head when you and I are with them."

She gasped. "Why didn't you say anything?"

Elijah blushed, a sight so unusual that Noah's eyebrows about jumped off his forehead. "Given some of the, um…"

Now all three sons stared at their father. Elijah Wright speechless? They didn't think it was possible.

"Spit it out, dear," Esther encouraged him with a kiss on the cheek.

"You've been a little moody and seemed to have, maybe, hot flashes," he said in a rush. "I thought it was just, you know, menopause."

Esther sighed. "Well, you're not wrong. That's what I thought too."

"The two may be related," Patty interjected, and everyone looked at her. She waved her hands around for emphasis as she explained. "As we're all aware, magical inclinations appear during puberty. That didn't happen for Esther." She grimaced. "Sorry for the bluntness."

"No need," Esther assured her.

"Why does that happen?" Patty asked, and nobody answered. "That wasn't really rhetorical," she said with a smirk.

Noah snorted and his brothers side-eyed him, which he ignored. "Our best guess is that the inclination appears during puberty because of the hormonal changes…" He trailed off when the implication hit him.

Patty pointed one hand at him and touched her nose with the other. "Bingo."

"It may be menopause that's triggering the magical development," Ben concluded for them and clapped his hands together. Noah almost laughed at the medical scientist in his brother, salivating at this *new witch thing*.

"Has that ever happened before?" Esther asked.

Noah and Patty exchanged glances before she jumped in to answer. "I don't think so, no. I've never come across anything like that in my own magical research."

Patty and the men stared with trepidation at Esther, waiting to see her impression of this development. She broke out in a wide grin.

"That might make going through menopause worth it," she declared. "How are we going to make it work right?"

Noah's worry evaporated at his mother's question. He should have known she'd not only take it in stride, but see it as a blessing from the Goddess. Noah grabbed Patty in a bear hug, which she enthusiastically returned. Her sweet vanilla scent filled his nostrils and he could almost rest his chin on her head.

He barely resisted kissing her, and his heart hammered that she'd gotten under his skin like that. If only she wanted more than a fling. He knew he wanted to date. The temptation of accepting her where she was – offering a fling – surfaced. No, that would only lead to dissatisfaction when he couldn't have more.

She didn't want to date. She'd asked for a fling. That broke the spell, and he held her at arms' length, offering a lop-sided smile, which she matched, confusion mixed with attraction clear on her face.

CHAPTER ELEVEN

PATTY

The unexpected hug threw Patty for a loop. Her body tingled where theirs had touched, a quite pleasant sensation. But she needed to focus on the issue at hand. Helping Esther get a handle on her new magic.

"Have you noticed any abilities that started around the time of menopause?" Patty asked.

Esther tapped her fingers on the table while she thought. "Not that I'm aware of."

"You mean you can't hear animals talking to you?" Aaron joked, and his mother smiled indulgently at him.

Patty ignored him. "Hmm, so either that hasn't manifested yet, or it's something not obvious."

"What does that mean for your plan?" Noah asked.

"Let's try to help the chaos calm down," she said with a quick nod of her head. "Perhaps that's why the magic hasn't manifested yet. The magic is still too chaotic." Her voice dropped as if she was talking to herself. A throat clearing drew her attention back to the family surrounding her.

"What do you need from us?" Ben asked.

"I need everyone but Esther and Noah to clear out," she said. "You're well-meaning, but your energy could mess with what we're trying to do," she added, softening the request.

"Understood," Elijah boomed. "Everyone else out." He kissed Esther on the cheek. "You got this, sweetheart."

"Thanks, honey," she whispered back.

Patty's insides melted a little at the exchange. One day she hoped to have that too.

Chairs pushed back from the table and chatter continued while the men left the room as instructed. A quiet descended when only Patty, Noah, and Esther remained.

"Are you ready?" Patty asked.

Esther chuckled nervously. "As I'll ever be. What do I need to do?"

"Noah, sit next to your mother," Patty instructed. Once they were seated, she sat opposite. "What we're going to do," she reminded Esther, "is combine Noah's healing power with my ability to see your aura to help direct you toward calming and organizing your aura."

Esther squinted. "Yeah, you said that before. Do you have any idea how to do that?"

Patty flushed at the direct question. "Kind of." She pointed at Noah. "I'll need you to verbalize what you're doing with the healing energy. That way I can direct you to push, pull, or otherwise redirect your energy when I see the impact on Esther's magical aura." She opened her arms wide, ignoring the anxiety racing up her spine. "Easy peasy, right?"

"Easy peasy," Esther echoed.

"Let's do it," Noah said.

"First, I'm going to open myself up to seeing your aura, Esther." Patty relaxed and allowed her mind's eye to open. Fuzzy and indistinct at first, a glow took shape around Esther's body. "We're all going to verbalize what we're seeing, doing, and feeling. Right now, I'm seeing a sort of murky white aura surrounding you, Esther."

"Doesn't white signify connection to the Goddess?" Esther asked, her voice trembling.

Patty nodded but frowned. "Except that when it's murky like this, and turbulent, it signifies instability, waiting for a specific change." Her face brightened. "Which makes perfect sense, if you think about it. Your energy is undergoing a significant change right now. It makes sense that your aura reflects that."

"What do you need me to do?" Noah asked, placing one hand over his mother's on the table, to still her nervous tapping.

Esther visibly relaxed at Patty's explanation and her son's touch.

"This is where we're flying by the seat of our pants," Patty admitted. "Noah, I need you to direct your healing energy at your Mom, and do what you do. Think organizing, healing thoughts." She offered a shrug. "Let's see what happens."

Noah faced his mother. Their eyes dilated, possibly with the intensity of the energy exchange.

"Don't forget to verbalize," Patty reminded him.

"Oh, right." Noah closed his eyes for a moment and then reopened them. "I'm asking the Goddess to direct my healing magic to surround my mother." He raised his hands, like he had with Bobby, and moved them over his mother.

Patty's fingers played the air like she was playing the piano. "Ooh, interesting, when your light pink and blue aura mixed with hers, Noah, the colors muddled, and as yours surrounds hers, now fluctuating tan is interspersing with the murky white."

"What does that mean?" Esther asked.

"I have a pink aura?" Noah asked.

"Light pink and blue. That makes sense too," Patty answered Noah first. "Both are common colors for healers, plus pink shows with gentle souls who place great importance on romantic love." Her eyes locked with Noah and a shiver traveled the length of her body.

Patty broke the connection and answered Esther's question, though she swore Noah's eyes remained on her. "Total guess here. If you've always had some kind of latent magic, which seems likely, tan might have been your magical aura color, since it represents the logical, analytical side of you."

"Analytical would be accurate," Esther agreed.

"Guess there's a reason you make a great Chief Financial Officer," Noah added.

"Thanks, son."

"This is good. Please keep going, Noah," Patty instructed, keeping her eyes on Esther's aura.

"Yes, ma'am," he said, offering a mock salute that drew her attention. "I obviously can't see what's happening, Patty, but I can sense something pushing back against the energy I'm floating around Mom."

"Hmm, okay," Patty said, peering at the aural changes. "The tan is… almost pulsing… bigger, then smaller, bigger again… as your energy surrounds her."

"What about the murky white?" Esther asked, her voice tremulous again.

"That's not changing. Which isn't necessarily a bad thing," she rushed to add, seeing Esther's stricken expression. "Remember that you're experiencing something totally unique, to my knowledge. I figured we'd need multiple sessions." She peered back and forth between mother and son. Beads of perspiration dotted Esther's upper lip. "How are you both doing?"

"I can keep going," Noah answered.

Esther remained silent.

"Do you need to stop?" Patty asked gently.

"Let's try one more time." Esther offered a tight smile. "It's hard to describe. It's almost like a tug-of-war. Not just in my mind, but throughout my body. I've never felt anything like it."

"Are you sure you want to keep going?" Noah asked, his brow furrowed with concern.

This time she patted his hand. "Yes, let's try one more time, and then we can stop for the day."

Noah resumed staring into his mother's eyes and lifted his hands. "I'm again directing my energy, through the Goddess, to surround my mother and help her find internal peace, to organize that which is chaotic."

Patty liked the archaic-sounding word choice. "Nice," she whispered.

"What?" Esther asked. The inflection in the single word combined with her rubbing her palms on the table hinted at tension or anxiety from the process.

Patty wanted to reassure Esther that everything was positive. "You're doing great. The tan is receding again, and it's being replaced by streaks of silver through the murky white." She sighed happily at the transformation. Esther's aura was unlike anything Patty had seen before. "It's beautiful."

"Is it okay that the tan is shrinking?" Esther asked.

"I think so." Patty hesitated to offer supposition, but decided she was in the best position to do so. "Another educated guess, but it's almost as if tan isn't the ultimate goal for your organized magical aura, if that makes sense."

"Am I going to lose my analytical mind?" Esther asked and Patty picked up on her half-joking.

"Nah, I don't think so." Patty patted Esther's hand on the table. "Remember that the magical aura represents your magical abilities, for the most part. I mean, it also telegraphs personality and emotions too. Really, it tells the story of who we are." She spread her hands wide. "But mostly it conveys our magical inclinations."

"That clarified everything," Noah said drolly.

Patty winked at him. "I try."

"What about the silver?" Noah asked.

"That could be a number of things," Patty said, as the tan continued to diminish and the silver streaks replaced it within the murky white. "It's connected to intuition, which may be connected to Esther's eventual magical gift."

"That would be lovely," Esther interjected.

Patty raised her eyes to the ceiling. "It also could be related to your... womanly systems."

Esther snorted. "You mean it could be because of the menopause."

Patty lifted one shoulder in a half-shrug. "It's possible." She directed her attention to Noah. "Is the pushback still there?"

"Not as much, no."

"Okay, good." The beads of sweat on Noah's forehead matched his mother's upper lip. "Time to wrap this session up," Patty declared. "Noah, I need you to withdraw your energy, and Esther, tell me how you feel."

"I'm pulling my energy back," Noah said.

"The blue and pink are flowing from your mother back to you," Patty confirmed.

"The tug-of-war in my body is dissipating," Esther said, exhaling loudly.

After Noah's aura settled back around him, Patty turned her full attention to Esther. "The tan is almost entirely gone now. The bit of silver is still there. And although the white continues to be murky, it's not churning as much as it was at the start."

"That's good, right?" Noah asked.

"Is that better?" Esther asked.

Patty nodded in answer to the simultaneous questions. "This was great progress. The colors have changed and the volatility has decreased."

"What happens next?" Esther asked.

"We take it one session at a time. Give it a bit to see how you feel, especially if you notice any… changes of the magical variety."

Esther chuckled. "Understood."

"Everybody good?" At their nods, Patty called out, "Gentlemen, you can return."

Elijah, Ben, and Aaron returned to the kitchen, and Esther, Patty, and Noah gave them the short version of what they'd done and the apparent results.

"That sounds great," Elijah boomed, running a hand through his thick, dark brown hair. "Thank you, Patty, for the suggestion and the progress."

Patty flushed at the praise. "You're welcome, of course."

"If you're done for the day, I'd like to walk you out," Elijah said.

The offer surprised Patty, and her eyes cut to Noah, whose expression reflected the same. That did not go unnoticed by Elijah.

"I have something I'd like to talk to Patty about," he said, offering no further explanation, but excitement fluttered through Patty.

The job offer! Phase I had been a smashing success. Maybe now he'd offer her a job. Her thoughts careened around in her head as she said her goodbyes and followed Elijah to the front door. The two stepped through to the porch and Elijah closed the door behind them.

He turned to her with his hands clasped together at chest height. "Great job you did in there. It sounded like a very positive first step for Esther."

"Thank you." She beamed back at him.

"I'd already been considering your proposal, and this confirmed how invaluable you could be, to the coven and the company."

Patty stayed quiet, though her body trembled inside with excitement.

"I'd like to bring you on, after graduation, as an assistant priestess to start."

Patty gasped. She'd never imagined he'd start her in such a prominent position. The possibility of being just a step away from the high priestess role right after graduation boggled her mind.

Elijah's laughter bounced around the porch. "Yes, I know. It's a big deal. But I believe you'd be great. You are a gifted witch and a forward-thinking businesswoman. What could be better for the role of assistant priestess?"

"Thank you, thank you so much," she stuttered, reaching out a hand to pump his.

His expression clouded. "There's only one condition."

"Name it." There was nothing that would stand in the way of her dream.

"Stop pursuing Noah."

Her mind blanked. She'd surely misheard him. "Come again."

CHAPTER TWELVE

NOAH

Noah's nerves thrummed as he drove his truck to Wildcrest Wizardry to pick up Patty. He'd waited long enough to say his goodbyes to his family, and then called to invite her along when he visited patients again that afternoon. But now, he had the ulterior motive.

Patty lifted her hand in greeting after he'd pulled into a parking spot in front of the building. An uncertain smile flitted across her face, causing his nervousness to skyrocket. She hurried to the passenger side door and, grabbing ahold of the bar assist, hoisted herself into the large truck.

"One of the challenges of being tiny," she quipped.

"You're the perfect size. Snack-sized," he joked back, and a sizzle of attraction electrified the air between them. He hadn't meant the comment like a double entendre. Oh well. Too late now.

Patty focused on buckling her seat belt. "Thank you for inviting me along again. It's great watching you work," she said, changing the subject.

He rolled with the change, thankful for the break from the tension. "Of course. Having your perspective offers a unique opportunity for me to see, so to speak, from the magical side, what's happening."

"Who are we visiting today?"

Noah explained the medical issue of the woman next on his list, cutting his eyes to Patty occasionally. He noted with surprise how she kept her face forward the entire time, nodding at points, but never glancing in his direction, that he witnessed. His explanation ended as they reached the outskirts of town, and he began to turn onto a dirt road.

"Noah, look out!" Patty threw her hands up on the dash and leaned forward.

He slammed on his brakes, even without knowing what caused her outcry. His heart thundered in his chest and he held the steering wheel in a death-grip. His gaze swung wildly to find the source of her distress. There. A desert tortoise languidly crossing the dirt path. Noah had almost hit the large brown reptile.

Both their breathing had become ragged with the near-accident. Now their breath slowed as they watched the tortoise finish crossing.

"Is it okay?" Patty asked.

"I think so," Noah answered. "It's too bad Aaron isn't here to ask." He patted his jeans pocket. "I could always call him to check in with the turtle."

Patty chuckled, the sound strangely nervous to his ears. "It doesn't seem necessary to bring in your family."

The formality of the response sounded even stranger than the chuckle. "Not my family. Aaron." Noah cleared his throat. "Honestly, though, the turtle's moving at a normal pace for his kind, and I don't see any physical wounds." His expression brightened. "I could attempt to heal his energy, just in case, if it would make you feel better."

Patty flushed. "That's unnecessary. You're right. I freaked out a little with almost hitting it."

Now he flushed to match her. This was becoming increasingly awkward. "I'm sorry I was distracted."

She met his gaze full on. "What had you distracted?"

Noah hesitated.

She fiddled with her hands in her lap. "Never mind. I'm sure you were thinking about your patient."

Noah almost took the out she gave him, but remembered his ulterior motive. To work with her again this afternoon, and when they were both relaxed and happy about helping his patient, he'd ask her out.

"Would you like to have dinner with me tonight?" He blurted out the question, kicking himself for veering off the plan.

She grinned for the briefest of moments before her expression clouded.

"I know I said I wasn't interested in a fling—" he said, rushing to fill the silence, assuming he was the cause of her discomfort. His words dried up when Patty placed a hand on his between them on the center console.

"I mangled my invitation before," she said, biting her lower lip before straightening up. "But I'm correcting that now. Yes, I would like to have dinner with you tonight." A shadow again crossed her face, and he wondered at its cause, now that she'd accepted his invitation.

"Are you sure?"

"Yes." She squeezed his hand. "I am."

"We can work out the details after this visit." Joy flooded him at the thought of going on an actual date with Patty.

She faced forward again and, if he wasn't mistaken, her mouth turned down a moment before thinning out.

Noah considered asking her again if she was sure, before realizing this might have nothing to do with him. She'd probably used a lot of energy helping his mother in the morning. The unexplained looks and body language almost certainly were related to that. Patty had done a phenomenal job, but this was all unfamiliar territory to the coven. She'd made her interest in him clear. After all, she'd asked him out first.

Satisfied with this explanation, Noah focused on the path before him and headed toward the next encounter.

CHAPTER THIRTEEN

PATTY

She'd said yes. An actual date with Noah. Not a fling, like she'd said before. Instead of excitement about this step forward, as she prepared for her date, Patty found herself beyond conflicted. The rest of the afternoon with Noah had been better than the awkward conversation in his truck. She could almost see him running through possible explanations for her bizarre behavior, and wondered what had worked to finally relax him. By the time they'd reached his last patient, it was almost as if they hadn't had the verbal exchange at all.

Patty pondered her appearance in the full-length mirror that leaned against her childhood bedroom wall. She wore a bright yellow sundress that skimmed the tops of her knees. Given that she was height-challenged, dresses always were a touch longer than she'd prefer. But the cotton fabric was nice against her skin and she smiled, watching the image in the mirror reflect the same. Her short hair curled around her face and showcased her hazel eyes. She looked good.

"Are you turning into Narcissus?"

She faced the desert owl perched on a sturdy fake tree in a darker corner of the bedroom and mock-frowned. "How is that helpful, Aveline?"

The desert owl hooted again and fluffed her wings. "Ooh, you used my full name."

Patty pursed her lips at her familiar and then shook her head. "Yes, I did, Ave." She'd brought the sandy desert owl up to speed when she'd first arrived home. From working on the chaotic magic with Esther and Noah in the morning to Noah asking her out when they spent the afternoon visiting patients.

"Did Elijah really say owls eat rabbits?" the owl asked.

"I couldn't believe it," Patty said. She paused in rubbing the vanilla lotion onto her arms, her mind flashing back to the morning's conversation with Noah's father at the front door.

After she'd questioned Elijah's proviso, he'd rushed to explain himself…

"I like you," he'd said, taking her hands in his. "You know that."

She'd pulled her hands away, speechless in the face of his request.

"I saw the interest when you and Noah hugged."

"And?" she'd bit out.

"You're not a good fit for my son."

She opened her mouth to question that statement.

"Even your familiars are enemies," he'd quipped.

"What?" Her confusion at that moment had been profound.

"Owls eat rabbits." He'd looked so pleased with himself for the little joke.

She, however, had not been pleased. "I'm going to need a bit more than that."

Elijah had the good grace to appear chagrined.

"Why don't you think Noah and I are a good fit?" She'd gripped the handle of the front door with one hand, the other planted against her hip.

Elijah placed a hand against the door, as well, almost like he was mirroring her. "He's worked to establish his practice and is ready to settle down. You're still in school and preparing to start your career." Now he clasped his hands in front of him.

Patty wanted to shake him from his relaxed stance. "Yes, I'm preparing to start my career. That doesn't mean I'm not ready…" She'd floundered a bit at the end. What *was* she ready for personally?

"I know it seems personal, but it's really not. One day you'll thank me for seeing what you couldn't," he assured her.

The certainty and openness in his tone and expression had flummoxed her. He really thought he was doing the right thing…

Aveline hooted again, bringing Patty back into the bedroom, where she recognized she was playing with fire. She'd accepted the job offer from Elijah, including the one proviso that she not date Noah. Ave, of course, being the nearly eternal being that she was, thought Patty was doing the right thing.

"He means well," the owl said.

"You think so?" Doubt dripped from Patty's voice.

Aveline fluffed her feathers. "I do."

"Then explain it to me like I'm a child. Because all I see is a parent trying to control a grown man," Patty grumbled, sitting on the cheery yellow comforter on her bed. She propped her head with her hands.

"It's like he told you, after the ridiculous thing about your familiars."

Patty could practically hear the eye roll in her familiar's words.

"You and Noah are at different stages in your lives, and you're on separate paths."

"But you support my going out with Noah," Patty interrupted.

"I do. I'm explaining why Elijah thinks he's doing the right thing."

"Oh yeah." Patty collapsed back on the bed, listening to Ave.

"As a father, since he believes you and Elijah aren't right for each other, he's encouraging you not to start down what he sees as a negative path."

Patty bolted upright and jumped from the bed. "You don't think he offered me the job solely to keep me from Noah, do you?" She struggled to keep her voice from breaking.

"I do not."

"Okay, good." She picked a brush off the dark wood dresser and ran it through her hair. The strands fell back into place.

"What's going through your mind right now?"

"It made sense to accept the agreement in that moment. Noah had told me no when I asked him out," she said, more to her reflection than to her familiar. "I didn't have anything to lose, and everything professionally to gain."

Patty met Ave's eyes in the mirror over the dresser and offered a wicked grin. "I'm dating Noah. By the time Elijah figures out what I'm doing, Noah and I will be a couple, and he'll never take the job from me."

Despite the assurance in her voice, the quiver in her belly told Patty she wasn't quite as certain of that outcome as she portrayed.

CHAPTER FOURTEEN

NOAH

"A date, huh?" Ben asked Noah. The three brothers stared at Noah's reflection in the bathroom mirror. "It's about time."

Noah cut his eyes to Ben. "Really?"

"Big brother, we all see the chemistry between you and Patty," Aaron said with a laugh.

"Why so nervous?" Ben asked.

Noah turned from the mirror and his younger brothers followed him through the bedroom to the kitchen. He stopped at the island and leaned against it. "I'm not sure," he admitted.

Ben sat on one of the island stools. "Walk us through it."

"He doesn't want to screw it up," Aaron teased, opening the refrigerator and pulling out a bottle of sparkling water. He grabbed glasses for the three men.

"Will you throw a pod in the machine? I have a late night at the hospital," Ben interjected. "Thanks," he added when Aaron complied.

Noah withstood the desire to roll his eyes at Aaron's comment. "You're not wrong, of course." He frowned. "It's more than that."

Aaron sat beside Ben, and the brothers stared at Noah. "Go on," Ben said.

"I don't remember where I left off with each of you, but she asked me out and I said no because it sounded like she only wanted a summer fling."

"Before she headed back to graduate school, right?" Aaron asked.

The scent of coffee wafted over the men.

"Exactly." Noah sipped from his glass of water and idly wondered if having a coffee would keep him up. "I'm of an age where flings aren't my thing."

Ben snorted. "Of an age? What are you, 50?" He jumped off the stool to grab his mug of coffee.

Noah flushed. "You know what I mean."

"You aren't that old and she's not that young," Aaron reminded him.

"I tutored her in high school," he protested.

"Aren't you over the few years age difference?" Ben asked.

"Yes, I am," Noah said, swigging from his water. "You're right."

"Then what's the problem?" Ben persisted.

Noah laid his hands flat on the quartz counter. "I sensed the attraction you mentioned, and after hanging out with her, decided to see if all she really wanted was a fling."

"That's good," Ben said, confusion in his voice.

"And she confirmed that."

"But…" Aaron said.

"But, after helping Mom with her chaotic magic this morning, something seemed off this afternoon with Patty."

"Could it be she was just magically drained?" Ben asked.

Noah pointed at him. "That's what I thought, too."

"Now you suspect it's something more?" Aaron asked.

"She was quieter all afternoon—"

"Which would happen with an energy drain," Ben interjected.

Noah ran a hand through his thick hair. "It's hard for me to explain. She seemed distant. I noticed she looked… almost sad, a couple of times."

Now Ben frowned. "Yeah, that wouldn't be from an energy drain."

"Did you ask her?" Aaron asked with a shrug. He was always the most direct of the brothers.

Noah flushed again. "Not exactly."

"So, no." Aaron shook his head and sipped some water.

"I double-checked she wasn't having second thoughts about the date."

"And she wasn't?" Ben asked.

"Not that she said." Noah sighed. "I do like her. Once I got past my age hang-up," he added with a half-smile.

"That was silly," Ben helpfully pointed out, and now Noah rolled his eyes.

"What can I say? I'm only human."

"My advice? Go on the date and have a great time." Aaron came around the island to slap his brother on the back. "You two have obvious chemistry. You'll probably find out tonight whether her behavior has anything to do with you."

That was what worried Noah.

CHAPTER FIFTEEN

PATTY

Butterflies actually fluttered in Patty's stomach as she stared at Noah across the table from her. He stunned in dark jeans, a gray button-down top, and a blue sport coat. She felt underdressed in her typical sundress, but if the glint in his eye was any indication, he liked the yellow dress just fine.

"You're beautiful," he blurted out, and relief flooded her at the confirmation. "I should have said that as soon as I saw you."

"Better late than never," she quipped and then cut her eyes away, pretending to take in the décor as if she'd never been to The Cozy Coven before. It was Wildcrest's only upscale restaurant, and where everybody went for first dates and anniversaries. She hadn't been surprised when he'd picked it. Plus, the food was amazing, an eclectic fusion of international cuisines. Even now, the scents of Italian herbs blended with spicy curries. The intoxicating combination made her stomach growl. Her gaze moved between the vaulted ceilings with the wood beams and the other white tablecloth-clad tables in the dining room.

"Good evening. My name is Jackson, and I'll be taking care of you tonight. May I get you something to drink besides water?"

Patty silently thanked the waiter for his appearance, saving her from further awkwardness. "Yes," she rushed to answer, before thinking to ask Noah, "Did you want to share a bottle of wine?"

Noah agreed, and they spent a moment deciding on a nice red, and then Jackson retreated to get the bottle, leaving them to decide on their meals. "When's the last time you were here?"

She wondered if this was his way of asking if she'd been on a date here before, and she bit the inside of her mouth to stop a chuckle from bubbling out. "In all honesty, I haven't been here too many times. I think the last time was when Shelly launched her business."

"It's a great place to celebrate." He sipped his water, his eyes never leaving her face.

She mirrored him and kept chattering. "It is! Shelly was so excited and nervous about branching out on her own. We were so proud of her. She's worked hard to make it a success. Once Shelly finished the coven website redesign, she got more work than she could handle. She's had to turn down work." Patty paused to breathe.

"That's so great for her. Being able to do what you love, and be successful at it, is important."

"That's why I'm excited that I have the job offer from Wildcrest Witches International," she said, and immediately wanted to retract the words.

"What? You got an offer? That's wonderful. Congratulations. I had no doubts," Noah said, reaching a hand forward as if to take hers, but then pulling it back. "You're definitely moving back to Wildcrest after graduation?"

"It looks that way," Patty said. Her tone must have been off because he tilted his head. But he said nothing. She wondered if he suspected she was hiding something. Except since he hadn't known about the job offer, he couldn't know about his father's proviso. If only she hadn't gotten herself in this mess to begin with—wait, she silently argued with herself. This wasn't her fault. Or Noah's for being so attentive, honest, and ruggedly handsome.

"What's the job?" he asked, interrupting her thoughts.

Before Patty could answer, the waiter returned to take their order. "We haven't even looked at the menu yet,"

Patty admitted. She scanned the Thai section. "If you still have the red curry with vegetables, I'll take that." When Jackson confirmed, she handed him her menu.

"I'll have the barbecue chicken platter," Noah added, handing his menu to the waiter as well. "Can't go wrong with good barbecue chicken."

The waiter promised the meals would be out soon and withdrew.

Noah lifted his eyebrows expectantly. "The job offer?"

She flushed. "Right. I'll be your father's assistant," she said, downplaying the offer by not providing the title.

He frowned. "Assistant? With a master's degree? That's not what you proposed to my Dad, is it?"

"Assistant priestess," she clarified, and his eyes widened.

"Now that's different," he exclaimed. "That's amazing."

She nodded, not meeting his eyes.

"Is something wrong? Do you not want the job?"

"Of course, I do. Accepting it is only a formality. It's just… jitters," she stammered.

"You'll do great. You've always been so intuitive—"

"I mean, I read magical auras," she interrupted with a self-deprecating shrug.

"That's not what I mean. Besides your magic. Like the way you're helping my mom. That's more than just your magic at play."

"You think so?" She'd believed it was more than her magical inclination, too. That also played a part in her desire to be the high priestess one day. It thrilled her to hear him express that belief as well.

"I do. First off, you thought of the idea when nobody else did. And, second, you're risking draining yourself to help, which not everyone would do."

His gushing embarrassed her. "It's not that big of a deal."

"Patty, look at me," he said softly.

She did so warily. While she enjoyed his support, not all of her choices were good ones, and the full force of his loyalty and encouragement created an uncomfortable tightness in her chest. She reminded herself she was doing the right thing, not telling Noah about his father's proviso.

"It is a big deal. Family is everything." He reached across the table and took her hands in his.

"Family is everything," she agreed, and her fingers tightened in his as guilt flooded her. No, it would be okay. Elijah would realize it was a mistake when he saw her with Noah. There would never be a risk of a strain in the two men's relationship from the proviso. "I'm glad I can help Esther," she said, focusing on the man before her.

"Me too." His thumb drew circles on her palm and tingles raced up her spine. "I'm glad I got past my hang-ups to ask you out."

"Me too," she agreed, swallowing the desire to blurt out his father's demand. Once Elijah saw how happy she and Noah were together, he'd relent.

Noah's aura flashed bright pink and green.

Patty watched the swirl of colors.

"What happened?" he asked.

"What do you mean?" she asked in response, still distracted by the unexpected flash, though now it faded.

"You're somewhere else."

She put her hands together. "You know I don't read auras without permission, right?"

He nodded.

"But sometimes they appear when there's a strong emotion."

"Ahh," he said. "You're about to apologize for reading my aura without permission."

"Kind of. Though in my defense—"

"You don't need a defense," he assured her. "I guess I can't hide that I'm interested in you."

"Not really," she said.

"What did it look like?"

Relief and joy swirled in her at his quick acceptance of her magical quirk. "It was the prettiest shade of bright pink and green."

"That's an interesting combination, but common with healers, right? Similar to what you saw when we were working with Bobby and my mom."

"Absolutely," she agreed, "and also when you're in love with someone who balances your energy."

His jaw dropped open.

"Oh, my Goddess, I didn't mean... it's probably more...," she stumbled over her lack of an explanation. Did she seriously just use the word *love*? What was wrong with her?

A low laugh rumbled in his throat. "It might be a little early for that, but I guess an aura doesn't lie."

"No, it doesn't," she whispered. They clasped hands again. Tender yearning filled her. She knew this was right. They were right together.

Now she needed Noah's father to accept it.

CHAPTER SIXTEEN

NOAH

Noah thought about Patty the rest of the night, and was still thinking about their date when he knocked on his parents' front door the next morning. It hadn't been a planned visit; his mother asked him to bring a box of books to Ben. There was no rush, but Noah figured, why not do it now before his afternoon patients?

Esther wrapped her arms around Noah and pulled him into the home. "Good morning, honey." She released him and pointed to a box sitting on the dining room table. "That's it. Not too heavy. They're mostly paperbacks. Not hardbacks."

Noah peeked inside and guffawed. "These are Ben's adventure books from when he was a kid. He wants these back?"

"I believe he's planning on donating them. Your father and I are cleaning out the garage," she explained.

"Ah, got it. No problem. I'll throw them in the truck and drop them at the house later."

A booming voice reached them. "Is that my eldest?"

"Yes, Dad. It's me," Noah hollered back. "Mom asked me to bring the books you found in the garage to Ben."

Elijah appeared around a corner and held open his arms. "That's fabulous. One less box in the garage. Your mother has me moving stuff around all over in there."

"It'll be worth it in the end," Esther pointed out as Elijah reached her and looped an arm around her waist.

Noah grinned at his parents.

"What has you all smiles this morning?" his mother asked him playfully.

He didn't even hesitate. "Patty and I went on a date last night."

"You what?" Elijah asked.

"I know, right?" Noah said. "I never would have guessed that would happen. She was always like a little sister to me. Until she grew up."

"That's wonderful, darling. I want to hear all about it," Esther said, leading Noah by the elbow toward the kitchen.

"Of course, Mom." Noah walked with his mother, his father a few steps behind. Once they sat at the kitchen table, Noah summarized his date with Patty. They didn't need all the details.

"She's so sweet," Esther said when Noah finished. "Isn't she, Elijah?"

"She's—"

"Patty told me about the job offer," Noah interrupted his father.

"She did?" Elijah's eyebrows lifted.

"Of course," Noah answered. "Why wouldn't she? She's so excited."

"Is she, now?" Elijah asked drily.

Noah tilted his head. "What's going on, Dad? She's a great fit for the job – and you offered it to her – why wouldn't she be excited?"

Esther joined her son in staring at Elijah, whose expression remained neutral.

"Why wouldn't she be, indeed." Elijah didn't elaborate after his inscrutable comment.

"C'mon," Noah said, "tell us what's going on. What do you know that we don't?" Noah suddenly worried that something had changed between last night and this morning. Had Patty changed her mind about the job?

Elijah stroked his chin but remained quiet.

Noah and Esther continued to stare at him, waiting.

"Perhaps I need to help her retrieve a memory," Elijah mused.

"I don't understand," Noah said. His father's magic was memory magic. He recalled all of his own memories since his magic manifested at puberty and could manipulate energy to retrieve others' forgotten memories, as long as the brain had coded the memory at some point. But Noah couldn't fathom what that had to do with their current conversation about Patty and the assistant priestess job.

"Elijah, quit being obtuse and explain yourself," Esther commanded.

Noah's father steepled his fingers together and looked between his son and his wife. He laid his hands flat on the white oak table and sighed. "I'm surprised to learn that she went on a date with you, son."

Noah furrowed his brows. "I was surprised feelings developed between us, too."

Elijah's eyebrows furrowed in an identical reaction. "That's not quite what I mean."

"What did you mean, then? You're kind of freaking me out here," Noah said.

"What exactly did Patty tell you about my offering her the job?"

This conversation with his father was maddening. "Not much. Just that you'd made the offer and she'll start after she graduates at the end of the year." He squinted at his father. "What are you dancing around?"

"You should call Patty and invite her over," Elijah said instead.

The non sequitur threw Noah. "Not until you explain what's going on," he demanded.

Elijah flushed, a sight which startled Noah and Esther.

"Elijah?" Esther asked.

"I told Patty the job was hers, with one proviso."

"What was that?" Noah asked.

"That she couldn't date you."

CHAPTER SEVENTEEN

PATTY

Noah sounded odd on the phone when he invited her over. Given their date had gone well, Patty wondered if there was a problem with Esther and the chaotic magic. He didn't say when she asked, only repeated the request. Of course, she'd go, but the brick in her stomach became heavier the closer to the Wright home she got.

Patty drove through the wrought-iron gates at the beginning of the driveway. Her mouth became cotton as she parked outside the ranch-style home. Esther surely must be fine. There wasn't a reason for her to have a problem related to the work Patty and Noah had been doing with her. Patty tapped her knuckles on the teal front door.

It flew open, revealing Noah.

Patty's wide smile died on her face. "Is everything okay with Esther?" she blurted out.

"What?" Noah asked, confusion clear.

"You sounded off on the phone. I assumed—"

"Please come in," he interrupted her, his voice clipped. His magical aura flashed a murky red and, without her desiring to, she now had confirmation of Noah's frustration and sadness.

She wrapped a hand around his bicep. Energy radiated off of him.

He didn't quite jerk away, but broke contact and strode toward the kitchen.

The acidic taste of fear burned her throat. Was this an issue with Esther? Or something else?

Esther and Elijah sat rigidly at the white oak kitchen table, their hands mirroring each other as they rested on the surface.

"Good morning, Patty," Esther said softly.

"Good morning, Patty," Elijah echoed in an inflectionless voice.

"What's going on?" Patty whispered her question. "Esther, are you okay?" Another possibility surfaced and Patty squashed it.

In an expression of confusion identical to her son's, Esther paused before shaking her head. "Nothing's changed with me," she answered obliquely.

Patty's head swiveled back to Noah, who stood tall at the side of the table. She found his angry and sad aura overwhelming. Had he found out about the proviso? "Please tell me what's happened," she whispered.

"My father and I talked about the good news of his job offer," Noah said.

The truth of the situation slammed home for Patty, and she swallowed hard. "I can explain," she said in a rush, stepping in his direction, but halting at the swell of his aura.

"Are you reading my aura now too?" he asked, sadness tinged with defeat.

"No," she stammered, "not on purpose. It's just very… prominent." The last word squeaked out.

"Please explain, Patty," Elijah said, his voice quiet but forceful. "I thought we had an understanding."

"An understanding that never should have been made."

The interjection by Noah startled Patty, and she realized that his anger was directed at his father, not her. Patty's arms dropped to her sides, and she rubbed her palms against the cotton of her sundress. "It wasn't like that," she said.

"How was it made?" Noah asked in a level voice that contrasted with his swirling aura.

"You said you didn't want to date me—"

"This is my fault?" Noah quirked an eyebrow.

She flushed. "Of course not. I just meant—"

"And to be accurate, I didn't want a fling."

Patty risked a glance at his parents. Esther's mouth was down-turned and her eyes glistened. With unshed tears? Elijah's face was stonier, but bits of gray shot through his aura, suggesting uncertainty. She wondered if he was regretting his proviso. She certainly regretted agreeing to it.

With a deep inhale, she tried again. "I went into my meeting with Elijah under the belief that there was no future with you."

Noah winced.

"When your father made the offer, then attached the proviso, at that moment, I had everything to gain professionally and nothing to lose personally."

"I can understand that," Noah said, surprising her.

"You can?" Hope bloomed in Patty that they could overcome this horrible situation.

"I can," he said, but his mouth remained a thin line. "What I can't understand is the decision to not tell me."

White hot heat of embarrassment raced through Patty at the comment. "I thought…" She hesitated. "I thought that if we showed your father—" She risked a glance at Elijah, whose expression hadn't changed. "—what a good fit we are, he would change his mind."

A mirthless laugh escaped Noah. "You didn't think I could be part of that plan?"

"I didn't think—"

"No, you didn't," he interrupted her again.

"Please stop interrupting me," she said, "if you want me to answer your questions."

Noah flushed, though at her rebuke, his aura calmed to invisible again. That meant his emotions were calming. She'd only see his aura now with effort, which she wouldn't do. "My apologies." He opened his arms wide. "Please continue."

"I mishandled the situation, I agree." She crossed her arms and then uncrossed them, fidgeting. "I should have told you." She risked another glance at his father. "Part of my thinking was avoiding this scenario."

Noah smirked. "Really?"

"Really," she said. "I know Elijah thinks he's doing what is best, but he's not. The only way I thought to correct this was to keep it from you until he changed his mind. Then it could be something we laughed about later."

Noah's eyes widened. Patty hoped it was at her inference of an ongoing relationship with her.

"I didn't want this," she waved her hand between them, "to cause a rift in your relationship with your father." She offered a crooked smile. "But I also wanted to be with you. That's why I asked you out so awkwardly to begin with."

Noah's stance softened. "I'll have to think about that," he admitted, the hurt in his voice wounding her. "It's hard for me to see past the idea that you didn't feel you could talk to me, or that you didn't want to." He reached out as if to take her hands, then dropped his arms to his sides. "But it's not all your fault." He squared off with his parents, his eyes lasers for his father's.

"Right now, what I mostly see is your betrayal."

CHAPTER EIGHTEEN

NOAH

Noah bit his tongue to keep from commenting about the hard expression on his father's face. Not just because that would be unhelpful, but because he thought he saw something reflecting in his father's eyes. Fear.

"Dad, if we could please chat in the living room," Noah said instead. With a curt nod, his father followed him out of the kitchen, leaving Patty and Esther behind.

Their boots made soft thumps on the red terracotta tiles. Noah stopped beside their white couch but didn't sit. He stared out the window at the expanse of the desert beyond, considering his words.

"Son," Elijah said.

"Yes?"

"I'm just trying to help you." Elijah spread his arms wide.

Noah remained facing the window, considering how to word his response.

"Son?"

The genuine question in the tone softened Noah and he turned to face his father.

"If you could understand what I was trying to do."

Noah quirked an eyebrow. "How is it helpful to give a woman I'm interested in an ultimatum, forcing her to choose between her personal and professional goals?"

"Well, she didn't choose, now did she," Elijah pointed out.

"Don't do that."

"Do what?"

"Lay the blame on Patty for what you started."

"But you told her—"

"How Patty and I choose to move forward is between us," Noah gently corrected his father. "Right now—" He waved his hand between them. "—this. This is between us. Your choice to try to control my life."

"I didn't try to control your life."

Noah raked his hand through his hair and stood even taller. "What would you call it?"

"Looking out for your best interests," Elijah retorted.

"How is that different from trying to control my life?"

His father stepped toward him.

"I'm a grown man." Noah stuffed his hands in his pockets and sighed.

Elijah grasped his son's shoulders. "I know that."

"Then why?"

"She's on a different path than you."

"What does that even mean?" Noah yanked his hands out of his jeans pockets and stepped away from his father. "You know what? It doesn't even matter. This isn't your decision to make, nor your situation to manipulate. Period." He held up a hand to stop his father from interrupting.

Now Elijah crossed his arms, not quite defensive, but getting there.

"I want your word that Patty's job offer has no more strings attached."

"Hmm."

"That's not your word."

"It's important to the coven that our priestess, including an assistant, has her priorities straight." Elijah picked nonexistent lint off his shirt sleeve.

Noah's mouth dropped open. "Are you joking?"

"Whatever do you mean?" Elijah asked.

"Are you really not going to lift the ridiculous proviso on the job offer?" Noah's voice rose in bafflement.

"I'll think about it," Elijah conceded.

Noah stared at his father. This made zero sense. He'd always been stubborn, but this seemed a strange hill to die on.

"If you think you can trust Patty now," Elijah added.

"That's enough." Noah realized the conversation wasn't going anywhere helpful. "Thank you for reconsidering," he stated. "I hope you make the decision that's in the best interests of the family and the coven." With that, Noah strode back toward the kitchen, the silence behind him deafening.

The women met his eyes when he reached the doorway, Esther sad and Patty stricken. His heart sped up at the sight. He couldn't deny feeling rejected by Patty because she agreed to his father's absurd demands and then lied to him about it.

Although technically it was a lie of omission, a tiny voice in his head pointed out. Really, one could argue she got caught in the middle. And she looked miserable. Unlike his recalcitrant father.

Patty approached him, reached for his arm, then let hers drop back to her side. "I'm sorry," she whispered. "This isn't at all what I wanted to happen."

"I know," he said. The tension between them physically hurt.

Patty glanced back at his mother. "Do you still want me to work with Esther, if she still wants me to?" Her hand fluttered at her throat. "I can leave if not."

Her small voice broke his heart, and he took her hands in his. "This issue with my father is separate from helping my mother," he assured her, his heart warmed by the bright smile that blossomed on her face. "I would very much like for you to continue working with her. With us."

"I'm glad," she said.

"Are you okay with doing it now?"

Surprise flitted across her face and she squeezed his hands. "Yes, if she is, absolutely."

CHAPTER NINETEEN

PATTY

Patty acknowledged that none of this had played out the way she'd hoped. She still believed she could make it work. Thank the Goddess that Noah realized she could still help his mother. Patty's goal remained attainable. She would win over both Noah and Elijah by helping Esther. Everyone would let go of the pain and miscommunications. Everyone would have a happily ever after.

She hoped she wasn't being naïve. Maybe she was delusional. But she'd focus on Esther, and the chips would fall where they may. Or whatever the expression was.

Patty sat next to Esther. "Are you ready?"

"I am, if you are," Esther responded, the question in her tone reinforced by a quick squeeze of Patty's hand. Esther's heart was so big, regardless of whatever was happening between her husband and her son.

"I am," Patty assured Esther. "Are you ready?" Patty directed this question at Noah, who nodded and sat opposite Patty and his mother.

"Let's do this," Noah boomed, though the confidence convinced neither woman. So much tension swirled in the room.

Patty took Esther's hands in hers. "Let's start where we stopped before."

Esther nodded.

"Look inside and find the ribbons of magic that have been manifesting," Patty instructed.

Esther's eyes closed and she rested her hands on her legs.

Patty watched the colors swirl around Esther, like before.

"What do you see?" Esther asked.

"It's white with silver streaks," Patty answered. She frowned.

"What?" Noah asked.

Instead of answering, she directed him. "Send your healing energy to your mother."

Noah's mouth thinned into a grim line. "Okay."

Energy swirled around the room, almost a physical presence for Patty. This wasn't going as well as last time.

She gasped as Noah's and Esther's auras tangled together. And they really were tangling. Instead of the light pink representing Noah's intuitive healing guiding Esther's spiritual white, Noah's darker red aura pulsed at Esther's increasingly cloudy aura.

Esther gasped in concert with Patty.

Noah's hands gripped the table. "What's wrong? What happened?"

"This feels off somehow," Esther said, beads of sweat breaking out on her forehead.

Dread filled Patty. Maybe this had been a mistake to try right now. "We should take a break."

"No, I want to move forward," Esther insisted. "It's just a bump in the road."

Patty bit her lower lip. "If you're sure?" Patty wished she had a better sense of manipulating magical auras like this. She didn't believe Esther was in any danger, but she worried that maybe she wouldn't know until it was too late.

"I am."

Esther's determination lifted Patty's spirit. "Noah, I'll need you to take some deep breaths," Patty said.

"Am I the problem?" he asked in response. Guilt telegraphed across his face.

"No." Patty swallowed. "I think it's a mix of all the tension colliding."

"Don't worry, Mom, I can relax." Noah flexed his fingers on the white oak table. He took several deep breaths, as directed by Patty. Nothing happened.

"How are you feeling?" Patty asked Noah, already suspecting the answer.

He flexed his fingers on the table again. "I'm getting there."

Patty worried her anxiety was contributing to the tension issues. She inhaled and exhaled slowly, in tune with Noah's steady breaths. Together, they breathed in concert, and the internal struggle abated for Patty.

The darkness of Noah's aura began to lighten, as well, though it still didn't look as light and lifting as before.

Esther stretched like a contented cat. "That feels better."

Patty watched Esther's aura continue to swirl. It absorbed some of the lighter pink resurfacing in Noah's aura, but the murky white coalesced around the silver and extinguished it. "Hmm."

"Hmm, what?" Esther asked.

"Now it's your turn to relax, Esther," Patty said.

Esther nodded and closed her eyes. Mimicking her son, she breathed in, held it to a four-count, and then exhaled. As with Noah, nothing happened at first.

Patty tapped Noah on the back of his hand. His eyes flew open. "Breathe with her," she mouthed the instruction.

Noah flipped his hand over to squeeze Patty's. They shared the warmth and connection for a moment, before he closed his eyes and joined his mother's rhythm.

Several iterations of mother and son breathing in unison occurred, while Patty tried to ignore how much she missed Noah holding her hand. She gave a silent head shake and focused on the swirling mother and son auras.

"This is looking good," she assured them. Noah's now-lighter-pink aura surrounded and buoyed up Esther's clearer white with the silver streaks. Blips of light yellow appeared, which Patty found curious but not alarming. The color was consistent with Patty's earlier suggestion to Esther that spiritual magic might be Esther's eventual outcome. It also fit with Esther's background as a smart, creative, natural leader. Patty wondered what the actual magical ability would end up being.

"This is nice," Esther said, hugging herself. "It feels… like home. I don't know how else to describe it."

Patty chuckled. "That's a great way to describe it. I think that's what's happening. Noah is helping your magic find its way home."

Noah quirked an eyebrow.

She shrugged. "I don't know how else to describe it, either." A weight lifted. "It's beautiful."

"That's great," Noah said and found Patty's gaze. His smile strengthened and then slipped a fraction.

Would this not be enough? Patty found herself distracted by the tension between herself and Noah. They broke eye contact, stared through the kitchen doorway toward where Elijah had gone, and the damage was done.

"Focus on your mother," Patty directed Noah, hoping to head off where the auras were going, as first Noah's aura darkened with grays of uncertainty, and then the shade found its way to Esther's aura. The white and silver aura became cloudy again, with murky red forming.

Esther glanced between Patty and Noah, her eyes widening. "What's happening? Something has shifted."

Patty wanted to cry, but she needed to focus on salvaging the session for Esther, so she inhaled and exhaled while Noah spoke to Esther.

"It's okay, Mom. Let's just refocus." Noah reached across the table to rest his hand on his mother's.

She yanked her hand back. "No. It's not okay. I can feel all the negativity." Her gaze swung around the room. "I don't understand what's happening. Why your father can't just—" She cut herself off and her hands formed fists. "And you." She glared at her son. "Why do you let your father get under your skin like that?"

Noah and Patty exchanged their own wide-eyed glance.

"Esther, are you okay?" Patty asked, knowing the answer, and dreading her role in the ongoing drama.

"I'm fine. This was a mistake. Until the three of you work through your nonsense, you won't be able to help."

With that pronouncement, Esther jumped to her feet and strode from the kitchen.

"Oh no," Patty mumbled, Esther's murky red and cloudy white aura burned into her magical eye.

"What?" Noah grabbed her hand. "What did you see?"

Patty pulled back, her mouth turning down. "Your mother's aura is too sensitive right now to respond well when we're still… working things out."

"What did you see?" Noah insisted.

Patty described the aura. "She was so close to her spiritual aura solidifying. But, the instant we, um, broke concentration, the immediate impact—" Patty's leg bounced against the floor. "As I said, her aura is too sensitive right now. We're too influential over it."

"Now what do we do?" Noah's voice sounded lost.

She came around the table to sit beside him. She touched his cheek, pleased when he leaned into the touch for a moment. "I saw where her aura might be heading, and it was good. But she's too emotional with us… not getting along." Patty stood and paced to the other side of the room. "We need to resolve what's happening between us and with your father."

"I agree," Noah said. He stood and walked to where Patty was rooted into the ground. He stared down into her eyes.

With everything out in the open, she waited for him to ignore his father's edict and forgive her for not being open with him. Then they could work together as a couple on helping Esther move forward.

Patty placed a hand on his waist.

He stiffened and stepped back.

"I thought you agreed," she said, confused.

"I did… I do."

"Then I don't understand."

"My father is right," Noah said.

"Wait, what?" Patty was certain she'd misunderstood.

CHAPTER TWENTY

NOAH

"My father is right," Noah repeated, straining against the desire to break eye contact with Patty. He'd do this right, no matter how painful. "Mom is struggling because our magic is… misbehaving," he said with a wave of his hand.

"That's not what I said. At all," Patty disagreed.

"Did you see what I did?"

"Of course."

"Mom was doing well and then our negative energy caused her to become frustrated and fail." He blew out a breath. This was much harder than he'd anticipated.

Patty slowly nodded her head. "Exactly. Once we work through our issues and settle things with your father, she'll be good."

"One way to work through our issues is to accept we're not on the same path." He ran his hand through his hair. "It's just like with my brother."

"Which one?"

"Aaron."

Now Patty grinned. "That just proves my point."

"It does?" Noah wondered what he was missing.

"Yes. Aaron and Laura chose their relationship over their misaligning magic."

"They got lucky. Laura was willing to accept the possibility her magic might never be restored. I won't do that to my mother. It's not my choice."

"Okay. Following your convoluted line of reasoning…"

He winced at her word choice.

"It should be Esther's choice, yes?"

Noah frowned. Patty had a point. But, no. The chances of something going wrong were too high. His mother's well-being mattered more than his love life. His heart constricted and he swallowed down the pain.

"I can practically see the wheels turning in your head," Patty said with a sad chuckle. "I'm not getting through to you, am I?"

"Look," he conceded, touching her elbow before pulling away. It wouldn't do to be too familiar with her if they were breaking up. Although, they never started dating. A single date did not a relationship make. "You have a point."

"I'm glad you recognize that."

"But," he stressed. "It's not enough."

"I don't understand. You like me, I like you. Your mother said to work through our issues, including with Elijah. She did not agree with your father that we don't belong together."

"Yes, but—"

"No, but," she interrupted. "I've known your mother my entire life—"

"Me, too." This time he interrupted her, and they shared smiles before replacing them with frowns.

"Do you really think she'd want you to sacrifice your happiness for a theoretical problem her magic might have with our negative energy?" Patty swung her arms out wide in apparent exasperation and then planted her fists on her hips.

She was so cute when she was mad. Wait, he couldn't go down that path. Oh, but he wanted to.

"See," she blurted, pointing at him. "Your aura just flashed pink again."

His face reddened. He hated that her power made him an emotional open book around her.

"I didn't peek on purpose," she assured him. "Your emotions are obviously running hot."

He sighed. "They are." Noah sat at the kitchen table and held his hand out for her to join him. When their fingers intertwined, a bolt of electricity ran through him. Maybe she was right.

"You're considering if I'm right."

"How do you do that? I know that's not visible in my aura."

"No, it's not," she said. Her eyes dropped to their hands resting on the table between them.

"I don't deny I'm interested in you. That ship has sailed." He disentangled his hand and placed it in his lap. "It doesn't change the facts. As long as my father doesn't want us together, there will be friction between the three of us, and that will impact my mother. I can't challenge my father at the risk of harming my mother."

"Even if it's not what she would want."

"You don't know that," he argued, though his heart wasn't in it. Patty was right. His mother said for them to work this out. Esther didn't say she agreed with Elijah. "Except she's an exceptional mother who will always put the needs of her sons over her own. I can't let her. I'd never forgive myself if something happened to her."

A tear escaped Patty's eye and tracked down her face.

Noah wiped it from her cheek. "I'm sorry," he whispered.

"Me too." Patty jumped to her feet and strode halfway to the front door before Noah even reacted. "I'll reach out to Esther about continuing to work with her. Solo," she called over her shoulder, pausing for a moment at the door.

"Okay," he announced into the silence after she quietly closed the door behind her.

CHAPTER TWENTY-ONE

PATTY

"Are you home?" Patty asked her sister over the phone, tears streaming down her face while she drove across town toward Shelly's apartment, hoping she'd be there.

"What happened?" Shelly responded in a sharp tone, the worry clear despite the tinny sound of the mobile.

"I'll tell you when I get there."

"Okay, and yes, I'm home. Drive carefully."

Patty smiled through her tears. The joke was she always drove her bright-red hatchback at precisely the speed limit. She'd never gotten a speeding ticket and, if the rumors that red vehicles drew the attention of cops were true, she didn't want to tempt fate.

Minutes later, she pulled into the parking lot of the apartment complex and parked in front of Shelly's building. Patty bounded up the stairs and rapped on the door.

Shelly opened it on the first knock and gathered Patty into a crushing bear hug.

"I can't breathe, big sis."

Shelly released her and held her at arm's length. "You've been crying." A statement, not a question.

Patty rubbed at her cheek, then glanced around. "I don't need everyone knowing my business."

"Of course not, come in." Shelly held the door and Patty headed straight for the turquoise dinette set off the small galley kitchen. "Wine's on the counter."

Patty glanced at her phone to confirm it was at least noon. She could have a lunch cocktail.

Shelly patted her on the back. "It's five o'clock somewhere."

"True enough." Patty grabbed two glasses and poured them both the red wine. "Out of white?" Shelly preferred white to red.

"Brought it over to Ben's house for dinner the other night," Shelly said.

"Makes sense."

The sisters sat next to each other, their knees almost touching. "Okay, spill," Shelly demanded.

Tears pricked Patty's eyes again and she took a swallow of wine. "Fortification," she said, and Shelly patted her knee.

"What happened?" She asked in a softer tone this time.

"Noah broke up with me."

Her sister's forehead crinkled in surprise. "You were dating?"

A laugh bubbled up. "Fair enough. We went on a date and were exploring the possibility of dating," she amended.

"He changed his mind? Why?"

"Because of his parents." Patty stifled the urge to roll her eyes. It was a childish response, but that's what this whole thing boiled down to. She explained Elijah's ultimatum, Esther's continued chaotic aura, and Noah's choice to stop things now before their misbehaving magic made things worse.

Shelly quirked an eyebrow. "Those Wright men don't make things easy, do they?"

Patty barked another laugh. "No, they don't." Shelly had had her own bumps in the road to happiness with Noah's brother, Ben. "That strengthens my argument."

"How do you mean?"

"He gave the example of Laura's misaligning magic as a reason he couldn't risk his mother's just as it's blossoming."

"Isn't Esther's chaotic magic the reason behind Laura's misaligning magic? So everything will be fine?"

"Exactly."

"Noah didn't buy that argument."

The corners of Patty's mouth dropped and she swigged more wine. "No, he didn't. He believes they got lucky figuring out the issue and solving it. He says he doesn't want to risk it with his mother."

Shelly tsked sympathetically. "That's a bind."

"Right? I can't be mad at him for caring about his mother's well-being. But," she said, and her expression darkened, "this all started because Elijah decided I wasn't good enough for his son."

"Elijah means well," Shelly said, "and that's not what he said."

Patty sighed. "I know." She jumped up, poured herself some water instead of more wine, and headed for a cabinet near the refrigerator. "Chips still in here?"

"Of course."

"Like with Noah, it's hard to fault Elijah for doing what he thinks is right. But, just because I'm a little younger and a little wilder—" She winked at her sister before retaking her seat and placing the chips on the table between them. "—doesn't mean Noah and I can't be a good match."

"No, it doesn't." Shelly chewed and swallowed a chip. She lasered in on Patty. "What are you going to do?"

"I'm still going to work with Esther," Patty asserted.

"Can you do that without Noah?"

Her confidence wavered. "I'm not sure. It helped a lot to see his healing magic, and since we've done it twice, I'm hoping there's some residual healing magic I can help her direct."

Shelly tilted her head. "That sounds difficult."

"What else can I do? I made a promise to help Esther."

"And what about Noah?"

Patty cradled her water glass in both hands. "I still think my plan can work."

"Which one?"

"Smart aleck," Patty said, swatting at her sister.

"In all seriousness, you do?"

Patty set the glass of water on the table, a spark igniting within her. "Yes, I do. Actually, it'll work even better now."

"How so?"

"Noah's objection is less about his father's problem with me and more about his concern for his mother."

Shelly nodded. "If you help Esther, it eliminates the source of his concern."

"Exactly."

"What's the next step?"

Patty fished her phone out of her dress pocket and texted Esther. "I'm going to fix this." She chugged the rest of her glass of water. Her phone dinged an incoming text. "Right now." She stood, and when Shelly did the same, Patty threw her arms around her. "Thanks, sis, for always listening to me work through things."

"Of course, little sister. Good luck."

"Thanks," Patty sang out as she headed to the door, down the stairs, and revved her car's engine. Time to restart the plan. This time, it would work. She was certain.

CHAPTER TWENTY-TWO

NOAH

"Oh," Noah said when he saw Patty standing on his parents' doorstep again. He groaned inwardly at his lack of eloquence. "What are you doing here?"

She smirked at his obvious discomfort. "Thanks for the warm welcome."

He flushed and held the door open. "Apologies. Please come in. What can I help you with?" He gave a slight butler-bow and winked. His reward was her giggle. "Better?"

"Much." She stood inside the doorway, fidgeting.

He withstood the desire to embrace her, his arms longing to wrap themselves around her and hold her close.

After what he'd said this morning and his stance on their relationship possibilities, he surmised it would be unwelcome. Although the glint in her eye made him wonder.

Patty entered the living room and glanced around. "Esther agreed to try another session with me."

"Oh," he repeated. This was going great. Such a scintillating conversation.

"Did you have a stroke?"

He laughed and she visibly relaxed; he guessed her attempt at levity was to reduce the obvious tension between them. "I don't believe I did, but in all seriousness, how are you doing another session?" His brow knitted in confusion. "Did you want me there too?"

"I don't think that's a good idea, given what happened this morning." She sank one hand in her dress pocket and pulled it back out.

Was she nervous? "Will it work without my healing power?"

"I don't know, but Esther's willing to give it a try."

"Good." He stared over her head and snickered.

"What's funny?" She stared at him quizzically.

"I was thinking about how short… I mean, petite… you are." The tips of his ears burned.

Her eyes darted to his ears, and then she was stuffing a smile, too. "All you Wright men are the same."

"Are we now?"

"Your ears turn bright red when you're embarrassed."

"Oh, really."

"I remember Ben's doing that around Shelly all the time. Yours, not as frequent. But, definitely right now." She gave a little finger point to the side of his head.

"Hmm." His conversational skills continued to excel this afternoon.

"This isn't about you," she said.

"I know," he replied, his tone defensive to his own ears.

"You do, huh?" She squinted at him as if trying to read his aura. "I'm not trying to read your aura."

Now his guffaw echoed off the walls and vaulted ceiling of the large space.

"What?" She appeared perplexed.

"How do you do that?"

"Do what?"

"Read my mind."

Now she mimicked his guffaw. "I wouldn't end up in half the situations I do if I could read minds."

"So you say."

"So I say." She broke eye contact.

The awkwardness flooded through him and cotton balls clogged his mouth.

"I know you don't want to see me."

"That's not quite right," he protested.

Patty tilted her head. "You don't want to pursue a romantic relationship," she amended. "In any event, as I said, I'm not here for you. I'm here for your mother."

"Yes, you said," he repeated, finally recognizing why he maintained the asinine conversation. He wanted to keep her with him, however possible.

"I made a promise to help her, so whether or not I lose you and the job, I'm going to do everything in my power to do so."

"We appreciate that." The butterflies in Noah's stomach became angry bees, and he crossed his arms. "I wish none of this had happened this way."

"None of it?"

The wistful tone caught him off guard, and his arms dropped to his side. "Not none of it. Just some of it."

"It's not over 'til it's over," she sang out and winked at him.

He narrowed his eyes at her. "What does that mean?"

"Is Esther ready?" she deflected.

A voice floated in from the other side of the home. "If that's Patty, no reason to give her a hard time. You can send her to the kitchen, Noah."

"I will, Mom," Noah called back, his baritone voice echoing in the room.

Patty pointed past him. "I know the way."

He ushered her through. "Of course." He followed behind her, surprised when he reached the kitchen that his father was there too.

"Patty," Elijah said in greeting.

"Gentlemen," she responded. "I'll need you both to clear the room, so I can work with Esther without… tension." She shrugged on the last word, but Noah understood.

"C'mon Dad, let's go," Noah said, grasping his father's elbow and leading him through the sliding glass doors to the backyard. "Let's give the ladies their space."

"Thank you, Noah," Patty said, her tone formal, but her body language suggesting a good mood. She surely couldn't have gotten over this morning already. His father closing the door behind them spared Noah having to respond.

CHAPTER TWENTY-THREE

PATTY

Patty hadn't lied to Noah when she said she wasn't trying to read his aura. Not exactly. She wasn't trying. But it had practically shouted at her. Then, when they'd entered the kitchen, his father's aura flashed. Although Patty never sought auras without permission, both Noah's and his father's auras were quite talkative.

Noah's flowing healing pink aura was so much stronger than that morning, leaving her wondering how much romantic feelings might be brightening it. Elijah's aura swirled a beautiful blue with lighter streaks suggesting acceptance. That buoyed her some. However, both men also had bits of black floating around, too. Black was often associated with negativity, which worried her. The little bits shrank in comparison to the happier colors as she watched. She wondered if her presence caused the reaction. She almost blurted out the auras' activity before the men left the room. Thank the Goddess she didn't. It wouldn't help, and it wasn't like she could be that precise on the meaning, anyway.

Patty perched on the edge of the seat next to Esther. "Are you ready?"

"I'm sorry I made things worse between you."

Patty waved her hand to dismiss Esther's comment.

The older woman captured Patty's hand in her own. "Don't do that."

"Do what?" Patty whispered the question.

"Act like this isn't a big deal."

Tears flooded Patty's eyes and she blinked them away. "I'm not. Promise. It is a big deal. I want the job Elijah offered. I want Noah." She rolled her shoulders. "But, more than that, right now, I want to help you."

"I know you do."

"Which is why you don't need to apologize. You did nothing wrong."

Esther pursed her lips. "I guess not. It just feels like, if I could get this unexpected magic under control, much of the drama would go away." Now she waved her hand dismissively, though her cheeks flushed.

"This is not your fault," Patty said. "Do you understand how rare and amazing you are?"

Esther shook her head. "I'm pretty self-confident, but I wouldn't go quite that far."

"You're the first person any of us has ever heard of to develop magic later in life," Patty enthused. "It's incredible."

"I got old, you mean," Esther responded, but with a light tone.

"I can only hope I'm as exceptional when I'm 'old' like you," Patty said, using air quotes.

"Of course, I don't actually have any magical abilities yet. Just the chaotic aura." Esther shrugged. "You believe the magic will manifest once the aura is under control?"

"I do, but I literally have zero to base that on, except my intuition." Patty's chest tightened at the idea she might be leading Esther on, getting her hopes up for something she'd never get. But Patty believed she was right about the aura and Esther's magic. She grabbed hold of that thought. "You're the one that has to do the hard work," she teased.

"I'm still game." Esther sipped from a glass of tea on the table. "Can you do this without Noah?"

"That I'm less sure of. I saw how close you were before…" She trailed off.

"I went magically nuclear?" Esther offered.

"It wasn't that bad," Patty countered. "There is such a thing as residual magic, so that's what I'm relying on here."

"Noah's magic might still be attached to my aura somewhere?" Esther's uncertainty shone through her words.

"That's the idea. Are you ready to get started?"

"Let's do this."

Patty guided Esther to focus on her inner energy and healing thoughts. A slight smile rose on Esther's face, reassuring Patty that they were on the right path. "This is great, Esther." The aura had bloomed the murkier white like at the end of the morning's session, but now it brightened.

"Think of yourself as connected to the world, to all the living beings within," Patty instructed.

"That feels nice," Esther murmured, her aura lightening further.

"I'm seeing those silver streaks and even the little bit of yellow like before."

"That's good?" Esther asked.

"Yes," Patty answered, concerned that the lightly asked question might mask more self-doubt.

"Okay, good."

Despite the positive statement, Esther's aura darkened. The silver streaks faded. "What are you thinking right now?"

"I'm... not."

"Esther, you need to tell me the truth." Patty straightened in alarm at the spreading darkness of the yellow in the aura.

"I'm worried," Esther admitted. Her hands clenched and unclenched in her lap.

Patty's hands closed over them. She dropped her voice lower, soothing. "Clearing your mind isn't the goal. Think about the connection to the world around you," she said again. "You are a bright shining light within it, whatever your ultimate magical ability may turn out to be."

Esther's aura brightened and then immediately darkened.

"Esther?"

"If I develop my magical ability."

Alarm bells rang loudly in Patty's head now. "Of course, you will. Why wouldn't you?"

"I… don't know." A tear slid down Esther's cheek.

"Would the Goddess gift you a magical aura without a magical ability to go with it?" Patty asked, trying for a joking tone to relieve the tension. It didn't work.

"Why would the Goddess give me a chaotic aura?"

"I don't know," Patty said, echoing Esther's earlier statement. "But." She stopped and stared, bringing Esther's wavering gaze to her own. "The Goddess doesn't do things without a reason. You won't find your reason until you learn to control your aura."

Esther yanked her hands free and stood from the table, though she leaned forward and braced herself against it.

"Are you okay?" Patty rubbed her back in circles.

Esther stood tall, pushed back a stray hair that escaped from her French braid. "I will be."

"Are you sure?" Patty asked. Esther's dark yellow aura screamed self-criticism, so Patty doubted Esther's answer.

"I'm okay," she insisted. "But we can't work on this until you, Noah, and Elijah figure out what to do."

Patty nodded, unsure what to say. Esther's aura was changing, despite what had happened. The yellow was brightening again to a healthier, supportive light yellow.

"It's an odd sensation," Esther continued, her eyes almost dreamy. "I know without question that I can't move forward until you three fix this. But I can't say exactly how I know that."

Patty tasted acrid fear, but a small part of her wondered if this was part of Esther's blossoming magical ability.

"I'm sorry, dear, that sounds terribly self-important. And I don't want to put any pressure on you."

"We've put all the pressure on ourselves, no doubt," Patty said. "We'll work it out." If only she had an idea how to do it. She was in a classic chicken or egg situation. The need to help Esther to remove that barrier to a relationship with Noah and convince Elijah to confirm the job offer. But now Esther was telling Patty that she needed those things to happen before Esther could move forward. *Gah!*

CHAPTER TWENTY-FOUR

NOAH

Noah and his father sat on side-by-side deck chairs. The silence weighed heavy. A slight growl drew both men's attention.

"It's okay, Richard," Elijah said to the gray wolf that had joined them and padded between their chairs on the deck. The wolf shook his head back and forth, his green eyes thoughtful yet alert.

"No, really, it is," Noah assured him, assuming the wolf would remain on alert until the tension between the men lessened. That was probably a holdover from the wolf's warrior days as a human.

Richard settled between them, dropping his head between his paws and letting out a harrumph that sounded human. The laughter it elicited from Noah and his father thawed the icy tension a little.

"Son."

"Father."

They shifted in their seats simultaneously, alike in so many ways. Noah had his father's striking looks and booming baritone. He hoped he wasn't as stubborn as the old man.

"Your proviso was asinine," Noah began.

"No."

Noah quirked an eyebrow at the absolute answer from Elijah, though he wasn't surprised. "That gives us nowhere to start."

"There's no starting here."

"There's not? Then you lied to Richard."

At his name, the gray wolf lifted his head and growled again.

"I did not," Elijah disagreed.

"You told him everything was okay."

"So did you."

"Yes, because I hoped you would be an adult about this." Noah winced even as the words left his mouth.

The stony expression on Elijah's face confirmed the mistake. "I'm not an adult?"

"That's not what I meant."

"Then tell me what you meant, son," Elijah said in a flat tone.

Noah tapped his foot. "I thought you'd be open to discussing the realities of the situation."

"What are those realities?"

"I like Patty and I want to be with her." The words slipped out so easily and quickly that Noah knew they were unstoppable.

"Indeed."

"And she's a superb choice for the assistant priestess position."

"Hmm."

"You know she is, or you wouldn't have offered it to her to begin with," Noah pointed out. "I don't believe for a moment you offered it to her specifically to convince her to stay away from me."

"Thank you for that." Elijah's softer tone still boomed around the backyard.

"You love the coven and want what's best for us."

"I do."

"And you think you're doing the right thing, trying to keep us apart, but you're not."

"She's young and still finding herself. You're ready to settle down."

"You act like I'm done living," Noah said with a snort.

"That's not what settling down is," Elijah said. "Do your mother and I look like we're done living?"

"Of course not." Noah groaned and realized what his father was saying about his stage in life. "That's where you're wrong, though."

"That your mother and I aren't done living?"

Noah laughed. "No, that Patty's young and still finding herself."

"She's not?"

"Dad, she's only four years younger than me." Noah could smack himself for thinking the same thing as his father in the beginning, that Patty was too young for him. It wasn't that far-fetched for his father to erroneously believe it too. "You also wouldn't have offered her the position if she was still finding herself."

"That may not be true. She's young and impressionable."

With a shock, Noah identified the reason behind his father's contradictory notion that Patty was young and impressionable, yet still the choice for Elijah's eventual replacement. "You wanted to create a mini-you?"

His father shocked him by reddening. "Maybe a little."

"That would never happen."

"I've accepted that Patty isn't nearly as impressionable as I'd thought. She is, however, even more capable."

"You're leaving the offer on the table?"

Elijah lifted his hands in surrender. "Yes, yes."

"Without the asinine proviso?" Noah deliberately left the word in there.

"Your mother told me the two of you weren't seeing each other anymore, anyway," Elijah said, sidestepping the question.

"When I saw Mom in pain…"

Elijah's hands tightened on the chair's sides. "Seeing my love like that.."

"No," Noah agreed. "I didn't want to be the source of that."

"Of course not."

"Much like you, though, with the asinine proviso." He didn't enjoy the discomfort his repeated use of the word caused his father, but the proviso had started a damaging series of unfortunate decisions. The magnitude of the fact needed to be recognized. Then he softened. "Like you, too, I'm a big enough man to admit when I was wrong."

"I never said I was wrong."

Noah side-eyed his father, who lifted his hands in surrender again.

"Fine. I was wrong."

"As was I with Patty. I made a mistake, but I'm going to fix it as soon as they finish this session." He stood suddenly, startling Elijah and Richard. "What am I doing? I should be in there helping Patty and Esther. Now that we've cleared the air and we're on the same page?"

"Yes," Elijah said. He joined his son, and they approached the sliding glass door.

"Something's wrong," Noah said. His mother braced herself against the white oak kitchen table. He opened the door and watched Patty comforting Esther. He waited until a small smile crossed his mother's face, and he knew she was okay, then he entered the kitchen to both fix his mistake with Patty and help his mother.

CHAPTER TWENTY-FIVE

PATTY

The sliding glass door opening drew Patty's attention. The smiles on both Noah's and Elijah's faces heartened her. She rushed to Noah, certain that they were meant to be together. "I'm so sorry," she blurted out.

"I need to apologize," Noah said simultaneously.

They both laughed.

"You go first," Noah said.

"Esther, could I talk to you in the living room?" Elijah asked. Esther took the hint and Noah's parents started to leave the room.

"Wait, Mom, you're okay, right?" Noah asked.

"Yes, honey, I am," Esther confirmed.

"Okay, good. I'd like you both to stay. You should hear some of this, too." His parents returned to sit at the kitchen table, and Noah grasped Patty's hands.

"I'm so sorry," she repeated. "Your father never should have made the proviso. But I never should have accepted it."

"You wouldn't have taken the job? Even though we weren't together?"

"No. On principle alone, I should have rejected his attempt to control me. The job enticed me, obviously, but no job is worth sacrificing your self-respect." At a sound from Elijah, she shot him a be-quiet look. "I'm not finished. I know that's not what your father was trying to do, but it's what in-effect he did." She placed her hand on Noah's chest.

Noah clasped her hand and brought it to his lips.

When he kissed her palm, a shiver of pleasure moved through her.

"I agree with all of that. My father meant well, but his belief that you and I were wrong for each other blinded him. He'll apologize later."

"Thanks for taking care of that for me, son," a sardonic voice interrupted from the table.

A low laugh rose in Patty's throat. "There was enough stupidity to go around."

"Indeed. My stupidity was in blaming you for not telling me about what my father did."

"No," she shook her head. "I should have. We're friends, and his proviso impacted us both."

"From that standpoint, yeah, I suppose. But how do you tell someone your father made an unacceptable proposal?" His eyebrows raised with the question.

"I want to officially date you," Patty said. "If you'll have me." She grinned impishly.

"What about school?"

"We can date until I leave for the fall. We'll have to stay long-distance until after graduation—" She side-eyed Elijah.

"You don't even need to ask. The job will be waiting for you when you get home," Elijah assured her, his voice gruff.

"I'm all in," Noah said, and Patty's heart soared. "Now that's out of the way, are you ready to help my mom?"

The couple faced Esther at the table. She gave an uncertain nod. "I'm ready if you are."

Patty and Elijah sat across from Noah and Esther.

Patty glanced between Esther and Noah. "You two know the drill. Noah, direct your healing energy at your mother. Esther, accept the healing energy of the universe and try to find the center of your developing magic. Our goal is to finish calming the chaos so your magical ability can manifest, your magic won't interfere with others, and maybe your menopause will improve." She threw in the last item as an added incentive to also break some of the nervousness she saw on Esther's face.

"That's all?" Esther asked, quirking an eyebrow.

Noah held his mother's hands and began talking through his internal actions. "Mom. I'm sending my energy to connect with yours."

As before, Noah's aura glowed, this time a gorgeous shade of healing pink. It mixed with Esther's murky yellow and white, which almost immediately lightened. When Patty relayed that information, the remaining tension drained from everyone's faces.

"Let's keep going," Patty encouraged them. "Esther, how are you feeling?"

"Light, almost like I'm floating. Everything feels positive, good." A blush of health rose on her cheeks.

"Your aura is continuing to transform," Patty relayed. "The yellow is growing stronger, but it's a sunny yellow, tied to intelligence—"

"That definitely fits," Elijah boomed.

"Shh, honey," Esther chided him.

"It also suggests creativity and a supportive nature. All of which fits your personality."

"What happened with the white?" Noah asked.

"Focus," Patty said, thinking just how much he was like his father. "The white is still there, but it's also transforming." She watched as rays of light formed; that usually signaled a connection to the higher self and the

Goddess Herself. The glow almost became too bright, it was so beautiful. As she shared that with the Wrights, Patty wondered just what magic Esther would manifest. It would no doubt be as unique and as beautiful as her aura.

Patty sighed happily. "We're almost there. Esther, your aura is so calm, you must sense that."

"I do. I've never experienced anything like this before. Is this what having magic is like?" she asked.

"Maybe?" Patty answered. "Everyone experiences it differently." She placed a hand on Noah's arm across the table. "You can start withdrawing your healing energy now. Do you feel the improved health in your mom's energy?"

His eyes shone with gratitude. "I do," he whispered.

"It's too early for 'I do's'," Elijah grumbled.

Patty ignored him. "Maybe one day," she whispered back to Noah, who curled his fingers around hers.

"One day," he agreed, and pulled her across the table to capture her lips with his.

On the tips of her toes, she used her hands to hold herself above the table, while she enjoyed the gentle pressure and sweet taste of Noah's kiss. They'd made it to their happily ever after.

EPILOGUE

NOAH

Noah watched from the corner of his eye as Patty spoke, resplendent in a purple dress with cartoon black cats on it. She had debated wearing the dress all week, bringing it up every time they video chatted, until she decided that this was her personality. The coven knew her, and they would accept it. And they did, of course. She'd come home from college for the weekend to lead the coven's Samhain celebration. Her job as assistant priestess wouldn't officially start until December, but his father had suggested she lead the ceremony. This would introduce Patty to the coven in her soon-to-be new role.

Patty stood in their coven circle, surrounded by their family and friends, in his parents' backyard. She would lead them through the Summer's End ritual, honoring those who had crossed over the veil, as well as celebrating members' hopes for their new year. As always with their sabbats, folding tables laden with food filled the expansive space outside the circle. Every member of the coven brought a dish that held special meaning for them, representing a lost loved one. In the evening's dusk, the scents of everything from macaroni and cheese to apple pie wafted over the witches.

Members of the circle had already called in the four elements of earth, wind, water, and fire. Although not always included in their rituals, Patty had also called a fifth element of spirit, since tonight the veil between worlds would be at its thinnest.

Noah squeezed Patty's hand in support and she flashed him a quick smile, eyes shining, before focusing on the circle.

"I ask for any of us who have lost a loved one over the past year, if you'd like to speak," Patty said. Her gaze traveled from person to person around the circle. They'd invited several solo practitioners to join them, so the group might have been thirty people strong.

A thin, older man stepped forward. "I'd like to remember my wife, Alyssa." The group listened in rapt attention as he described his thirty-year marriage and her recent passing.

Since they were a small town, even with adding the solo practitioners, the celebration advanced quickly to the witches' plans for the future. Several members of his and Patty's families had looked ready to burst, so he had an idea that they would have a few memorable announcements.

He wasn't wrong.

Patty asked the assembled circle if they had expectations for the next year. His brother, Ben, and Patty's sister, Shelly, exchanged a quick glance and said in unison, "We have an announcement."

"You're not pregnant, are you?" Grace Newsome asked in her husky voice. All eyes swung to the thin, petite woman. Patty's mother threw her head back and howled with laughter, her curly red hair bouncing around her face. Then she winked a purple eye, and added, "I'm just being a smart aleck."

"Thanks for trying to steal our thunder," Shelly joked before she glanced again at Ben. "We're getting married!" they shouted simultaneously.

Congratulations rang out at the news, and Patty jumped in. "This is only the first announcement, everyone. Let's try to stay calm." At her direction, the chatter dropped.

"I'm thankful for my new magic," Esther jumped in next, "and I look forward to continuing to hone it over the next year." She clasped her hands in front of her chest before retaking Elijah's and Aaron's hands on either side of her. "And, in honor of this news, I'd like to offer as my wedding gift, fixing Shelly's misfiring magic." Gasps greeted her offer.

"Great. What am I supposed to get them?" Elijah grumbled good-naturedly.

"We all know I was responsible for Laura's magic misaligning with Aaron's," Esther continued as if her husband hadn't interrupted. "It occurred to me that since my magic is a connection to the divine, including a connection to the organizing energy of the universe, that I can help disorganized magic." She nodded at Shelly. "I believe I can heal your magic, too."

"That would be amazing," Shelly said, her voice thick with emotion.

A high-pitched whistle sounded from a tall tree about twenty feet from the circle. Noah stared at it, but in the dark could not see his mother's familiar perched there. Evelyn, a magnificent bald eagle, had appeared when his mother's magic manifested. Evelyn told the family she was a distant cousin from the 1950s but had been a devout believer, and they figured this was why she'd returned as his mother's familiar.

"Since we're announcing relationship goals," Aaron said, his deep voice rising above the hubbub, which quieted the circle. He locked eyes with his girlfriend, Laura, the redhead stunning as always in what Noah had been told was a designer pantsuit.

"Aaron is moving in with me," Laura interjected with a happy squeal.

"Into the house I helped her find," Aaron added.

The members of the circle maintained their contact, but lifted their hands in support for the happy couple.

After much fast and furious sharing by other members of the circle, the tempo slowed and Patty opened her mouth, possibly to thank them and close the circle.

"I have one more announcement," Elijah boomed into the night. All eyes zoomed to him. "For those of you who weren't aware, Patricia Newsome performed this evening's ceremony at my request. I've offered her the role of the assistant priestess once she graduates with her master's degree in two months. My intention was for her to become the high priestess upon my retirement."

Another lifting of conjoined hands in support of Patty followed. Noah's heart swelled with pride for his girlfriend.

"However," Elijah continued, "recent events have caused me to reevaluate my commitments. More details will be forthcoming, but I plan to go to half-time when Patty graduates, with full retirement by this time next year." Gasps greeted this statement.

"That's unexpected," Patty murmured.

Noah heard the anxiety in her voice.

"And terrifying," she added, confirming his guess.

"You've got this," Noah assured her, squeezing her hand. "Plus you'll have my family and yours there to help, every step of the way."

Elijah kissed his wife's forehead. "I plan to spend all my time with my wife, Esther. At least until she gets tired of me."

"Never," Esther said, wrapping one arm around Elijah's waist and leaning into him.

"Aw, that's sweet," Patty whispered, more for Noah's ears than for the circle.

Understanding dawned for Noah. His father was stepping back to be there for his mother with both the magical manifestation and menopause.

Noah squeezed Patty's hand again. His parents' love never ceased to surprise and warm him. Now, his brothers were moving forward with their happily ever afters. Noah leaned down so that his mouth was at Patty's ear. "We're definitely next," he whispered. Patty's head turned, and she kissed both his cheeks before placing the sweetest kiss on his lips.

"Absolutely," she breathed.

THANK YOU!

Thank you so much for supporting my work and reading this book.

If you liked the book, please consider leaving a review online.

Just a few lines would be great. Reviews are not only the highest compliment you can pay to an author, they also help other readers discover and make more informed choices about purchasing books in a crowded online space. Thank you so much in advance.

If you didn't like the book or have concerns, please email me directly at
heather@heathersilvio.com

ABOUT THE AUTHOR

Heather Silvio writes fun, fast-paced, supernatural mystery & flirty romance. She sometimes strays from that to write non-supernatural fiction, and even the occasional nonfiction book. Heather is also an actress and clinical psychologist who channels her inner flapper as a 1920s jazz and blues singer when she isn't working.

Visit https://www.heathersilvio.com for more information and to sign up for her Theatrical Thursdays Newsletter.